Playing With Stars

'Where are we most likely to find a Scorpio?' asked Zoe. 'They're supposed to be highly-sexed, aren't they?'

I laughed. 'That's an understatement. Even the quiet ones are closet sex maniacs.'

'A porn cinema, then, or perhaps a strip-show or a sleazy lap-dancing club?'

'Mmm. There'd probably be loads of Scorpios in those places but I don't fancy going somewhere like that at the moment. Besides, supposing I got one who was into SM or something peculiar?'

Little did I know then that, by nightfall, I would be dressed in fetish wear in the dungeon of one the kinkiest Scorpios in town. And loving every minute.

Playing With Stars

JAN HUNTER

BLACK
lace

Black Lace novels contain sexual fantasies.
In real life, make sure you practise safe sex.

First published in 2001 by
Black Lace
Thames Wharf Studios,
Rainville Road, London W6 9HA

Typeset by SetSystems Ltd, Saffron Walden, Essex
Printed and bound by Mackays of Chatham PLC

ISBN 0 352 33653 6

Contents

Chapter One
The Challenge

My father, the famous astrologer, Gerry Hathaway, died at a New Year's Eve party. He was drunk, of course, but having a whale of time when he suddenly slumped to the floor in front of everyone and died almost instantly of a massive heart attack. His nubile young girlfriend, Anna, was by his side when it happened. He was only 59.

I was thrashing about wildly beneath my gorgeous boyfriend, Ryan, on the verge of orgasm, when the mobile phone by the bed started ringing out its sweet Bach melody.

'Shit!' Ryan cried, arching his back. 'Don't answer it!'

I had no intention of doing so. It was two o'clock in the morning, for Christ's sake, and I was enjoying myself. Ryan continued pumping away inside me, while the phone kept ringing. Then it stopped. Ten seconds later, it was off again.

'They're not going to give up,' I said resentfully when the precious orgasm didn't materialise and Ryan's erection started to dwindle. 'It might be important.'

Ryan groaned and dragged himself off me.

I reached for the phone. 'Hello,' I said gruffly into the mouthpiece. Then I was quiet, a stunned expression on my face. 'I'll be right over,' I said at last, and put the phone down.

Ryan sat up, his face full of concern. 'Something wrong, Ellie?'

'My father's just died,' I said dumbly. 'That was Anna. I've got to get to the hospital straightaway.'

The funeral took place a week later. It was very well attended. Lots of well-known celebrities who had consulted my father about their birth charts on a regular basis came to pay their respects.

Beautiful, leggy Anna – who was making a name for herself as a sexy hostess on a well-known quiz show – sobbed her heart out throughout the service. She was only 21, poor thing, a year younger than me. I came to the conclusion that she was either a very good actress or she had truly loved my father. But I liked her, so I gave her the benefit of the doubt. I knew my father had been besotted with her during the three months they'd been seeing one another.

Personally, I hated crying in public. I left most of my grieving until later, when I was alone. I had loved my father very much, and he had doted on me, especially after my mother died when I was just two years old. I was an only child and grew up to be very precocious. Recently, my father had been teaching me astrology and introducing me to some of his best clients so that I could take over from him when he retired. He was good at his work and had made a niche for himself in the world of the rich and famous. I wanted to emulate his talent.

Two days after the funeral I went to see my father's solicitor, Bernard Enright, about his will. Bernard had told me over the phone that I was the only legatee, so I was a bit puzzled as to why he should ask me to go to his office.

Bernard shook my hand formally. 'Please be seated, Miss Hathaway.'

I sat down, crossed my legs enticingly over my short skirt, and gave him my sweetest smile. 'Please, call me Mariella. Or even Ellie, if you like. That's what all my friends call me.' I knew I was waffling but I couldn't help it. For some reason I was rather nervous. Had Anna contested the will?

Bernard Enright got down to business quickly. 'To be honest, er, Mariella, I've asked you here because your father's will is not at all straightforward.' He coughed loudly. 'It's very strange indeed, and somewhat embarrassing, to say the least.'

He coughed again, and I felt like laughing, but I kept my cool. I was intrigued. 'Why is it embarrassing, Mr Enright?'

'Your father was an astrologer, I believe?'

'Yes?'

'And he was training you to take over his work?'

'Yes. But I'm nowhere near as good as he was – yet.'

'Well, your father has made a certain stipulation in his will about your astrological studies. He wants you to write a book about the sexual habits of males born under each of the twelve star signs, and to do this he asks that you, er, experience each sign sexually.'

I stared at him for a few seconds, then burst out laughing. 'How do you mean? Does he want me to actually have sex with twelve different men?'

Bernard Enright was agitated. 'That's what he says, yes. Here, read it for yourself.'

He thrust the will at me. I quickly scanned through the legal jargon until I came to the relevant bit, then started to read slowly.

I hereby request that in order to inherit all my wordly goods and possessions, my daughter, Mariella Jane Hathaway, must write, and complete in

3

one year, a non-fiction book relating to the sexual habits, preferences and techniques of each of the twelve star signs. To do this she must physically experience at least one man from each sign of the zodiac during the thirty days when the Sun is travelling through his sign. For example, Aries man to be experienced between 21 March and 19 April, Taurus between 20 April and 20 May, and so on. She must start her year of experiences during the sign of Aries and finish during the sign of Pisces the following year, whereupon at the end of this sign on 20 March she must hand the completed book to the solicitors for scrutiny. Providing everything is completed to my word and the solicitor's satisfaction, my assets can then be duly released to my daughter.

I stopped reading. I didn't want to know what would happen if I didn't complete my task. I would do it. My canny father knew just what to do to make me get off my backside and do something with my life. At the end of the year I would be a brillliant astrologer, ready to follow in his footsteps. And I would have a lot of fun in the bargain.

Bernard was staring at me whimsically.

'I'll do it!' I cried, grinning from ear to ear. 'And I'll have that book on your desk pronto, no later than the twentieth of March next year.'

Bernard gave a watery smile, stood up, and offered me his limp, pudgy hand to shake again. 'Well, good luck to you then, young lady. I hope you enjoy yourself.'

'Oh, I will. Don't worry.' I jumped up from my chair and careered out of his office into the sharp, wintry air. It was 10 January. I had exactly ten weeks to get myself sorted and pan out exactly how I was going to tackle this crazy adventure. I couldn't wait!

Chapter Two
Aries: The Horny Stud

20 MARCH

*I*t's 20 March, and I'm eager to begin my mission. Last week I left the office where I had been bored to tears for over a year working as an accounts assistant for a stuffy old sod who never laughed or said 'thank you' and always called me 'Ms Hathaway'.

I don't have much money in the bank, so I reckon I might have to do some casual work or get a loan until I get hold of father's money and can live in his rambling, old mansion in Sussex. But I'm happy, and more than ready to seek out my first conquest: an Aries man. I have thought long and hard during the past ten weeks about my tactics. How and where can I find suitable blokes in such a short space of time who don't look like Quasimodo, and who fancy me? More to the point, I've got to fancy each one enough to feel horny. I know it's not going to be as easy as it sounded when I first read the will. Luckily, I still have a boyfriend!

In the beginning, Ryan ranted and raved at me and begged me not to do it, but I managed to win him round when I told him the value of my father's estate and how these men would mean nothing to me other than a means to an end. A bit of a fib, I know, but what else could I tell him? Ryan is a Sagittarian: fiery, sexy, adaptable and not at all possessive, so I'll be all right when it comes to December. In the end he agreed to help me as much as he could. A few days ago he proudly presented me with a list of all his mates with their occupations and birth data.

I have made copious notes of what I know about each sign and where I am most likely to find my prey. When reading through the Aries data, several unsavoury (to my mind) facts stick out a mile. This man is supposedly hot and rampant – no problem here! – an all-brawn-and-no-brain type, with very little sensitivity or under-standing of the female psyche. A typical 'wham bam, thank you ma'am' guy who loves the chase but tires of his conquests easily. I can see I'm going to have my work cut out. If I try to seduce him, he might not be interested, so I have to make it look as if he's doing all the running. Where am I likely to find this type of guy? Well, I know that Aries men love uniforms and like to be in on the action, so policemen, firemen or army officers might come up trumps. But how am I going to approach them, let alone find out their birth signs? It's exasperating. I know I've got to get out there and forget about niceties and the fact that I can be a bit shy when approaching people I don't know. Sure, I'm going to get plenty of rejections and find it difficult, but what the heck. I'm desperate to get on with my task quickly so I'm tempted to take the easy road, first time, and go through Ryan's list.

There are 21 guys on it, most of whom I know by sight, but only two of them are Arians: Clive, a short-arsed, cocky bloke in his late twenties who I can't stand, and Jason, a young lad of nearly nineteen who is taking a year out after his A levels to earn some money before going to university. He must have some brains, then. But at the moment he's working as a bricklayer for

Ryan's building company. I've never spoken to him, but I've seen him, briefly, from a distance, and he certainly looks passable. Not much of a choice, I know, but I've got to start somewhere and notch up an Aries, so I've made up my mind I'm going to try Jason for starters. If we don't hit it off, I can always find someone else for the main course, can't I?

That night I spoke to Ryan and asked him to introduce me to Jason. He agreed, albeit reluctantly. I don't think he likes the idea of me having sex with a randy young stud. As for me, I was getting used to the idea and feeling pretty horny already.

The following evening six of us met up in the pub. Ryan had decided it would be less obvious if he brought some other mates along for the ride, one of whom was an ex-girlfriend of his called Gemma. We sat in a circle, with me placed strategically next to Jason, showing a great deal of leg and even more cleavage. Gemma and Ryan sat huddled together, opposite us. In between were Tony and Aaron, two of Ryan's buddies from school-days. At first I eyed Gemma and Ryan coldly as they flirted outrageously with one another. I tried not to notice when Ryan put his hand down the back of Gemma's trousers and she responded by wriggling her arse upwards so that he could get his hand down further. If Ryan thought he was going to make me jealous, he had another think coming. I was here to work. So I turned my attention to Jason. Close up, he was not particularly good looking. He had typical Arian features: an irregularly shaped face, slightly reddish hair and a large nose. But he had a cheeky grin and a gorgeous physique, and as he chatted animatedly with Aaron, I decided that he was good enough to make a play for. But there was no way I could ask him outright if he'd like to fuck me; that would turn him off.

They were talking about football – surprise, surprise

– a game I hated and knew nothing about. I heard Jason say he supported Chelsea. Quickly I butted in with, 'Oh, that's my team too!'

Jason turned to me and gave me his lopsided, cheeky grin. 'Really? Do you ever go to watch them play?'

'I used to. But I haven't been for a long while.' I made my voice sound as wistful as possible.

'You ought to go again. They're playing at home this Saturday.'

'Are you going?'

'Yep. And Aaron. Why don't you come along with us?'

I smiled and feigned delight. 'I'd love to.'

After that we chatted, and I found myself beginning to feel a bit horny at the prospect of a good shag coming up. But by the end of the evening it looked as if I was going to have to wait until after the football match before anything happened. He was very friendly and couldn't keep his eyes off my tits which were virtually spilling out onto the table, but he didn't make a move.

Halfway through the evening, Ryan and Gemma disappeared together for about fifteen minutes. Gemma came back first, looking hot and flustered, followed by Ryan, a minute or two later, looking like the cat who'd got the cream. I felt like screaming out at him 'You bastard!' but Jason was nattering on about a top Chelsea player and I had to appear interested.

On the way home with Ryan in the car, I let loose.

'What do you expect?' he said, shrugging his shoulders. 'It was either that or sit and watch you ogling Jason all night.'

'But I'm doing this for a reason. It's a job!'

Ryan wasn't impressed. 'Look, I've agreed to help you. Supplied you with the first guy, even, but don't expect me to stay at home like a good little boy whilst you're out on the razzle getting shagged by every Tom,

Dick and Harry. I still want to be your boyfriend, but I'm gonna have some fun too.'

What could I say? I slumped in my seat miserably. Inwardly, I was seething with emotion. 'Nothing's happened with Jason,' I said at last. 'But it's promising. He supports Chelsea, so I'm going along to the match with him on Saturday.'

Ryan guffawed with laughter. 'You at a football match? You can't stand the game. You'll be bored to tears after five minutes.'

'No I won't. Not with Jason next to me. He's very fit. I'm looking forward to it. Only three days and I might have my first conquest under my belt.'

Ryan slammed his brakes on, coming to a sudden halt outside my flat. 'I won't come in,' he said abruptly. 'Have a good time on Saturday. I'll give you a ring on Sunday.'

When I got out of the car he was off like a shot. I wondered momentarily if he was rushing back to see Gemma. I sighed deeply. It looked as if things were going to be tougher than I thought. Roll on Saturday!

It was an icy cold day, and I was wrapped up to the nines, trying to look sexy in my thick coat, hat and scarf. I met Jason outside the grounds at two o'clock. To my delight, Aaron hadn't turned up. He had a bad cold, poor thing. Jason seemed very pleased to see me and ushered me into the stands. After waiting what seemed like ages before the kick-off, and then standing, shivering for three-quarters of an hour in the middle of a crowd of yelling louts who swore every time the other team came close to scoring a goal, the whistle blew for half time.

I looked up at Jason and suddenly felt faint. As I teetered, he put out his arms to steady me and I collapsed against his sturdy chest. I wasn't putting it on. I was absolutely knackered.

He put his arm around my shoulders. 'Are you all right?'

'Yes, I'm fine. Just a little tired with all this standing.'

He seemed relieved. 'Great match, isn't it?'

'Yes,' I enthused, thinking I had rarely been so cold and bored in all my life. If it wasn't for Jason holding me tight against him right now, I would be out of those gates as fast as my feet could carry me. 'Shame there haven't been any goals,' I said, just to show interest.

'There will be in the second half. I predict Chelsea will win two nil.'

The thought of another three-quarters of an hour of hell made me feel nauseous, so I snuggled up to Jason's chest and he seemed quite happy to have me there.

The second half came and I was slowly dying on my feet, my eyes closed, when Jason's arm moved abruptly and there was massive cheering all around us. Chelsea had scored. I looked at Jason's delighted face and couldn't help but feel happy for him. He turned to me, grabbed me to him and planted a huge kiss on my cheek. I was pleasantly surprised by his sudden action – typically Aries – but wanted more. When he let go I stared meaningfully into his eyes and he pulled me to him again and this time showed me what he was really capable of. His long, probing tongue thrust urgently into my mouth, filling it with a combined taste of tobacco and chewing gum. But it wasn't unpleasant. After a few seconds I began to respond, opening my mouth as wide as possible, greedily sucking his tongue into the back of my throat, imagining it was his cock. He quickly got excited and before I could come up for air, he was unbuttoning my coat and squeezing his cold hands against my breasts, over my jumper.

He cursed as he tried to drag the thick jumper up and get his hands onto my naked flesh. He was brash, and totally lacking in finesse, but I was strangely excited, possibly more by his lack of awareness about the crowd

10

and what was going on in the match than by anything else.

He managed to get my jumper up and then push my bra up over my tits. My nipples were standing out like big, red buttons. He pulled hard on them, hurting me. 'I want to fuck you,' he whispered into my ear.

I looked around me, aware that some of the men close by were more intent upon watching us than the match. Jason was pressing his body against me, the bulging erection in his trousers begging for action.

The men around us started to leer. 'Go on, give her one, mate,' one of them cried.

I decided I'd had enough – for the time being anyway. There were goose bumps on my naked flesh and a randy old sod close by was masturbating himself through his trousers. I pushed hard at Jason's chest. 'What about the match?' I asked breathlessly.

'I've got better things on my mind now,' he answered cheekily, yanking me back towards him.

'But I'm freezing and there are too many people around.'

'So what? Let's give 'em something to look at.' In one speedy movement, he put his hand to my waist, unzipped my jeans and thrust his hand down my front. His fingers immediately found my swollen clit. I was at last experiencing the red-hot passion of a typical Aries. He wanted me, and nothing was going to stand in his way.

And I wanted him. My juices were flowing like mad and my knickers were soaked. But I didn't want to be fucked on a cold, stone floor in the icy wind, being ogled by lots of dirty old men. Somehow, I had to be strong. I knew that pushing him away and making him wait wouldn't ruin my chances. In fact, it should make him even hornier.

Gaining my strength, I yanked his hand out from my trousers, pushed him away again and quickly buttoned up my coat. 'I don't want to do it here,' I said. 'Why don't we go back to my place?' With that I walked away, praying that he would run after me.

He did. I smiled to myself as he caught up with me and grabbed my arm. 'I hope you don't live too far away,' he said, 'because something's going to burst out of my trousers soon.' He pointed proudly to his rampant cock.

I laughed. He wasn't exactly a budding Romeo, or at all skilled in his actions, but he was young and enthusiastic and behaving just like an Aries should.

I drove him in my car. He didn't have one; he was saving all his money for university. It was a slow drive, heading out of the London traffic towards the suburbs of Wimbledon where I lived. Throughout the journey Jason kept touching me – and himself – keeping us both horny. By the time we got back to my flat, my jeans were halfway down my bum and my bra was gaping open. As I put the key in the door, Jason was already unzipping his trousers. I hardly had time to close the door before he pushed me against the wall and started tugging at my jeans. As he pulled them down I reached out for his very large, swollen cock, and began to stroke it. I was almost as excited as he was. This was something very different to my regular sex with Ryan. Jason had a fantastic body and his cock was even bigger than Ryan's.

Jason was groaning. When I was free of my trousers he roughly pushed my legs open very wide and, before I could tell him to slow down, he was thrusting away urgently inside my gaping hole. I gasped with delight and began to move with him, but less than a minute later he exploded into me, shrieking out with pleasure. Then he quickly pulled himself out and sank to the floor in delirium. Bemused and disappointed, I stared down at him, and then at my thighs, as what seemed like half a pint of come ran down my legs. My pussy was still aching with desire.

Slowly, I turned away and went to the bathroom to clean myself up. I was very angry. I ripped the rest of my clothes off, stepped into the shower and started scrubbing at my body. I was tempted to masturbate but that would defeat the purpose of my mission. Besides, I wanted to have an orgasm with Jason inside me.

When I emerged from the bathroom ten minutes later, my hair wet and a towel wrapped round me, he was waiting outside the door.

He gave his cheeky grin and I began to melt a little. 'You are something else,' he said wondrously. 'Just give me another ten minutes and I'll be ready to give you another big thrill.'

The arrogance of him! I had intended to use him as my starters, but instead he was using me. Hopefully, I would get more satisfaction from the main course.

I dropped the towel from my body and stood in front of him naked, my large breasts, with their elongated nipples, jiggling proudly at him. He grabbed at them and pulled me by my nipples towards him. It was obvious I wasn't in for a night of sweet, sensuous passion, but I was so aroused I didn't care.

'Take me to the bedroom,' he ordered hoarsely. 'I'm gonna be ready sooner than I thought.'

This time we both had our clothes off. I ran my hands excitedly over his strong, young flesh. There wasn't an ounce of fat on him, but he was far from skinny.

'You've got a great body,' I said, and kissed his nipples.

'I do weight training four times a week at the local gym. You ought to come along.'

'Mmm,' I murmured, knowing full well that wild horses wouldn't drag me there. I got enough exercise in bed.

He pushed my head down towards his half-erect

penis and I took it into my mouth. Within seconds he had a full hard-on once more. I continued sucking and stroking and licking the head of his cock as he moaned and writhed in ecstasy. When I'd had enough he shoved me onto my back, sprang on top of me and tried to thrust his cock inside me. He was, without doubt, a very selfish lover. I pulled away. 'No, not yet. Touch me.'

He knew what I wanted. His hand went down to my clit and he started rubbing it, far too hard. I moaned, not with pleasure, but with annoyance. He instantly took it the wrong way and before I could stop him, he was inside me again, pumping like mad, his hands on my buttocks, pulling me up from the bed onto his rock-hard cock. I felt as if I was going to burst. Pain was turning into pleasure once more. I grabbed his hand and put it back on my clit, but after a few moments he pulled it away again, arched his back, gave a terrific moan and slumped down on top of me.

I couldn't believe it. It was great to see him enjoying it so much, but what about my orgasm? But I should have known. Aries men can't wait, and they don't appear to have a thoughtful bone in their body when they get into the bedroom.

Jason clambered off me. 'I must have a fag,' he said, rummaging through his trousers.

I stared resentfully at him. I wanted to say that I didn't allow smoking in my home, but I kept quiet as he lit up a cigarette and inhaled deeply. Then he plonked himself on the bed beside me. 'That was even better than the first time,' he crowed.

'I didn't come,' I almost hissed at him.

He looked at me in surprise. 'Do you need to, then? I thought girls only came once in a blue moon, or pretended to have an orgasm.'

I was shocked. Didn't he know anything about women?

I was just about to tell him to sling his hook when he turned to me and said, with genuine feeling, 'I'm sorry, I didn't realise. I really thought you were enjoying it as much as I was.'

'I did enjoy it,' I said begrudgingly. 'If you'd kept going a bit longer and touched my clit more carefully, I would have had a fantastic orgasm.'

He scowled. He didn't like being told that he was lacking in some way. 'I'll try to make it better next time, madam,' he muttered.

I wanted to throw him out. I realised we didn't have much in common apart from a love of sex, but I was committed to at least trying to get him to satisfy me, and learn more about his sexuality, and he was rather cute when he smiled.

I said nothing, turned my back on him and pretended to go to sleep.

He puffed away on his cigarette silently for a few moments then suddenly he said, 'You've got a lovely arse,' and his hand came crashing down onto the tender cheeks of my buttocks.

I jumped out of my skin and turned on him angrily. 'Bugger off,' I shouted. My cheeks were stinging like mad. He was a strong guy.

Jason started to laugh. 'I like you even better when you're angry.'

I should have known. Arians liked a bit of spunk from their women. It boosted their ego if they were able to control and dominate it. I knew that if I fought back, he would get aroused again very quickly, and I wasn't sure if I was ready for dessert!

I sank back onto my pillow and ignored him.

He started to get irritated. 'You were begging for it at the football match. I don't even know what the final score was.'

'It'll be on Ceefax. Put the telly on and find out,' I said coldly.

'All right, seeing as you've become such a misery guts, I might as well.'

He stomped out of the bedroom and a minute later I heard the loud tones of the television.

I sighed. No orgasm, no cup of tea, and now no bloke. What had started off so well was turning into a dismal failure. But at least I had something to write about.

I opened my eyes to the sound of snoring. It was very dark. I fumbled for the bedside lamp and turned it on to find Jason lying naked on his back, fast asleep beside me. I stared at his broad, young body with a mixture of resentment and admiration. I realised that I still felt very horny. Gently, I touched his flaccid penis and it began to move a little. But he kept on snoring. A wave of anger swept over me and I grabbed his cock and began to pull on it, hard. A bit of tit for tat, I thought gleefully.

Jason's cock sprang into life, and so did he. 'What are you doing?' he shouted groggily, trying to sit up. His breath smelt of drink and I realised he must have found Ryan's beer in my fridge and helped himself whilst I was asleep.

'What does it look like?' I shouted back, angry that he was taking me and my home for granted.

'Ouch!' he squealed as I gave the nub of his penis a little pinch. 'That hurts.'

'Like you hurt me when you mauled my clit.'

He stared at me for a second or two then suddenly grinned. 'OK, OK, carry on, I like it.'

I was furious. It was obviously hurting him, but his cock was still expanding and he was starting to get that glazed look of desire in his eyes. What could I do to make him take notice and see me as a person with needs as strong as his?

The next moment was purely instinctual. I took my hand away from his cock and began to slap him, hard, with both hands, first on his chest and then all over his body.

He was stunned to begin with, but then he sprang up and grabbed my hands, laughing. 'What a little spitfire you've turned out to be.'

Using all my strength, I broke free and began my assault again. I was in a frenzy of anger and passion. I hated him, but I wanted him badly. Then I leaned forward and, without thinking, I sank my teeth into his shoulder.

He cried out, and I bit him again on the chest, and again, and again. I didn't really know what I was doing, I was so frustrated. And he accepted it all, laughing, growing more excited as I became more violent. Then suddenly, I was sitting astride him wildly, pulling at his cock and thrusting it towards my hungry pussy. It slid in like a dream and I groaned with pleasure. Jason made no move to help me, so I started bouncing up and down on him, holding his cock steady with one hand while I masturbated myself with the other. I was moaning like mad, almost there, when he reached up and pushed me off him and I tumbled ungracefully onto the floor. In an instant he was beside me, turning me onto my front and yanking me up into the doggy position. Then he entered me savagely from behind, his finger rubbing roughly at my clit. I yelled out in ecstasy, as I began to feel the crescendo of my much-awaited orgasm.

Jason kept going, thrusting so hard I thought I would split open, and I kept coming and coming. Then he came too. I wanted to deny him the pleasure, but I had no control over my actions. Afterwards, we sank together to the floor, fighting for breath.

'That was fantastic,' he said, after a while.

'Yeah, it was great,' I agreed. 'Now you can go.'

He frowned. 'Just like that? Don't you want another session? Give me half an hour or so.'

'No thanks, I've had enough,' I said coolly, dragging

myself up from the floor. 'I'm going back to bed. I'll give you ten minutes to get your clothes on and leave.'

I lay on the bed and closed my eyes as he fumbled around the room. I didn't want to look at him and be sidetracked once again by his body. I wanted to go to sleep, and get up bright and early in the morning and start writing. I'd learned a lot about Aries man, some good, some bad, but most of all, I'd learned that he wasn't what I regarded as good relationship material. Fantastic quick fucks, yes, emotional satisfaction, no.

When I opened my eyes ten minutes later, all was quiet. He'd gone.

Chapter Three
Taurus: The Hungry Bull

20 APRIL

*H*ow time flies. It's the first day of the sign of Taurus and I'm ready to start stage two of my quest. I haven't been idle since the escapade with Jason. Apart from completing the first section of my book, I've been getting in plenty of hands-on experience with Ryan, who seems hornier then ever. Although he won't admit it, I think he's actually turned on by the thought of me having sex with other guys.

At the beginning of April I began to rack my brains to think of a good way to meet a half-decent Taurean guy. Then I had a brilliant idea, simple really: I would advertise in the lonely hearts column of the local paper. The next day I placed the ad, saying I was an attractive but lonely Capricorn. I'm not really, I'm a Sagittarian, like Ryan, but Capricorns are supposed to be more compatible with Taureans than Sagittarians. I said I was looking for a physically active Taurus male to share leisure pursuits with. I had to be cryptic with the wording – it was, after all, a local freebie paper – but I felt confident I'd got the message across. Sure enough, immediately the ad appeared, I was inundated with

19

replies. After sifting through the dross I ended up with three wannabes who had sent me their photos and looked quite 'presentable'. I decided I would have to twist the rules a little and meet all three as soon as possible so that I could suss them out. I reasoned that if I didn't have sex with any of them before the first day of Taurus, I wouldn't actually be breaking the requirements of dad's will.

The first guy, Colin, was a real drip. He was about as sexy as a soggy lettuce and twice as boring. Pity, because his photo had looked so promising.

Jerry, the next bloke, was exactly the opposite. His photo was just about passable but the moment I saw him, tall and broad, with a thick mane of black curly hair, I was hooked. He put his arm round me immediately, bought me a drink and asked if I'd like anything to eat. Typical Taurus, I thought, always thinking of their stomachs. I'd already eaten. I didn't want to stay too long: I might be tempted to seduce him. But I had problems getting away. He kept stroking my hands and my arms, and kept trying to stroke my thighs. Reluctantly, I had to push him away. 'I hardly know you,' I said coyly, wishing I could grab his hand and place it inside my knickers to show him how wet I was. I could see the bulge in his trousers getting bigger, and licked my lips in anticipation, but knew I had to wait. When I finally managed to drag myself away from him, he asked to see me again the next day. It was only 7 April. There were still two weeks to go before I could start my Taurean work experience, so I had to think quick. I said the first thing that came into my mind. 'I'm off to America tomorrow, for a couple of weeks. I'll ring you when I get back.'

He seemed very disappointed. 'Whereabouts in America?' he finally asked, obviously just to show interest.

I had to lie again. Well, only a little fib, really, but in

order to succeed in my quest, it's going to be necessary to twist the truth occasionally. So, before you could say Jack Robinson, I was going on a tour of California with a mate (Zoe, my real best friend) visiting Hollywood, San Francisco, Santa Barbara and all the sights I constantly dream about but can't afford to go and see.

Jerry was impressed. When I finally managed to give him a chaste kiss goodbye, he wished me a good holiday, and said he would ring me the day after I got back to hear all about my travels.

I was delighted, knowing that I more or less had my perfect Taurean in the bag, ready and waiting, but not so pleased that I had lumbered myself with some geography revision. The next day I made a trip to the library and picked up all the books on California I could find.

I did meet the third guy on the list, Daniel, an older man in his late thirties. He was OK, quite sweet really, but not horny like Jerry. I decided to put him on the standby list just in case Jerry did a runner.

So, it's now only two days to go before I speak to Jerry again. I'm getting very excited and can't help but feel that I'll have a better time with him than I did with Jason.

Every time the phone rang, I prepared myself to hear Jerry's voice, but the day moved on relentlessly without a word from him. At midnight, I crawled into bed alone, feeling bitterly disappointed and very frustrated. I'd put Ryan off so that I could be with Jerry.

The next day I was in a right tizz. Should I ring him, or wait for him to ring me? At three o'clock I picked up the phone and dialled the work number he had given me. After all, I had a job to do and limited time to do it in.

Jerry was a deputy manager in a small renovating company. I got through to his secretary. 'Mr Johnson is away in Scotland on business at the moment,' she informed me in a posh voice.

I was dismayed. It was so unexpected. 'For how long?' I managed to croak.

'I'm not sure. It's a rush job. Two weeks, maybe three. Would you like to leave him a message?'

'No, no thank you.' I flung the phone down and burst into tears. All my best-laid plans were kaput. I couldn't afford to wait three weeks. We'd be almost into Gemini by then! After a five-minute bawl and stamping of fists on the table, I calmed down and forced myself to face facts. Reluctantly, I dragged out my standby file and found Daniel's phone number. I had told him I was going away too, but had never really imagined I would be ringing him back as I'd promised.

Daniel ran a struggling hardware shop on the edge of town. He picked up the phone almost immediately and seemed delighted to hear from me. 'Mariella! I didn't think you'd ring.' He was more perceptive than I thought. 'Of course, I'd love to see you again. A meal tonight? Yes, that's fine. I'll call for you about eight. Is that OK?'

'No!' I felt like screaming at him. It wasn't OK. I wanted to meet horny Jerry, not dippy Daniel. But I had no option, so I agreed.

Daniel was dressed in a smart, charcoal suit with shirt and tie, whereas I'd dressed down, still making sure I was wearing one of my shorter skirts, of course, with a silky black thong underneath. It was irritating my arse like crazy, but unfortunately a little bit of suffering is a necessary evil when practising the art of seduction.

Daniel stood on the doorstep, small and stocky, only my height, with a big smile on his face. He was far too dapper for my liking, but he was trying hard, and would no doubt be eager to try out his cock later on.

22

'I thought we'd go to Bellini's,' he said eagerly as we walked up the driveway to his car.

Good start, I thought. Bellini's was the best Italian restaurant for miles around. And he'd actually booked a table, yet another brownie point. I was beginning to enjoy myself.

The waiter danced attendance on us. We had the best wine and a glorious three-course meal which bloated me out and made my skirt too tight, but no matter how many innuendos and little seductive sighs and glances I made, Daniel seemed content purely to eat. Even my risqué comment about undoing my skirt and taking it off led nowhere. Daniel just kept on piling food into his mouth. I know Taureans love to eat, but they usually love sex just as much. I could see I was going to have to be a bit more obvious. After I had finished my coffee and he'd paid the bill, I edged my chair closer to his and started stroking his thigh. 'That was a wonderful meal, Daniel. Thank you so much,' I purred in my best husky voice.

Daniel stared down at my wandering hand. He seemed more embarrassed than excited.

I persisted. 'What would you like to do now? The night is young. We can go anywhere, do anything we want.' My fingers were moving upwards, almost touching his cock. I couldn't make it more obvious.

Daniel shifted. He looked unhappy. 'I, I don't –' He stopped and stared at me.

'You don't what?' I said gruffly, pulling my hand away with a sinking feeling in my heart.

'Er, nothing.' He stood up abruptly. 'Come on. Let's go.'

Once in the car, I decided to try again. I wasn't going to give up that easily. I needed this man to fulfil my quest. I leaned back into the seat and opened my legs wide. I was beginning to feel quite turned-on. Immediately I wished I was with Ryan or Jerry. I imagined

Ryan's large cock pushing into me and I moaned loudly.

Daniel kept his eyes averted and started the car up. 'I think I'd better take you home,' he said stiffly.

I turned on him, my frustration getting the better of me. 'I thought my ad was clear enough,' I said. 'Physically active, into leisure pursuits. Doesn't that spell out S-E-X to you?'

Daniel sighed and stopped the engine. We were still in Bellini's car park. 'I'm sorry, Mariella. It didn't occur to me you wanted sex. I thought you were just a lonely lady looking for company like I am. I don't think I'd be much good to you. I've never had a proper girlfriend. I think I might be gay.'

'You think! Don't you know for sure?' I asked incredulously.

Daniel shrugged. 'I've never had a boyfriend, either. I just don't seem to be very interested in sex. I did try, once, with a prostitute but I couldn't do it so she ended up wanking me off. I quite enjoyed that, but as far as anything else goes . . .' He shrugged his shoulders again.

'You're nothing like a Taurean,' I said sulkily.

'Ah! I have a little confession to make. I'm not a Taurus, I'm a Virgo. I just wanted to meet you and talk to you. You sounded so nice.'

I was fuming. What a waste of my precious time and energy. But it was no good crying over spilt milk. I forced myself to smile at Daniel. It wasn't really his fault: it was mine for being so gullible, and placing such a silly ad in the first place. Besides, I'd just been treated to one of the best meals I'd ever had. Surely that was worth something.

'You'd better take me home now,' I said quietly.

Panic set in. Ryan came round the next day and I droned on and on at him about how things weren't working out. Where on earth was I going to find a decent

Taurean now? He suggested I use his list again, but I was loathe to do that twice in a row.

Eventually Ryan shut me up by grabbing hold of me by my hair, pulling my knickers down and putting me over his knee to give my bottom a good spanking – not too hard, I might add. After a minute or two, when my wobbling cheeks were covered in red fingermarks, Ryan pushed two fingers into my pussy to see if it was wet, which of course, it was. He knew I loved being spanked. Then he made love to me in typical Ryan style, aggressively but considerately. Ryan was willing to do anything to give me an orgasm. It didn't take long before I was panting and moaning and begging for more.

When we'd finished Ryan sat me, naked, on his lap and jogged me up and down like a baby. 'There now, do you feel better?' he crooned.

I had to laugh. Feeling much happier, I planted a noisy kiss on his forehead before rushing off to find my clothes, which were scattered all over the kitchen floor.

'Get that list out, Ryan,' I called from the kitchen, 'and I'll make us a cup of tea.'

Ryan knew quite a lot of Taurean blokes, four in fact. Unfortunately, one was nearly fifty, another was married with two young children. Yet another, who sounded quite suitable, was on holiday in Tenerife, so that left just one available prospect: Mick, his best buddy, who was a bit of a jack-the-lad. I knew him quite well but had never fancied him and felt it would be a bit of a cheek to ask him to have sex with me.

'I'm sure he'd love to oblige,' Ryan said.

I was pleased. 'Does he fancy me, then?'

'Probably. But you know what he's like. Mick loves pussy. Anybody's. If I ask him to shag you, he won't let you down.'

'I'm sure he won't. But that last girlfriend he had was a real bimbo. Why on earth do you like him?'

'He's a good laugh.'

'If we ask him, will you ever speak to me again?'

'Course I will.'

'Will you speak to him again?'

Ryan grinned. 'I'm not sure about that. It's one thing asking him to shag my bird, but another thing him actually doing it and you actually enjoying it.'

'I don't think I would enjoy it.'

Ryan sighed. 'Make your mind up. We're going round in circles here and I'm getting bored.'

'OK,' I said reluctantly. 'Talk to him. Tell him what it's all about and that it'll only be a one off. And don't make any arrangements for a few days. I can't face him just yet.'

It would appear that Mick was a very busy man. He couldn't fit me into his hectic social calendar until the following week. But that was fine by me; it would give me time to do some writing and decide how to find and handle conquest number three, Mr Gemini. Ryan arranged a date for me and Mick for 9 May. I sat back and waited.

The day before I was due to see Mick, the phone rang late in the evening. It was Jerry. I was in bed, luxuriating in the aftermath of a mammoth shagging session with Ryan and waiting for him to finish in the shower.

'Jerry!' I squeaked with pleasure. 'I thought you were in Scotland.'

'I was until a few hours ago. I've just flown back from Edinburgh. I thought I'd ring you immediately, just to let you know I'm still interested, and to say I'm sorry for not ringing you before.'

'You could have rang me from Scotland,' I said petulantly.

'I know. But I've been working solidly almost twenty-four hours a day so that I could get back as soon as possible and see you.'

He sounded so sexy. I remembered how much I'd been looking forward to getting to know him. 'OK,' I said, pretending to relent, whilst grinning from ear to ear.

'Can we still get together then?' he asked eagerly. 'How about tomorrow? A meal, the theatre or the cinema? Whatever you want. Your wish is my command.'

'Anything will do me,' I said, and felt like adding, 'as long as it's followed by a good shag.'

Jerry laughed. He knew exactly what I wanted. 'I'm sure we'll work something out. I'll call for you tomorrow, about 7.30 then. OK? Right now I'm ready to hit the sack. Bye.' He blew a kiss into the phone and hung up.

Ryan came in, rubbing his hair dry. 'Who was that?'

I sprang out of bed and danced around the room in the altogether. 'That, my dear Ryan, was Jerry! He's back earlier than expected. We've made arrangements to meet tomorrow night.'

I pranced towards the shower, my boobs with their large, swollen nipples bouncing in front of me.

Ryan caught my arm. 'What about Mick? Aren't you seeing him tomorrow?'

Damn! I'd forgotten all about horny Mick. But Jerry was a much better proposition. 'Sod Mick,' I said gruffly. 'At least I fancy Jerry.'

'Thanks a bunch! After all my planning. Mick'll be devastated.' Ryan was a bit cross.

I knew he wouldn't stay cross for long. I leaned forward and rubbed my hardening nipples against his hairy chest. 'I'll make it up to you, I promise. Keep the bed warm.'

* * *

I was dressed to kill in a very short, clinging, black dress which left virtually nothing to the imagination. The Wonderbra I was wearing made my tits look huge, and the new thong – which had cost me a fortune – seemed pretty comfortable for a change. A visit to the hairdresser had turned my unmanageable shoulder-length blonde hair into stylish curls. I felt very sexy.

When he saw me, Jerry eyed me up and down and whistled appreciatively. 'You look great. I think we'd better go for a meal.'

I didn't care where we went, so long as I was with the gorgeous Jerry. We went to an Indian restaurant on the outskirts of town.

As we walked into the restaurant, Jerry put his arm round me possessively and lightly brushed my left breast with his hand. A shiver of delight ran through me.

'I love Indian food,' I said, as we were led to a secluded table in the corner of the room.

'I thought you would. It's supposed to make you feel sexy. Mind you, I doubt whether you need it.'

I laughed appreciatively. 'I don't think you do either, Jerry.'

We smiled knowingly at one another, and I felt that wonderful, familiar sensation in my pussy as it started to get damp.

The waiter handed us menus, but my eyes kept glazing over. I was far too aware of Jerry's close proximity, and the way his left hand was gently caressing my knee under the table.

'Are you having a starter?' I asked, at last.

Jerry's eyes locked into mine. 'Of course. I couldn't manage without a starter. I fancy a nice bit of pussy.'

As he spoke his hand moved slowly up my right leg to my thigh, until it reached the edge of my thong.

'Ah, I think I've found what I want,' he crooned and

began to rub my pussy very lightly through the flimsy material.

Waves of pleasure ran through me.

When the waiter came up to take our order, Jerry looked him boldly in the face and ordered for both of us, still stroking my pussy. My clit was pulsing and my thighs were wet. I was terrified the waiter could see what was going on, but I was so excited I could hardly breathe.

When the waiter had gone, Jerry pushed my legs open a bit wider and began rubbing my clit with the back of his thumb, whilst glancing casually around at the other customers.

The waiter brought us some poppadoms with a choice of dips. Jerry pulled his hand away and studied his fingers. They were soaked. 'Mmm, I'd like to taste some of that later on,' he said, staring at me with his large, brown eyes. 'But for now, I'll have to make do with a poppadom.'

I closed my legs reluctantly. My pussy wanted more. 'Let's make this a quick meal then,' I said huskily.

Jerry gave me a knowing smile, and thrust a large bite of poppadom covered with chutney into his mouth. 'There's no hurry,' he said. 'The two biggest pleasures in life are food and sex, and we can enjoy both of them here.' He leaned forward and lowered his voice a shade. 'Why don't you, my lovely Ellie, take yourself off to the ladies and get rid of that stupid bit of material covering your crotch, and then come back and enjoy your meal.'

I was speechless, utterly mesmerised by him. Obediently, I clambered out of my seat.

Jerry reached for my handbag from the floor. 'Don't forget this,' he said, handing it to me. 'You'll probably need it.'

I grabbed it from him and stumbled towards the loo. In the privacy of the cubicle I took off my thong, did a

29

wee, and wiped myself dry, my hands shaking with pleasure at the promise of things to come.

Jerry leaned forward and placed a forkful of chicken tikka masala in front of my mouth. 'Open wide,' he said.

Obediently I opened my mouth and my legs. With his left hand Jerry popped the forkful of tikka masala into my mouth. With his right hand he reached under the tablecloth, put his hand up my dress and thrust three fingers into my pussy.

'Is that nice?' he asked, looking at my mouth.

'Mmm, lovely,' I murmured, wriggling my arse and opening my legs as wide as I dared.

We'd been playing this game for over half an hour. Jerry was making me taste every mouthful of the dishes he'd ordered, before eating them himself. At the same time he was working me up into a state of frenzy. With every mouthful he was teasing me a bit more. He had started with one finger, pushing it in gently halfway, then thrusting it all the way in, gradually working his way up to three fingers.

Every so often I would glance round to see if anybody was watching us but the tables were emptying and the waiters seemed oblivious.

When he took his fingers out, Jerry would give them a little lick and say he liked the taste, before moving onto the next mouthful of food.

My legs were soaked, my dress was stained – luckily it was black – but I didn't care. I just wanted more. I pushed against his fingers and his thumb started to rub me again.

'Lovely little button,' he murmured between mouthfuls.

I was almost at the point of no return. I forgot where I was and gave a little moan. Jerry pulled his fingers out, and I stared round the room in embarrassment in case anybody had heard.

Jerry seemed unconcerned as he licked his fingers again and put a large mouthful of prawn curry into his mouth.

'Try this,' he said, turning to me with another forkful of something different.

'I can't,' I whispered. 'I'm full up.'

'No, you're not.' Jerry pushed the forkful into my mouth and thrust what felt like four fingers into my gaping hole. I gasped with a mixture of pain and pleasure.

'Ah, I think you are full up now,' Jerry said, his eyes looking at me innocently.

'Please, don't.'

'Don't what?'

'Stop. I think I'm going to come,' I said desperately.

Jerry's fingers carried on pumping into me whilst the nub of his thumb continued to massage my clit.

'No, no,' I murmured, feebly trying to push him away whilst my eyes locked into his, begging him to carry on. Then my whole body started to shudder. I hardly knew what I was doing as I tried desperately to cover up my movements. I wanted to moan out loud, but instead I let out a few little whimpering noises, closed my eyes and momentarily entered the gates of heaven.

When I opened my eyes a few moments later, Jerry was sitting calmly, his hands in his lap, smiling at me. 'That was a lovely meal,' he said. 'I think it's about time we paid the bill and left.' He glanced at his watch. 'We might just have time for dessert somewhere else.'

I nodded, stood up in a daze and tried to smooth out the lower half of my crumpled dress.

The waiter came up with the credit card bill for Jerry to sign. Whilst Jerry bent down to sign it, the waiter's eyes turned to me and purposefully made a beeline for my crotch. He smiled at me lecherously and an acute shaft of embarrassment shot through me as I realised he knew what we'd been up to and had probably been watching us all the time.

Jerry left him a huge tip and we hurried out of the nearly empty restaurant.

'He knew, the waiter knew,' I babbled as we closed the door behind us.

Jerry gave his charming, placid smile. 'Of course he did. Couldn't keep his eyes off us. We must have brightened up his evening no end.'

Stunned, I wondered how many other people had known what we were doing. But I didn't have time to ponder on it. Jerry was bundling me into the car as quickly as possible.

'Where are we going now?' I asked as he drove off at a speed. I was glad he'd only drunk one glass of wine.

'I know a nice little place where we can finish our meal,' he said.

I reacted immediately. 'You're making me wet again,' I whispered, lounging back in my seat. I pulled my dress up to reveal my swollen pussy.

Jerry laughed. 'You're insatiable. Looks like you're just about ready for dessert, and I'm still ravenous.' He took one hand off the wheel and reached down to stroke his cock through his trousers.

I watched his cock spring to life. Suddenly, I wanted to pleasure him too. I leaned over and unzipped his trousers. He had no pants on and his hungry cock burst out immediately, thick and hard, ready for action.

I put my head down, thrust my bare arse into the the air, and took him into my mouth.

'I think I'm really going to enjoy dessert,' he said after a few moments.

Jerry drove into a little clearing in the woods. Before I had time to protest, he was pulling me out of the car into the cold night air. I began to shiver but he took no notice. Instead, he pushed me up against the car, yanked my dress up over my head and pulled it off so that I was naked. My nipples shrunk and stuck out like two small buttons.

'There's a blanket in the boot. I'll get it. Stay there,' he ordered.

He got the blanket and wrapped it tightly round me. It was thick and warm.

'Come on,' he said urgently, and pushed me towards the trees.

I trusted him completely. It felt strangely sensual to be walking along beside him with nothing but a blanket and a pair of shoes to cover me up.

After a few minutes we reached another small clearing, with short dry grass and the sound of flowing water nearby. He'd obviously been there before.

He pulled the blanket from me and laid it on the grass. Then he picked me up and gently laid me down.

He stood over me, yanking at his clothes and throwing them to the ground until he too was naked. He had a lovely thick-set body, a bit hairy, but one hundred per cent male. I watched him, mesmerised, forgetting how cold I was.

'Do you like doing it under the stars?' he asked, towering above me, his rigid cock pointing towards me.

'Yes, but I've never done it on such a cold night with only a blanket to keep me warm.' I started to shiver again.

Jerry sank down and laid his warm naked body over mine. 'I'll keep you warm,' he murmured, rubbing his rock-hard cock against my tummy.

I reached down and grabbed him, suddenly longing to feel him in my hands. He gave a loud moan when my cold fingers encircled him, but when I started to masturbate him, he pulled away.

'Not yet. I want my dessert. You taste so lovely.' He

rolled off me and gently started to lick and nibble my neck around the throat.

I shuddered with delight. Then, with slow, sensuous flicking movements of his tongue, he began to taste my body. When he reached my nipples he rolled each one round his tongue and bit them gently, so that I cried out in pleasure. When he poked his tongue into my navel I felt another shaft of ecstasy. He was gradually transporting me into a different world. As he neared that part of me which was again wet and hungry, I began to get impatient. I pushed his head down onto my sopping-wet pussy, but he quickly pulled away.

'Naughty Ellie,' he crooned. 'You must learn to be patient. The best things come to those who wait.' And suddenly he flipped me over and started moving downwards with his tongue over my back. When he reached my arse, he gently pulled my cheeks apart and slid his tongue down my crease until he found the nub of my anus where he stopped and started to suck harder.

My mind flipped. This was something else. I started to moan with pleasure, thrusting my arse into his face for more.

He started getting rougher and I loved it. Without warning he yanked me up onto all fours and finally thrust his tongue deep into my open pussy from behind. I cried out in pleasure and begged out for more, so he moved faster, pushing his tongue in and out with slick, sharp movements, finding my clit, sucking it, leaving it and then thrusting his tongue into my pussy over and over again until it began to hurt and I thought I was going to burst.

Suddenly he stopped and I felt his cock rubbing my anus and I thought he was going to enter me there – and I would have welcomed him – but he didn't. Instead, with one clever movement he pushed me onto my back and thrust himself deep inside me, making me scream out with pleasure.

From a distance I heard my own voice yelling at him, 'Fuck me, you bastard. Harder, harder,' as I rubbed myself.

And he did, so hard that I felt myself coming again and again.

Then he came too, spilling his load into me, calling me a bitch and a whore, before he sank down with exhaustion onto my naked body.

I loved the feel of his heavy body tight against mine, keeping me warm. Gently, I ran my fingers through his hair and kissed his head. 'Thanks, Mr Taurus,' I murmured. 'You'll come pretty high in my ratings, I'm sure.'

He didn't stir. He had no idea what I was talking about.

I sank into bed, knackered and cold, at 2 a.m.

I have promised to see Jerry again. He really does want to hear about my holiday in America and I'd love to tell him all about it, but I doubt whether I'll have the time. Besides, I really must move on. Mr Gemini beckons.

Chapter Four
Gemini: The Double Act

21 MAY

Well, here I am on the very first day of the sign of Gemini without a whiff of a Gemini bloke, and I haven't panicked once. That's because in two days time I'm off to Ibiza on a Club 18–30 holiday for two weeks with my best mate, Zoe, who has convinced me that I'm sure to find a suitable candidate for my quest amongst the horny, young studs in our group. If not, the clubs are bound to be full of eager Geminis.

Zoe is a wonderful mate. She's a bit barmy, says what she thinks, and loves to show off, but she has a heart of gold and will do anything for me. She's great looking – a bit on the thin side with hardly any boobs at all – but she has a lovely smile and gorgeous big, blue eyes. She oozes sex appeal and blokes love her. But as far as I'm concerned, the best thing about Zoe is her love of sex. She can shag more men in one day than I can in a week. She's experimented with just about everything, including orgies and S & M. She enjoys doing things that I've never done, like dressing up in black leather and whipping stupid blokes' arses, but she enjoys a good shag even more. She hasn't got a regular boyfriend at the moment so she's really horny. Having Zoe with me on holiday should make my life a lot easier. She's promised to ask any suitable men what star sign they are and help me get to know them.

I'm a bit sorry to be leaving Ryan, but he understands I need to get away and do my own thing and find a Gemini. Besides, I'm sure he won't be on his own for long. His tarty ex-girlfriend, Gemma, is still coming on to him and seems willing to drop her knickers any time. I know Ryan is just using her to get his own back at me, and there's nothing I can do about it, but I can't help feeling jealous. Ryan's my bloke and I want to keep him. But I want to finish my task, too. I suppose it's just too much to have my cake and eat it. Roll on Ibiza.

Zoe grabbed my arm, waking me up. 'Ellie! Look at him, over there. He's drop-dead gorgeous. I think he might be in our group.'

We were waiting in the departure lounge at Gatwick airport. It was 10 p.m. The flight should have left at 9.30, but the information on the board was still showing DELAYED, WAIT IN LOUNGE. I was really pissed off.

Zoe was jigging about in her seat, craning her neck to keep an eye on the fit bloke she had just spotted. 'I think I'll go over and introduce myself,' she said.

'Zoe!' I wasn't in the mood to encourage her. I just wanted to get on that plane.

'Be back in a mo.' Zoe dumped her backpack in my lap and dashed off towards the duty-free area.

I slumped back into my seat and closed my eyes again.

I opened my eyes. For a brief moment I was confused, wondering where I was. Then I remembered. The departure lounge had emptied out a lot and I was sitting alone in my row of chairs. Zoe was nowhere in sight. Her backpack was still in my lap.

Panicking a little, I glanced up at the information board, but there was no change. I began to get the hump again. Zoe had deserted me, and it looked like we were never going to get to Ibiza.

A few moments later, Zoe appeared. She looked flushed and excited, her short, spiky hair in disarray, her eye make-up smudged.

'Oh, Zoe! You haven't?' I gasped.

She grinned. 'I have. He's fantastic. Knows how to shag too. I feel well and truly fucked.'

'Where?' I asked, beginning to feel a bit horny myself.

'In the gents' loos. He sneaked me in when no one was there. It was quite a knee-trembler, I can tell you.'

I started to laugh. 'You're incorrigible, Zoe.'

'Big word, Ellie. You must be jealous.'

'You bet I am. What sign is he?'

Zoe frowned. 'I forgot to ask. Come to think of it, I don't even know his name, but he's on our flight, so I'll find out then.' She looked up at the information board. 'Still the same, then. Great! That means I've got time to go and clean myself up.' She grabbed her backpack off my lap and dashed off to the ladies.

The flight took off at eleven, two hours late. Everybody was puffing and moaning, feeling tired and hungry, but very relieved to be on the move.

Zoe had a window seat. She loved flying. I was a bit more nervous.

I sank back into my seat next to her and closed my eyes, still tired.

But there was no peace. Zoe nudged my elbow hard and whispered excitedly, 'Ellie, that's him. He's in the aisle next to us.'

Reluctantly, I opened my eyes and glanced across. A tall, slim, good-looking guy was putting his hand luggage in the overhead compartment. When he turned round to take his seat, he saw Zoe gesticulating at him and grinned with delight.

'Fancy meeting you here.'

Zoe didn't seem to mind the corny line. 'Hi – again,' she said, almost shyly.

Two more guys stopped in the aisle and sat down noisily beside Zoe's man.

He leaned across. 'These are my mates, Ben and Steve. I'm Tony, by the way.'

Zoe was in her element. 'I'm Zoe,' she shouted across. It was getting a bit noisy. People were still piling onto the plane. 'And this is my best mate Mariella, but everybody calls her Ellie.'

Three pairs of eyes raked us up and down. Ben and Steve were nowhere near as good-looking as Tony, and I didn't fancy them.

Ten minutes later the plane finally took off. The seat next to mine was empty.

We had barely unfastened our seat belts before Tony plonked himself down beside me. 'You don't mind, do you, Ellie? Zoe and I met at the airport.' He smiled knowingly, his eyes darting towards my enticing Wonderbra cleavage.

Zoe turned to me. 'Perhaps we could change seats, Ellie. Better still, why don't you go and sit with Ben and Steve?' She smiled at me, her beautiful, large, blue eyes pleading.

I had no option. Sighing, I got up and squeezed past the hunky Tony, who only seemed to have eyes for Zoe (and my boobs) and went to sit on the end seat, next to Ben. He grinned at me. 'Looks like our Tony's got it made,' he said loudly, ogling me up and down.

I gave a watery smile and turned away. Even if he was a Gemini, I was totally turned off. And Steve looked no better, with his stupid grin and outdated wedge haircut.

I ignored all attempts from both of them to flirt and

eventually they took the hint. After eating a dry, taste-less roll with plastic ham and a limp salad, followed by a slimy creme caramel, washed down with weak, cold coffee thrown at us by a miserable air hostess, I sank back in my seat and once more closed my eyes.

I was woken by funny little noises coming from across the aisle. I looked over at Zoe and Tony. They were covered by a blanket with only their heads showing. Zoe was wriggling and giggling.

'No guesses what they're up to,' said Ben.

Zoe saw me watching and winked, before ducking her head back under the blanket. I suddenly felt very lonely. I wished Ryan was with me. He always managed to get his hand inside my knickers when we were on a plane. The thought of him doing it to me now was almost unbearable. I felt so horny.

Ben must have been aware of my feelings, because he suddenly put his hand on the inside of my right thigh and started to caress it, slowly moving towards my crotch. For a moment I was tempted. My pussy was still burning with thoughts of Ryan. Then I remembered that I didn't fancy Ben and was saving myself for a Gemini. I picked up Ben's calloused hand and dumped it in his lap. 'I'm not interested,' I hissed.

I looked across at Zoe and Tony again. Zoe's eyes were tightly closed, a spasm of ecstasy etched on her face. Her body was jerking wildly beneath the blanket. Tony seemed spaced out. For a split second I hated Zoe, and the gorgeous Tony who, I had to admit, I fancied like crazy. Then I felt guilty. Zoe was my best mate and she deserved him. I was bound to find a fit Gemini soon.

It was 4 a.m., and ironically I couldn't sleep. Zoe was whacked out, lying naked on the bed on her back with her legs wide open, lightly snoring. It was a hot night and the room appeared to have no air-conditioning.

Still, what did one expect on a cheap Club 18–30 holiday in San Antonio.

Feeling fed up, I decided to take a walk. The hotel was very close to the beach and I was longing to feel the sand beneath my feet and watch the waves coming in. I threw on a pair of shorts and a T-shirt and sneaked out of the room. It was eerily quiet in the corridor. But when I reached the bar area downstairs, there were still several people milling around.

As I reached the front entrance, somebody tapped me on the shoulder. 'Hi, Ellie. Fancy meeting you here.'

It was Tony. I'd know that voice and that same old chat-up line anywhere. I spun round to face him. 'I'm surprised you're not shagged out,' I said caustically.

He laughed. 'Yeah. Zoe's quite a girl. But I can't sleep. Probably too excited. How about you?'

'I slept too much at the airport and on the plane. Now I'm wide awake. I'm going for a walk along the beach.'

'Mind if I come with you?'

My heart started to beat a bit faster, but I played it cool. 'Please yourself.' I turned on my heels and let him follow me out of the swing doors.

It was dark, but warm and humid. After a few minutes walking in silence, Tony said, 'You're going the wrong way. The beach is that way.' He pointed in the opposite direction and stared at me with a half smile on his face.

I was furious, but desperate not to show it. 'OK, Mr Clever Clogs. You lead the way.'

He took my hand and pulled me along. I liked the feeling. When we reached the beach, I flung off my sandals and dug my feet deep into the sand. Tony copied me, laughing. Then I ran towards the sea and waded in up to my knees. The water wasn't as warm as I thought it would be, so I dashed out again, gasping. Tony copied me again, imitating my movements, squealing at the cold water.

41

After a few more moments of laughing and frolicking around the water's edge, I ran back onto the dry sand and flopped down. Tony followed me and sank down beside me, pulling me into his arms and kissing me hard, his tongue delving deep into my mouth.

It felt good. For a few moments I responded, darting my tongue in and out of his mouth, thrusting my body against him to let him know how eager I was to be fucked. Then I suddenly remembered Zoe, and pulled away. I wasn't into the habit of doing the dirty on my friends. 'Bastard,' I said, and rubbed my lips. 'What about Zoe?'

He sat up and shrugged. 'What about Zoe? I like her, she's great, but I like you too. The first moment I saw you on that plane I thought, "What a cracker."' He turned to stare at my boobs. 'You've got great tits, you know. I'd love to suck them while I'm fucking you.'

My nipples sprang into action, straining against the thin T-shirt. I desperately wanted a good shag, but Zoe would kill me if she found out. Sighing, I said, 'I fancy you like mad, Tony, but I'm not going to spoil things for Zoe.'

Tony put his arm round my shoulders. 'Please. It's a lovely night. We could do it here. Nobody would see us.' His hand found my right breast and began squeezing.

I surrendered for a few seconds, then pushed him off again. 'No, I can't do it.'

He pouted. 'OK. Have it your way. I won't touch you again.'

I stood up and made a half-hearted attempt to run off, but he ran after me and yanked me back down onto the sand.

'Don't go. Stay here and talk to me,' he pleaded.

'What about?' I was shaking.

'Have you got a boyfriend?'

'Yes. His name's Ryan.'

'Doesn't he mind you coming away on your own?'

'No. We've got a good thing going. He does his thing, I do mine. I suppose you'd call it an open relationship.'

'Lucky you. So why won't you let me shag you?'

I stared at him incredulously. 'You know why. Because of Zoe. She's a good mate. For some reason – I can't think why – she likes you a lot.'

Tony grinned. 'So do you.'

I played the innocent. 'So do I what?'

'Like me, of course.'

'I think you're very good-looking, and very horny, and you turn me on, but I don't think I like you very much.'

'So, I turn you on, do I? Wouldn't you love to have my cock inside you right now, sliding up and down your wet pussy, making you come?' He started rubbing his crotch.

I tried to ignore him, tried to hate him, but my pussy was already embarrassingly wet with desire.

After a few moments of rubbing himself, Tony unzipped his shorts and pulled out his huge cock.

I gasped and looked away quickly. It was too much. He was teasing me. He knew how much I wanted it.

He started to masturbate himself vigorously. 'I want to stick it in your hot, sweet pussy,' he crooned, staring at me with round, blue eyes. 'I bet you feel lovely, really wet and horny.'

I was mesmerised by the movement of his hand on his cock. My pussy was wide open, begging for it. I knew I should run away, stop myself from doing something I would regret later, but I couldn't. So I just sat there, watching him.

'Take your T-shirt off. Let me see those beautiful tits,' Tony demanded.

Like a zombie, I obeyed.

Tony eyed my breasts, with their elongated nipples begging to be plucked and sucked, with delight. 'Lovely,' he murmured, pulling on his cock harder.

I leaned towards him, my mouth open, my nipples rock hard and tingling, and my shorts sopping wet.

He backed away, smiling that infuriating half smile of his. 'Hey. Steady on. You mustn't let Zoe down. You can only imagine you're being shagged. Take your shorts off and make yourself come.'

I shook my head, suddenly feeling resentful. How dare he tease me by tossing himself off without giving me anything in return. I wanted to feel his fingers on my clit. I could do it to myself any time.

Tony started moaning. 'Ellie, Ellie. I can feel myself inside you. You feel so good, so soft, so warm, your cunt is grabbing at my cock sucking it in, oh, so slippery. Ahhh.' He came with a long moan, spilling his creamy juice into his hand.

I stared at him, trembling, wondering where all the spunk was coming from after his sessions with Zoe. Suddenly I was glad that he hadn't touched me, glad that I wasn't a traitor to my best mate. But it had been a close shave. I'd wanted him so much, still did. My pussy was desperate to be filled and my breasts were aching. I had to find my Gemini soon.

Tony recovered quickly. He handed me my T-shirt. 'Put it back on quickly, before those gorgeous tits of yours get me going again.'

I slipped it on. 'Thanks for not doing it with me,' I said. 'You won't tell Zoe anything about tonight, will you?'

'Of course not. Sorry you didn't come, but it was your choice.'

'I know.' I stood up awkwardly, feeling tired and depressed.

We walked back towards the hotel in silence.

As we reached the main door I remembered something. 'Oh, by the way, what sign were you born under?'

Tony gave me a funny look. 'Why do you want to know?'

'No real reason. I'm an astrologer.'

'I'm a Gemini. The sign of the twins. I am a bit of a Jekyll and Hyde, I suppose.'

My heart somersaulted. A Gemini! And I'd asked him not to shag me. Now it was too late. Tears sprang to my eyes.

'See you later then,' Tony said. 'I'll only have eyes for Zoe, if that's the way you want it.'

I nodded dumbly and watched him stride purposefully towards the lift. I had really mucked up this time. Tomorrow I would have to start looking for another Gemini who I fancied and get him to shag me properly. Suddenly I laughed. Tony had just proved what a typical Gemini he was by talking his way through an imaginary shagging session with me. I had something to write about already. If the real thing was half as good with the next Gemini, I'd be a very happy bunny indeed.

Zoe and I had been at the hotel for three days now and I still hadn't found my Gemini. Feeling very guilty about deserting me for Tony on the plane, Zoe had excelled herself on my behalf during the next few days by finding out the sun sign of every available man on our trip. Besides Tony there were two other Geminis but they did nothing for me. My pussy remained stubbornly dry when I tried to chat them up, so I gave up on them. Ben and Steve were still buzzing around me like hungry flies in their wasted efforts to turn me on. I had warmed to them a bit and found some of their antics amusing, but no way did I want either of them to shag me. Besides, they weren't Geminis.

I began to get a bit worried that my hormones were up the creek and I'd never feel randy again. Then I met André, one of the waiters. He was half-French, half-Spanish, and very sexy indeed. Every time his big, brown eyes locked into mine, my heart flipped and my knickers got wet. It was a relief to feel normal again.

On the third evening Zoe and I were going to a club. She had reluctantly agreed to leave Tony behind in order to help me in my quest. Right now she was meeting him in the bar for a pre-club drink before whisking me off into the moonlight.

I was standing in front of the mirror, painstakingly putting my make-up on, when she burst into the room.

'Guess what?' she said excitedly.

'You and Tony want to get married,' I joked.

She laughed. 'No way. It's André, your waiter. He's a Gemini.'

I spun round. 'What? How do you know?'

'He's having a birthday party tonight on the beach. We're both invited. And Tony, of course.'

I ran over and hugged her. 'Zoe, you're an angel. He's got to be the one.'

'What about the club? I take it you don't want to go tonight.'

'You bet I don't. I'm going to get myself all dolled up for André. I know he fancies me too. If I haven't shagged him by this time tomorrow, I might as well give up and go home.'

Zoe laughed. 'Good luck. I'll go and tell him we'll be at his party.'

When she'd gone I started jigging round the room with excitement. Suddenly, everything seemed much rosier.

I looked up into André's eyes and teetered over. André reached out and caught me before I fell onto the sand. I was drunk, but not too blitzed to feel a tingle of excitement as André's arms encircled my waist. All I was wearing was a skimpy red dress. No bra, no knickers, not even a thong. The feel of the warm air blowing up my dress and embracing my naked pussy and buttocks was really making me horny. I had latched on to André from the word go. Now, several hours later with a dozen or so vodkas inside me, I was ready for anything.

I didn't want André to let me go. I flung my arms around his neck and pushed my tits against his chest. 'Dance.' I giggled, tottering around in the sand, pulling him with me. The music was still going and there were plenty of other revellers trying to move their weary, drunken bodies in time to the music. I could see Zoe and Tony standing up clasping one another on the outskirts of the crowd, pretending to dance, whilst Tony's hands raked over Zoe's bare arse. She didn't care. Another couple I didn't know were humping away on the sand with quite an audience around them.

I wanted some of it too. I reached out for André's hands and placed them on my buttocks. He grabbed my cheeks and squeezed them. I knew we were well on our way.

After a few moments of smooching, I pulled away and took André's hand. 'Let's go somewhere a bit more quiet,' I said in my best sexy voice.

He resisted. 'No. I stay to end. It's my party.'

Damn! Of course he had to wait until the party was over. At this rate it would probably be daylight before I could sample his wares, unless he was willing to shag me in front of everybody, and somehow I didn't think he was the type. He seemed quite shy for a Gemini.

I ran my hand through his long, dark hair which was usually tied back, but was flowing loose tonight. 'OK. I'll wait.'

I decided not to drink any more so that I didn't end up flat on my back, incapable of enjoying myself.

The party raged on. I watched André circulating around his guests, flirting with every girl around, and I nearly threw up with jealousy. But he always came back to me, his sensual lips brushing mine, his eyes full of promise.

Zoe and Tony ended up giving a full-blown shagging exhibition. Zoe was so zonked out she didn't know whether she was coming or going. I hated Tony for using her in that way, but I know she didn't mind. Once in the throes of sex, Zoe was oblivious to everything.

André watched Tony's naked buttocks heaving up and down over Zoe's body. 'Isn't that your friend?' he asked.

I nodded, feeling a bit ashamed, glad now that I hadn't pressured André to shag me in front of everybody.

André moved behind me and put his arms round my waist. I could feel his cock pressing against my bum. 'I would very much like to do that to you later on,' he whispered into my ear.

I gave a small shudder of delight, and nodded, pressing my arse back against his cock.

The party wore on, slowly. I was desperate to get it off with André, and he knew it.

About six in the morning, with daylight already on its way and virtually everybody gone, I turned to André expectantly.

He nodded and took my hand, leading me off in the opposite direction to the hotel.

'Where are we going?' I asked.

'To a house nearby. There's somebody I want you to meet.'

I was intrigued. 'Who?'

'Wait and see.'

André began to move very fast, pulling me along behind him. I had difficulty keeping up. Then we arrived at a small, white house up a side road, just off the beach. He pushed open the door.

'Allo! Phillipe,' he called.

A door swung open and a man swept through in a wheel chair. I gasped with shock. His face was exactly the same as André's, but his long, dark hair was tied back into a ponytail.

André gestured proudly. 'This is my twin brother, Phillipe. Phillipe, this is Mariella. She's from England.'

Phillipe smiled at me. He had the same warm, sexy eyes as his brother.

'Hello,' I said, unsure of where this unexpected turnaround was heading, but having a shrewd idea.

'Phillipe was injured in a car accident five years ago. He can't walk, but in every other way he is a normal man.' André stared at me pointedly, and I knew for sure what he wanted.

Phillipe moved his wheelchair nearer. 'You are very beautiful, Mari –'

'Call me Ellie,' I said, wondering what on earth to do. I wasn't sure how to handle a guy in a wheelchair.

André put his arm round me. 'Phillipe and I share everything,' he said. 'I owe it to him. I was driving the car that made him like this.'

There were tears in André's eyes. 'Please, Mariella. We'd both be honoured if you would share our bed.'

He placed his hand on my neck and started running his fingers lightly down my arm, until he came to my breasts. With a slick, darting movement, he brushed his fingers across my nipples. Then without a word, he took my hand and led me into the bedroom. Phillipe followed in his wheelchair.

The bed was huge, and I wondered if the brothers always slept together. Part of me wanted to run – I wasn't prepared for this – but another part of me was beginning to feel excited.

So I stood in docile acquiescence whilst André slipped off my dress and made me stand naked in front of them. Both eyed me appreciatively, the same look of desire on their faces.

André picked me up and laid me on the bed. Then he helped Phillipe, who was still fully dressed, onto the bed beside me. Finally he undressed himself and paraded his fine body in front of us. He was tall and slim, like most Geminis, but well-muscled and brown. His cock was already standing proud and erect.

I breathed in deeply, suddenly feeling very excited. As André lowered himself onto the bed on the other side of me, Phillipe reached out and touched my breasts. My nipples sprang to attention and I started to respond to his gentle touch. André reached down and put his hand between my legs, gently pushing them apart. Then he thrust a long, narrow finger deep into me. My juices drenched his finger as he explored inside me. I closed my eyes and relaxed. Phillipe continued to roll my nipples between his thumb and fingers, whilst André gradually extended his finger-fucking to three fingers and speeded up his movements.

I began to gyrate my body, encouraging them, egging them on to do it a bit harder. I was thoroughly enjoying the feeling of having my tits and pussy pleasured at the same time.

After a few moments André pushed me onto my side so that I was facing Phillipe who had undone his trousers and was proudly displaying his cock. I glanced down at it, engorged and ready, and felt pity for him, a man of his youth and looks relying on his brother to bring him some pleasure. I took his cock in my hand and began to caress it. He moaned softly.

From behind, André pulled my left leg up and held it so that my pussy was wide open. 'Put Phillipe's cock in there,' he whispered into my ear.

I did as I was told. Phillipe helped as much as he could but his wasted legs made it difficult for him. He used his hand to help push his cock up and down inside me. It felt good. André continued to hold my leg in the air so that Phillipe could move as freely as possible. With his other hand, he massaged my buttocks and ran his fingers along the crease of my anus. Phillipe began to moan more heavily. He was close to coming. As Phillipe finally spurted his creamy spunk inside me, André found the nub of my anus and pushed a finger into the tight hole. I shuddered with delight as the heavenly feeling of being invaded in two places at once began to take hold.

But it was all over too quickly. After Phillipe's ejaculation, the brothers pulled away from me. I was very disappointed. Then suddenly André was on top of me, pushing me down against the pillow and thrusting his rigid cock into my spunk-filled pussy. He raised his body a little and fingers began to rub my clit. A few seconds later I realised they were Phillipe's, not André's. My body was on fire.

I started to moan for more, sucking André's cock deep inside me, willing him not to stop. He thrust into me harder, making me scream out with pleasure. I arched my back and crushed my tits violently against his chest. I was on the brink of exploding. André suddenly came, loading my pussy with yet more cream, making it shudder with delight. All the while Phillipe's fingers were gently massaging my swollen clit, helping to bring me closer to heaven. Just as André started to relax, I felt myself go. Huge shudders of exquisite delight racked my body. André reached up and pulled on my hardened nipples, whilst Phillipe continued his relentless teasing of my engorged button. For a few moments I was in seventh heaven.

I put my dress back on. Phillipe and André sat on the bed, side by side, watching me.

'You don't have to go,' André said quietly. 'You could sleep with us, here, in this bed. We'd love you to stay and keep us warm.'

So they did sleep together. Funny set-up! I declined their offer. 'Zoe will be wondering where I am,' I said lamely.

Phillipe's large, brown eyes locked into mine. He looked very happy. 'Merci, Elleee.' His English was not as good as André's. I was beginning to see the differences between the two of them now. But I couldn't get involved. Didn't want to get involved. I had writing to do.

André saw me to the door. It was already daylight so I would have no problem finding my way back to the hotel on my own.

'Thank you for being so kind to Phillipe,' he said, 'and for giving me so much pleasure. You are a lovely girl, Ellie. Perhaps we could do it again before you go back to England?'

I shrugged. 'We'll see. I'll be around the hotel for a while yet, so I'll let you know.'

André smiled wistfully. He knew the final curtain had been called and that I had no intention of repeating this night's fascinating performance.

Chapter Five
Cancer: The Water Baby

22 JUNE

*T*he day after I got back from Ibiza I began my search for Mr Cancer. I had a feeling he was going to be a bit elusive so I wanted to get a head start.

Now we're into the first day of Cancer and I'm no further ahead. I know what Cancerians like: water, water and more water. I've been down to Brighton, strolled along the pier and the front, driven to the Marina and looked at all the boats, and even gone into a boatyard and expressed interest in a boat I didn't like and couldn't afford, even with the money from my father's inheritance. I've walked along the Thames, visiting umpteen pubs on the way, mostly with Ryan, and enquired about a possible membership to a yacht-ing club, but seeing as I don't have a clue about boats, my enquiry was not treated seriously.

Cancerians are also very domesticated creatures. They often end up in the catering profession. I thought about going to cookery evening classes – god knows, I need them – but upon enquiring at the local school I was politely informed that the term was just ending and they would not be starting up again until September. I felt like a right plonker; I only left school four years ago. Mind you, I didn't go to university. After achieving one measly A level in English lit, I gave up the idea of being a high-flyer and got a job as a dogsbody in an office. In my spare time, which has been precious little since I met Ryan just over a year ago, I helped my father out with his astrology, learning as much as I could in the process. But my knowledge of astrology doesn't make it any easier to find out a bloke's birth sign. I can't just go up to guys in the street, or anywhere come to that, and say, 'Hey! What sign are you?' Zoe doesn't mind doing it, but then I'm not Zoe and I can't keep asking her to find me the right bloke.

So I'm stuck and I'm beginning to panic. I've got to find a way round the problem without resorting to Ryan's list and the lonely hearts column again. I'm also broke. I'm going to have to find some work soon, otherwise I'll be thrown out of my flat. But I'm trying not to worry about it. I just want to get on with my task. Today I'm doing a round of the local estate agents. Cancer men like working with property or buildings, so who knows, I might strike lucky. If I can get some of those sexy negotiators I've seen through the windows into chat-up mode, it won't seem so crass to ask them what sign they were born under.

It was a futile day. I managed to chat up a few friendly blokes but I think they were more interested in selling me a property than getting me to open my legs. One guy in particular seemed very nice and he looked like a Cancerian: lovely eyes, a pale complexion and caring manner. He wasn't busy so we chatted for ages. I decided I really liked him, but when I asked him what sign he was, he turned out to be a Pisces. I congratulated myself on being close – he was at least a water sign like Cancer – but it wasn't close enough. I left soon after. It was no good wasting precious time. But at least I could keep him in mind for next March when the sign of Pisces finally arrived.

I got home, flaked out and irritable. I had arranged to meet Ryan at the pub later, so I made myself a quick ham and tomato sandwich and then stuffed down a huge bar of Cadbury's milk chocolate in five minutes flat. It made me feel sick but at least I wasn't feeling so sorry for myself.

When I got to the pub, Ryan was already there, but he wasn't alone. That cow Gemma was with him, hanging onto him for dear life, smiling as if butter wouldn't melt in her mouth.

'What's she doing here?' I shrieked. It was still early and the pub was nearly empty. My voice echoed round the bar.

Ryan looked embarrassed. 'All right! Keep your hair on. She's here to help you.'

Gemma pressed her breasts into Ryan's shoulder. She obviously had no bra on; her nipples were pushing hard against the thin material of her T-shirt. She was wearing the shortest skirt I'd ever seen. From the right angle you could see her knickers – what there was of them. The guy at the bar seemed to have the best view. His eyes were almost popping out of his head as Gemma moved her butt provocatively and uncrossed her shapely legs.

I stared at her resentfully, making no move to sit down.

'Don't you want to hear what I've got to say?' Gemma drawled in her sickly, sweet voice.

'Not really. I don't think there's anything you can do to help me, apart from getting the hell out of here and leaving Ryan alone.'

Gemma pouted and looked to Ryan for support. When he gave none, she stood up angrily. 'I think I'd better go then.'

Ryan grabbed her arm. 'Don't be stupid.' He turned

to me. 'Sit down, Ellie. Gemma's got some interesting news.'

Reluctantly, I sat down, and so did Gemma, smiling smugly at me. Ryan was in his element with a girl each side of him. He placed an arm around my shoulder but I shrugged it off.

I turned to Gemma. 'Say what you've got to say, then go. I know you were fucking Ryan whilst I was away but he's still my bloke. Got that?' I was itching for a fight. I hated her.

Gemma glared at me. 'Oh, really? I was going out with him long before you were. I've known Ryan since we were at school together.'

The truth hurt. I sprung towards her, fists ready, but Ryan pushed me back.

'Girls, please!' he said. 'If you don't stop it, I'll leave you both here.'

Gemma and I sank back into our seats, sulking. I had to admit that she seemed pretty keen on Ryan. If I wasn't careful, I would lose him.

Ryan turned to me. 'If you won't listen to Gemma, listen to me. Gemma's brother is a Cancer, and she thinks he might be persuaded to go out with you.'

'Oh yeah,' I quipped. 'She'd do anything to get me away from you.'

'No, seriously. I've told her all about your quest, and she wants to help. She's got a picture of him in her bag. Show Ellie the photo, Gemma.'

Gemma obediently delved into her bag and brought out a crumpled photograph which she handed to me.

I stared at it. An attractive, fair-haired man on a boat grinned back at me. He was a bit overweight, but certainly not unappealing.

'Well?' Gemma said. 'What do you think of him?'

'He looks OK, I suppose. How old is he?'

'He's nearly thirty-four. A bit old, I know, but he's young at heart. He got married when he was twenty-one, but she left him two years later. He's been divorced and on his own for nearly ten years now. He hasn't had many girlfriends and I think he gets a bit lonely. I'm sure he'd love to meet you.'

I wasn't sure I wanted to meet him. 'Does he like boats?' I asked eventually.

'Mmm. He loves them. He's got a small yacht that he takes out most weekends. He's been all over the Med in it.'

'By himself?'

'Mostly, yeah. I went with him on a trip to France once, but the weather was awful. I puked up so much it put me off boats for life.'

Nerd, I thought, but I smiled at Gemma for the first time. Annoying though it was, her brother could be the answer to my prayers. I decided I would give him a go.

'What's his name?' I asked.

'Calvin.'

'Unusual.'

'Yeah. He's an unusual sort of guy, but very nice,' she said quickly.

Ryan was beaming. 'So you'll meet him then, Ellie?'

'I suppose so. I haven't got much choice, have I?' I hated being indebted to Gemma, but beggars can't be choosers.

'I'll speak to him tomorrow,' Gemma said, 'and try to arrange a date for the day after. OK?'

'Fine.' I waited for her to leave, but she sat there, smiling at me and Ryan, knowing we were putty in her hands. She kept stroking his arm, fawning over him. I felt so jealous. I wanted to tell her to bugger off, but I kept my cool.

Eventually, Ryan made a move. 'Sorry, Gem, but Ellie and I have to go. I'll speak to you tomorrow.'

Gemma pouted, but thankfully Ryan ignored her. As we left the pub I looked back. Gemma was already propped up against the bar, flirting with the barman. I didn't doubt that by the end of the evening, she'd have another conquest under her belt. I was glad. At least it kept her out of Ryan's hair.

Brother Calvin seemed very keen to meet me. Two evenings after my session in the bar with Ryan and Gemma, I was sitting in the same pub with Calvin. Initially, I'd been very disappointed. He looked a lot older than he did in the photo. His hair was thinning badly and he was now the proud owner of a large, shiny, bald patch. He had also gained about two stone in weight, most of which seemed to be centred around a clearly defined beer gut. As he strolled towards me I was tempted to walk away, but I remembered I had no other Cancerian in line and time was running short. Then he smiled at me, his face lighting up with pleasure, and I thought he looked quite cute. So I stayed.

He wasn't the best conversationalist in the world. I had to drag everything out of him. It was hard work, but I put it down to shyness. I know that good talkers don't necessarily make good lovers, so I reckoned it must work the other way round too. He'd probably lose all his inhibitions when he got horny and excel himself on the job.

Gradually, as the evening wore on and Calvin showed signs of livening up, I talked myself into accepting the challenge. I didn't fancy him very much, but I didn't not fancy him either. And, most important of all, he seemed to like me. I'd dressed more conservatively than normal. I thought my knee-length, purple flowery skirt with matching pink top would be more in line with his tastes. I had, however, put on my Wonderbra and was exhibiting a fine cleavage. Cancer men are usually breast men, sometimes to the point of fixation. It seemed to work. By the end of the evening Calvin, tanked up with numerous pints of lager, was positively drooling over my boobs. At one point I thought he was going to bury his head in them.

When he told me he was taking his boat over to the Channel Islands at the weekend and asked if I would like to go with him, I immediately accepted the offer. A whole weekend alone with him on a boat should provide all the action I needed for the next chapter of my book. By the time we parted, and had made arrangements for the weekend, I realised he had grown on me. He certainly wasn't my usual type but there was something about him I liked.

That night in bed, I started to plan my approach. I needed to brush up on my seduction techniques for Cancerian men. I was beginning to look forward to sunning myself on the deck of Calvin's boat and enjoying all the pleasures that came with it.

The wind was howling and the rain was lashing down. It was the last weekend in June, but it felt more like March. The boat was bobbing up and down in the grey sea, a tiny blob in a huge expanse of angry water. Calvin was at the helm wearing a large, waterproof yellow jacket and black so'wester, loving every minute of it, whilst I was in the cabin heaving into a bucket. I thought of Gemma and felt a moment's compassion for her. Now we had two things in common: Ryan, and a dislike of sailing.

Calvin burst into the cabin, rubbing his hands gleefully and dripping water all over the floor.

I heaved up again, expelling the remnants of my breakfast.

Calvin rushed over, full of concern, showering me with water in the process. 'Ellie, are you all right?'

Of course I wasn't, the silly sod.

'Come and get some fresh air; it'll do you good.' He started to help me up.

I pushed him away. 'I just want to lie down and die,'

I moaned, collapsing onto the bunk. 'I can't take a whole weekend of this. I want to go home.'

To give him his due, Calvin was totally unfazed by my outburst. 'Don't worry,' he said soothingly. 'We're nearly there. In an hour or two we'll be mooring up at St Peter Port.'

'Is that in Jersey?'

'No, Guernsey. I like it better there. It's more quiet.'

'But it's bucketing down with rain, and so cold.' I shivered, as if to prove my point.

Calvin took the duvet off the other bunk and gently placed it over me. 'You stay here then, in the warm, and try to get some sleep. I've got to make sure the boat's on course.'

He picked up my bucket of sick and left the cabin. I watched him go, and found myself thinking how sweet he was. I imagined him touching my body gently, and making love to me. Hopefully tonight, when I felt better and the weather had calmed down, I could put my seduction plan into action.

Three hours later, after I'd had a nap and freshened myself up, we were still at sea. It had calmed down a lot and so had I. I no longer felt sick, but I was really cheesed off with the bouncing around. I longed to be on dry land. I put on my coat and ventured out into the air for the first time since early that morning.

Calvin was delighted to see me. 'Feel better now?'

I nodded. 'You said we would be in Guernsey in an hour – three hours ago.'

'We're nearly there, now. See the land?' Calvin pointed into the distance.

I looked up and saw Guernsey and, for the first time since I had stepped onto the boat, I felt a small thrill of pleasure. Calvin had got us here all by himself. I was impressed.

I tucked my arm into his. The yellow jacket was cold

and stiff, but at least it had dried out. He smiled at me and reached down to pat my hand affectionately. Together we stood like an old married couple watching Guernsey get closer.

I really fancied wandering around St Peter Port to find a good restaurant for dinner, but Calvin wanted to cook for me, so I let him.

The meal was pretty basic: steak, jacket potatoes and mushrooms followed by strawberries and cream, washed down with a cheap bottle of red plonk – all of which he'd brought with him – but he cooked it well and I enjoyed it.

Halfway through the meal, I started to get horny. I was fed up with all the niceties. I wanted some action.

I leaned towards Calvin, tantalising him with my breasts which were almost popping out of their Wonderbra. Either I was putting on too much weight or I needed a bigger cup.

Calvin couldn't keep his eyes off them, but he made no move to touch me, or kiss me.

When we were eating the strawberries and cream, I toyed around with the thick cream on my spoon. 'There's lots of interesting things you can do with cream,' I said, staring into his eyes.

He laughed. 'Such as?'

'Well, you know, you could lick it from somewhere nice.'

'From between your legs, you mean.' Calvin stared back at me.

I was stunned into silence. It was so unexpected. My heart gave a jolt and my pussy started throbbing. I actually started to blush like a silly teenager. 'But you don't want to, do you?' I said at last.

Calvin reached out for my hand. 'It's not that I don't want to. I think you're lovely, but –' He turned away, unable to continue.

I prodded him in the elbow, forcing him to look at me. 'But what? I want to know.'

He bit his lower lip. I noticed for the first time how full and red his lips were against his pale skin. He obviously had a very sensual side to his nature which he was keeping under lock and key at the moment. I didn't understand him at all.

He didn't answer. Then, out of the blue he reached across and pulled me towards him. 'Sit on my lap, Ellie, and I'll tell you about the only girl I've ever loved, still do, in fact.'

'Your ex-wife, you mean?'

He laughed, settling me onto his lap and placing his arm tightly around my waist. 'No, not Sarah. I hated her in the end. She left me because of Louise, the girl I'm talking about, the one I loved.' He stopped, unsure whether to continue.

'Carry on,' I urged. I was very curious as to where this was leading.

'I met Louise whilst I was still married to Sarah and fell hopelessly in love with her. We were soul mates. We both liked the same things. All Sarah ever wanted was to be fucked, over and over again. She never thought about what I wanted. Louise was different. She was my baby, my mother and my lover all rolled into one, and I was her baby.'

He stopped and looked at me pointedly. Then his eyes dropped to my breasts. I could see the desire welling up inside him and at last I was beginning to understand what he wanted, what he was really like. He was obviously a bit mixed up, but no more than most men.

I wrapped my arms around his neck and pushed my breasts into his face. 'Go on then, baby boy, my titties are all yours,' I murmured.

He went quite still as if he didn't believe what was happening.

I sighed. 'OK then, mummy get one out for you.' I pulled up my top, squeezed my right breast out from the bra cup and stuck the nipple into his mouth.

For a brief moment he was stunned. Then he started sucking on my nipple greedily, making little slurping noises like a baby. I watched him, fascinated. If this was what it felt like to feed a baby, it was very pleasant.

After a while his hand reached up and grabbed at my other breast, pulling the bra away. 'Baby want this one,' he said in a totally different, high-pitched voice.

He let go of my right breast. The nipple was elongated and red. I pushed the nipple of my left breast into his open mouth and he started to suckle me again.

From then on he changed nipples every few minutes and they began to get very sore, but something interesting was happening down below. My pussy had decided it liked breastfeeding and was pulsating with pleasure.

I wanted it to be more authentic, with Calvin on my lap instead of me on his, so without disturbing him too much, I manoeuvred myself onto the bunk and sat against the wall, straddling him across my chest like a baby and tucking my breasts, with their red, elongated nipples, into his mouth, one after the other. As he suckled and whimpered, he pressed his body against mine so that I could feel his erection against my legs.

I tried to open my legs, but his weight on me was too heavy, so I gave up and relaxed into the pleasure of being a mother.

After a while, he stopped and sat up, his plump, round face very red, his lips wet with saliva. I was fascinated and repelled at the same time. 'What's the matter, baby?' I crooned, playing his game.

'Nappy needs changing,' he said in his baby voice. He stood up and waddled to the wardrobe where he found a very large, terry-towelling nappy and some pins.

Christ! I thought. He wants me to put a nappy on

him. I'd seen a programme on television a few years ago about a man who had this fetish and I'd laughed. But I wasn't laughing now. I wasn't sure whether I was apprehensive or excited, but I would soon find out.

Calvin handed me the nappy and pins. 'Mummy, undress me,' he said, standing in front of me.

In a daze I undid his shirt and slipped it off. The skin on his chest was white and smooth, with small rolls of fat, like a baby's. His beer gut melted into the rest of his body, making him look like a round blob. But I wasn't repelled. Far from it; his body seemed to fit his fetish beautifully. It would have been much harder to carry on had he been a macho type with a hairy chest and bulging pecs. I reached for his trousers, feeling quite horny, and unzipped his flies. His trousers fell to the floor and he stepped out of them. Finally his pants. As I pulled them down, his fat, little cock sprang to life and got even fatter. I stared at it, fascinated. Calvin put his thumb in his mouth and started to suck noisily.

Part of me wanted to laugh, but I knew it would spoil it for him if I did, so I kept a serious face. I laid the towel out on the bed. I had no idea how to put a nappy on but I was willing to have a go. 'Get on the bed, darling, and mummy will put your nappy on,' I said, smiling at him.

He did as he was told, carefully lying down on the towel in the right place, and opened his legs for me.

I reached between his legs and gently caressed his balls. His cock started twitching and expanding a bit more. I pulled the towelling up between his legs and tried to do one side up with a pin. It was a bit small for Calvin so it took me a long while. All the time he was looking at my tits, which were jiggling about freely, close to his chest, and sucking hard on his thumb. When I finally managed to get the other side done, the nappy was very tight, his erection straining hard against the rough, towelling material.

He sat up, whimpering, and grabbed at my breasts again. 'More milk, mummy.'

He suckled me again, kneading my breasts with his hands, pulling hard on my nipples with his mouth and giving them little bites so that I cried out in pain – or was it pleasure? I didn't know. He kept pushing his nappy-covered groin against mine, getting more and more excited in the process.

I was getting quite excited myself. My pussy was wet and craving for release. Anything would do.

Calvin suddenly stopped sucking and gyrating and sat up. 'Mummy take nappy off. I done a wee wee.'

I gulped. Surely he hadn't really done one? I gingerly touched the nappy. It didn't feel wet. I undid the pins and took the nappy off. It was dry. I was unsure what to do, so I played it by ear. 'Naughty boy,' I said. 'You haven't done a wee wee.'

Calvin pulled a shameful face. 'Mummy smack me,' he said and turned over onto his stomach.

His pale, fat buttocks wobbled enticingly at me. I brought my hand down and hit them, hard, making my hand sting.

Calvin let out a baby wail and wriggled for more.

So I did it again, and again, and again, until my hand was sore and red and his cheeks were covered in red marks. All the time he was whining and whimpering, his hand down his front, caressing his cock.

When I stopped spanking him, he turned over and held his cock towards me. 'Sit on it, mummy. Make it feel nice.'

I pulled my skirt up and straddled across his legs. With a quick, sharp movement, he reached up, pulled my knickers to one side and thrust his cock wildly at my pussy. 'Help me, mummy,' he pleaded.

I guided his stubby, little cock into my wet hole. He

moaned with delight, reaching up to grab my breasts again. I leaned foward and dangled them into his face, whilst I jogged up and down on his cock. He was very excited, but couldn't seem to come.

After a while I began to tire of bouncing up and down. I found his balls and squeezed them gently. No joy. I pushed my tits together and thrust the two nipples into his mouth at once. No joy. I even managed to get my hand underneath his fat backside and poke two fingers into his arsehole, but although he writhed with pleasure, he still he didn't come, and neither did I.

Eventually I stopped and pulled myself off him. 'It's not working,' I said wearily.

Calvin sat up, grabbed his cock and pulled on it hard. 'It will, it will,' he cried. 'You lie down on the bed.'

Bemused, I did as I was told. Calvin loomed over me, cock in hand, and placed it between my boobs. Then he started rubbing himself against me, pressing his cock against my breasts, building himself up into a frenzy. As he was about to come he pointed his knob at my tender breasts, and gave a very loud groan. His rich, creamy spunk fired onto my excited nipples. He was in a mindless world of his own.

Almost immediately he dropped his cock and began rubbing his juices into my breasts with his hands, mois-turising them with squeezing, pummelling movements until I gasped with pleasure. When the sticky juices started to dry out, he licked my breasts clean, carefully and tenderly, like a mother cat. I was enthralled, watch-ing him. He really was a strange man.

Finally he stopped and flopped down, exhausted, on top of me. I cradled him in my arms and we both dropped off to sleep.

I woke up with severe cramp a few hours later. It was dark outside. Calvin was a dead weight on top of me. I wriggled about until he began to stir, and then managed to push him off.

He woke up and stared at me for a few seconds. Then he hung his head in humiliation. 'I'm so sorry, Ellie.'

'What for?'

'Everything. Making a fool of myself. Not giving you an orgasm. Falling asleep. I know I've disappointed you.'

'Don't be silly. I didn't do anything I didn't want to do. I've had a very interesting evening. We don't always need to have an orgasm to enjoy ourselves, you know.'

'That's not what Sarah used to say.'

I sat down on the bed beside him, hugging the duvet to my naked breasts. It was a cold night. 'What about Louise. What happened to her?'

'She left me too, in the end. She got fed up with the same old games. I tried hard to be different, I really did, but I can't seem to come unless I'm being a baby. I loved her, I cared for her in every other way. I did all the housework and the cooking during the short while we lived together, but it wasn't enough.'

I felt sorry for him, but what could I say? It was great fun being a mother to a full-grown baby for one night, but every night? No way.

'Does Gemma or the rest of your family know about your sexual preferences?'

He looked horrified. 'Of course not! Besides, didn't Gemma tell you, my mother died when I was born. Gemma's my half sister. My dad's second wife – Gemma's mother – is my stepmother. She hated me when I was a little boy.'

It all became crystal clear. Poor Calvin. He desperately needed a mother. I was glad I'd given him a few hours of pleasure. I took his head into my arms and cradled it against my breasts. His mouth opened instinctively. He slipped a nipple onto his tongue and sucked on it gently. I started to get aroused. I took his hand

and placed it against my pussy, but he immediately pulled away.

'I'll give you an orgasm tomorrow, I promise,' he said in a muffled voice.

And he did. An almighty crescendo of an explosion, which made me hit the roof. We were on our knees, naked, facing one another on the deck of the boat just after setting sail to come back to England. The sun was out for a change, and the air felt deliciously warm and sensual on our skin. Calvin had produced a vibrator, a big, thick one, which he pushed up and down and over my pussy, whilst he suckled my tits, which he had insisted on covering with cream. Afterwards we lay on the deck sunbathing. It was a glorious ending to a very different weekend.

Chapter Six
Leo: The Lusty Lion

23 JULY

*I*t's that time of the month again – and I don't mean my period. They're more or less extinct at the moment, as I'm taking the pill most of the time. When I finish this challenge next March, I think I'll come off it and try for a baby with Ryan. We were talking about it the other day and he seems quite keen.

But less of that and more about Leo. I'm really looking forward to this one. Leo is another fire sign, like me, and we're supposed to be suited. I haven't nabbed him yet, but I'm halfway there, thanks to Anna, my father's ex. I've spoken to her a couple of times since the funeral, but only very briefly. Then somewhat to my surprise, she rang me up a few weeks ago, sobbing her poor heart out. Despite the fact she's got herself another sugar daddy, she can't stop thinking about my father. We arranged to meet and have a chat to cheer ourselves up and talk about old times.

Two days later, whilst drinking coffee in Fortnums and Masons – her choice, not mine, I'm broke – she seemed to have recovered from her grief and was brimming with smiles and confidence. She's been offered a marvellous job on a new TV quiz show similar to *Who Wants to be a Millionaire?* which starts in September. Naturally she's very excited about it. We got on like a house on fire. I found myself telling her about the terms of my father's will and his unusual challenge. She was fascinated and offered to help me in any way she could. It was then that I remembered one of the most important things about Leos. They are natural celebrities and are two-a-penny in the showbiz world. Anna was sure to know lots of them. With mounting excitement, I asked her. She didn't know offhand of course, not being an astrologer, but she said she would try to find out some birthdates and get me an introduction to any men who seemed suitable. I could have kissed her feet. What a stroke of luck!

So I sat back and waited. Sure enough, true to her word, Anna rang a few days later. She really had been working hard on my behalf. She had found six Leo men, all of whom would be 'delighted' to attend one of her famous dinner parties and meet me. She hadn't let them know about my quest, of course. She told them I was a famous astrologer who would tell them their fortune. I don't know about that. Anna seems to think astrology is akin to looking into a crystal ball.

The dinner party is tonight at Anna's country cottage near Shere in Surrey. She's invited me to stay the night. I've got masses to do before I leave, so I'd better stop waffling and make a move. I need to study the map to find out how to get there, pack a few essential items – better not forget my thongs – and doll myself up for the big event.

I arrived at Anna's cottage early, looking gorgeous – I hoped – in a knee-length, gold evening dress decorated with a fringe at the bottom. The top half was strapless and low-cut, but not tarty. Leos like glitz and glamour and adore dressing up.

Anna hugged me warmly. 'You look wonderful, Ellie,' she enthused, boosting my ego.

She was wearing a plain, high-necked, black silk dress, which revealed very little flesh but somehow hugged her figure to perfection and made her look remarkably sexy. Her short, fair hair was cut in the latest style, casually spiky and supposedly unkempt, giving her sweet face an innocent baby look which added to her sex appeal. I felt a stab of jealousy but it quickly passed. I tossed back my long, blonde hair and stepped into the hall with confidence.

Anna's new man, Lester Graham, who used to host a quiz show back in the 1970s, was waiting in the lounge. He stood up to meet me and smiled with welcome, but I was so shocked by his wrinkles and grey hair that I stood for a few moments in limbo, mouth wide open, gawping at him. I knew Anna had a penchant for sugar daddies, but this one looked years older than my father.

Anna linked her arm into Lester's and smiled at me expectantly. I pulled myself together and gave Lester one my nicest smiles. He leaned forward and gave me a peck on the cheek. 'It's lovely to meet you, Ellie.'

The three of us sat on the sofa, Lester in the middle beaming at both of us. I felt awkward with him there. Inside I was bristling with dislike. I wanted Anna to myself.

'The boys won't be long,' Anna giggled, nuzzling her head against Lester's neck. 'Dinner will be at eight.'

It took me a few seconds to realise that 'the boys' were my Leo guests.

After half an hour of stilted conversation, dominated by Lester's dreary voice, my first Leo arrived.

By the time Anna had served up dessert, the eight of us – one of my merry men hadn't turned up – were in full swing. All five Leos were good company and one of them, a man in his early forties called Marlon, had us in fits of laughter with his raucous jokes. But I was instantly attracted to number five, the last candidate to arrive, a relatively quiet, dark-haired, young man called Warren. As the evening wore on, he livened up and told a few jokes of his own which were much nearer the mark than Marlon's. I felt my skin tingle with anticipation every time he stared pointedly at me. I felt convinced he knew why I was there. It turned out he was a 'would-be' actor, struggling to get his first decent role. Anna had met him through a friend of a friend of a friend.

On my left-hand side was a bright young spark, who did nothing for my senses. His name was Richie. Marlon was on my right-hand side. Every so often he would fondle my knee and smile at me. When he told a joke he looked at me for approval and I couldn't help liking him.

Warren was opposite me with two other hopefuls whose names I'd forgotten and who were only marginally more appealing than Richie.

Anna was a brilliant hostess. The meal was supplied by caterers but nobody, except for me (and Lester, I presume), knew it. Everybody kept congratulating her on her marvellous cooking. She accepted the praise gracefully, bowing her head and smiling sweetly. I thought she should have been an actress herself.

Lester didn't look quite so wrinkly as the evening wore on, but after goodness knows how many glasses of wine and lots of smutty jokes, almost anybody can look good. Anna seemed besotted with him. So much for missing my father! Several times Lester made a point of openly fondling her breasts whilst he was talking to the group. It was obvious he was telling us that Anna was his property. Anna let him do it, her nipples hardening like buttons as she gazed lovingly at him with her big, adoring eyes. I didn't like Lester, but it was her life, so I gave her my blessing.

At midnight the two hopeful wannabees whose names I'd forgotten gave up the chase and left, leaving me with Marlon, Richie and Warren. The remaining six of us retired to the lounge for coffee. Anna put on some soft music, whereupon Marlon promptly fell asleep on a sofabed in the corner of the room, grunting softly to himself from time to time. After a half-hearted game of Trivial Pursuit – which seemed twice as difficult as usual because everybody was a bit pissed and nobody knew the answers – Anna and Lester decided to hit the sack, leaving me alone with the three musketeers. Marlon was still zonked out. Although I didn't really fancy him, I couldn't help feeling a bit peeved about his lack of interest in me after such a promising start. So I made do with Richie and Warren who were still vying for my attention.

Richie came and sat next to me on the couch. 'You're very attractive,' he said, eyeing me provocatively.

Nice words, shame about the face, I thought, wondering whether I should tell him straight out I wasn't interested. I looked at Warren. He was slouched in his chair, staring at me with sleepy slit-eyes. He reminded me a tired lion, half asleep, but ready to pounce.

Richie took my silence as a positive sign and placed an arm possessively round my shoulder. When I didn't object, he began to kiss my neck with short, pecking movements. I decided enough was enough. I shrugged him off. 'Sorry, Richie, I'm not interested.' I thought I'd said it very nicely, but Richie didn't seem to think so. He took it badly. I remembered, too late, that Leos can't bear being rejected.

After a moment of stunned silence, he grabbed my arm and shook it. 'Fuck you then,' he shouted, shocking me with his sudden aggression. 'Bloody tart, leading me on.' He stood up and spoke to Warren. 'I'm getting out of here. I reckon you should too. She's just a cock-teaser.'

Warren eyed me speculatively. He seemed unsure what to do.

'Don't go, Warren,' I said. 'Just because I don't fancy Richie, it doesn't mean I don't –'

He didn't give me a chance to finish. 'Fancy me, you mean?' he smirked, and suddenly I didn't fancy him any more. I didn't like the smug expression on his face, and the assumption that I was ready to fall at his feet.

Richie stomped out in anger. Warren stayed put.

Warren sank back into his chair, legs wide apart, eyes gleaming with desire. 'Come and sit on my lap,' he ordered, patting his knees.

I began to dislike him intensely, but I needed him. There was only Marlon left and he was still fast asleep at the other end of the room. I wavered with indecision. Should I go with my gut feelings and tell him to follow Richie out of the door, or should I make an effort, let him shag me and get my stint with Leo over and done with?

'Well? Come on then. Do you want me or not?' Warren was getting impatient.

The answer was definitely 'not', but I stood up and walked over to him.

Warren grabbed me and pulled me down onto his lap. His thick, wet lips clamped onto my mouth, pushing it open. Then he thrust in his tongue, moving it in short, sharp movements towards my throat, making me gag.

I hated it. What was wrong with me? I'd really fancied this guy a few hours ago. Now I wished he'd crawl into a hole and leave me alone.

I tried to respond, but when his hand pulled at the front of my dress, tearing at the fabric to release my breasts, and his fingers began to cruelly squeeze my nipples, I knew it was no good. Another time, another guy, I would have been panting for it, but I didn't want

Warren. I pulled away, yanking my dress back up over my breasts.

'What's the matter?' Warren croaked.

I realised for the first time how drunk he was. 'I'm sorry, I can't,' I mumbled, clambering off his lap, and I ran back to the couch.

Warren focussed his slit-eyes on me. He was a very angry lion now. It looked like I'd made another gaff. 'Christ!' he roared. 'First of all you give Richie the come-on, then send him packing, saying you fancy me. Now you're giving me the same treatment. What gives you the right?'

He stood up and came towards me, clenching his fists. I was beginning to feel frightened. 'I'm sorry. I didn't mean to lead you on.'

'Yes you did, you bitch.'

He lunged towards me, but before he could do anything, a strong arm grabbed him from behind and pulled him back. Marlon had woken up.

I cowered in the corner of couch, watching Marlon handle Warren as if he was a puppet. 'I think you'd better sling your hook, mate,' Marlon said gruffly, dragging the unsteady Warren towards the door. 'The lady doesn't want you.'

In the end Warren went peacefully. Marlon came back into the room, rubbing his hands with glee. 'Well, that's him gone.'

I was very grateful. 'Thanks, Marlon. Good job you woke up when you did.'

'Oh, I've been awake quite a while, watching the show. First Richie, then Warren. You're quite a lady. What made you change your mind about Warren?'

It seems I'd underestimated Marlon. 'His ego, I think. I don't really know for sure.'

Marlon sat down beside me. 'Sorry I went to sleep. We were getting on quite well at dinner, weren't we?' He pulled his face into an expression of mock sorrow.

I couldn't help smiling. He was a bit old for me, but I liked him and he had saved me from Warren. 'We still could get on,' I said softly.

He took my hand in his. 'I was hoping you'd say that.'

We smiled at one another. Then he took me into his arms and kissed me, deeply and tenderly. We stayed like that for a long time, locked in each other's arms, his kissing becoming more intense as I responded. When he let me go I felt giddy with desire. He stroked my neck gently. 'I think it's a bit late to get all worked up now, don't you? Will you go out with me? Be my girl?'

His choice of words was bit archaic but quite romantic. I couldn't tell him I already had a steady boyfriend, so I nodded in acquiescence.

He beamed delightedly. 'I'll book some tickets for a show or the theatre for Saturday.'

I wanted to say it didn't matter about the theatre, but I changed my mind. It would make a change to be taken out somewhere nice before we got down to the nitty gritty.

Marlon left soon after 3 a.m. I was exhausted. I crept up to the spare bedroom, careful not to wake Anna and Lester up, and flaked out on the bed, still in my glitzy, gold dress.

I was rudely woken up at seven in the morning by the sound of loud grunting and groaning coming from Anna and Lester's bedroom. I listened in fascination, wondering what on earth Anna saw in the randy old sod. Eventually Anna gasped out. Lester was obviously doing something right. I felt a bit sorry that I hadn't copped off the night before, but when I remembered what had happened, I was glad. Marlon seemed a nice guy. I was looking forward to seeing him again.

* * *

I woke up again later with a dry mouth and a thumping headache. I managed to crawl off the bed, take off my crumpled dress and throw on a pair of jeans and T-shirt, before going downstairs for breakfast. Anna was in the kitchen cooking eggs and bacon, still in her nightie. She had a glow about her which made her look even prettier than usual. Lester was at the table reading a newspaper.

'Hi, Ellie,' Anna chirped. 'Want some breakfast?'

I could see Anna's big, round nipples through the thin nightdress, and the vague outline of her bare crotch. She was the only one not dressed. The smell of the bacon cooking made me feel nauseous. 'Just a slice of toast please, and some paracetamol if you've got some,' I said.

Anna looked at me with concern. 'Did you have a bad night, or is it too much booze?'

'Both.'

Anna glanced over at Lester who was still engrossed in his paper before leaning forward and whispering to me, 'Who did you end up with? Warren?'

'No way,' I said indignantly, forgetting I'd made a play for him throughout dinner.

Anna was surprised. 'Who then?'

'Well, I didn't get off with anybody, but Marlon is taking me to the theatre on Saturday.'

Anna flicked two eggs and a mound of bacon onto a plate. 'Marlon's lovely. I'm glad you chose him. You'll have to tell me all about it later,' she said, taking the plate of food out to Lester.

I followed her. Lester looked up from his paper, noticing me for the first time. 'Good morning, Ellie. How are you?' He beamed at me knowingly and once again I felt that same feeling of dislike I'd had when I first met him.

'Fine.'

'A bit worn out by last night, eh?'

Anna laid a hand possessively on Lester's shoulder as she put the plate down in front of him. 'Take no notice of him, Ellie.'

Lester looked at me slyly. Then with a very obvious movement he slid his hand up Anna's nightie and started squeezing her bare buttocks. Once again he was proclaiming Anna as his territory.

Anna ruffled his hair and tried to back off, but Lester held on to her tightly. 'Show Ellie your rings,' he said.

Anna seemed a bit put out. 'But I –'

Lester reached forward, yanked Anna's nightie up, and proudly pointed to two gold rings pierced into Anna's pretty navel.

My eyes were riveted to Anna's lower half, but it wasn't really the rings which were claiming my attention: it was her beautifully clean-shaven pussy, all puffed up and ready for action. 'Very nice,' I murmured. 'When did you have it done?'

Anna opened her mouth to speak but Lester spoke first again. 'Do you mean the rings, or the shaved pussy which you seem so interested in?' he sneered. He was still holding Anna's nightie tightly at her waist, but his other hand was now moving between her legs from behind, opening up her pussy with his long fingers.

I stared at Anna, lost for words. She looked back at me, embarrassed but making no move to stop Lester from invading her body. When his fingers started pushing inside her, I knew I should look away, but I couldn't. My own pussy was beginning to tingle and get wet, just as Lester intended. My feelings were in a turmoil. I felt Anna's humiliation deeply, but was excited by her body and what Lester was doing to her.

Lester's eyes were gleaming with sensuality as he stared at me, and for the first time I began to see what Anna saw in him. He was a ruthless man, very much in command of himself, and others, who knew exactly what he wanted and how to get it. Anna stood beside him submissively, whilst his fingers explored her pussy, his thumb nudging against her swollen clit. Then, with his other hand, he tapped her bottom and, like a zombie, Anna reached up and took her nightie off. She had lovely breasts, big and swollen, ripe for squeezing and sucking. I held my breath, mesmerised by the show being put on for my benefit.

'Tell Ellie the good news,' Lester said suddenly, reaching out to stroke Anna's flat stomach.

Anna looked down at him, a soft, loving expression on her face. 'We're trying for a baby,' she said.

I was surprised. My stomach lurched. Was it only yesterday morning that I had felt broody too?

Lester pulled his fingers out of Anna's wet pussy. 'We won't make a baby this way, will we, darling?' he said, staring up at her meaningfully. With a quick movement he unzipped his trousers and proudly pulled out his cock, making sure I saw it, before he pulled Anna down on top of him and plunged it into her. Then he fucked her, whilst I watched, fascinated, unable to move. Relentlessly he drove into her, silently this time, his eyes glued to mine. He seemed to have the energy of a man half his age. Finally he burst inside her, allowing himself one short, loud gasp as he released himself. Anna did not have an orgasm.

When the show was over, Lester thrust Anna away, telling her to go and get dressed whilst he tucked into his cold eggs and bacon. He didn't even glance at me.

I ran upstairs after Anna to apologise for watching.

Anna smiled at me. She was still naked. Her nipples were huge and the tops of her legs were glistening with moisture. 'Isn't he wonderful?' she said. 'I love him so much.'

'Do you really? Look, I'm so sorry. I shouldn't have stayed.'

Anna shrugged. 'Lester wanted you to be there, you

know that. He wanted you to see that he's not just an old man who's past it. He's quite sensitive about his age, you know. He thinks you don't like him.'

'So he tries to make me like him by getting me all worked up whilst he shags you in front of me,' I said indignantly.

Anna looked horrified. 'No, of course not. He wasn't trying to get you excited. He was just trying to prove a point.'

I nodded, slowly relenting, 'Well, he made his point, all right. He's got more spunk than Ryan – and that's saying something.'

Anna smiled proudly. 'He loves me, Ellie. He wants to marry me as soon as possible.'

I suddenly felt very sorry for her. 'Do you really want a baby?' I asked.

'Yes, of course. Lester's desperate to have another child. He's got two grown-up daughters from his first marriage, but he'd love a son.'

'But do you really want to be tied down with a baby? You've got a great job. You're going places.'

Anna turned away and started to get dressed. 'I can manage both. Lots of women do.'

'I know, but will Lester allow it?'

Anna shrugged. 'I don't know. He hasn't said. Look, I'm bored with this conversation. Tell me more about you and Marlon.'

'There isn't a me and Marlon – yet. Ask me again on Sunday.'

Anna laughed. 'I will. I'll want to hear all the gory details.'

I felt close to her again. I wanted to be her friend, to help her, but it looked like I'd have to accept Lester in the process.

When I left later that day, Anna hugged me tightly and begged me to come back and see her soon. Then Lester pulled me into his arms. As he clung to me I

80

could feel his erection pressing against me, but all I felt was sadness for Anna.

I started to yawn. The play was boring. It was Shakespeare's *Henry V* and I'd hated most of Shakespeare's plays ever since being forced to do *Julius Caesar* for my English lit GCSE. Marlon was loving it though. He was definitely a theatre buff, having acted in quite a few plays himself when he was younger.

I glanced at the people around me. All eyes were riveted to the stage. I felt a bit ashamed. Was I the only person in the world who didn't appreciate Shakespeare? I stared down at Marlon's crotch. No sign of life there, of course. I put my hand out and stroked his knee. He smiled at me, took my hand in his, then turned his attention back to the stage. I wished he'd taken me to see a film. I could get all steamed up watching tasty guys like Ralph Fiennes or Ewan McGregor.

I started fidgeting. My legs were aching and my thong was pushing into the crease of my arse, making me itch. I had to get out. Quietly I stood up and whispered to Marlon that I was going to the loo. He nodded, hardly aware that I was leaving my seat.

I found the ladies and ripped off my thong. I was beginning to appreciate the freedom of going knicker-less more and more. I was quite modestly dressed for once in a tight, black, knee-length skirt and a pink blouse. Nobody would know I had nothing on underneath, so I undid a few buttons on my blouse to reveal some cleavage and make myself feel sexier.

Back in the vestibule, all was silent. I didn't know what to do. I was reluctant to go back to my seat, but I had no intention of standing around waiting for the play to finish.

'Hi, there,' a voice said behind me, making me spin round with surprise. 'Are you looking for something?'

An attractive, dark-skinned young man in a blue

usher's uniform was grinning at me. My instant reaction was to tell him I was looking for a good shag, but I held my tongue and smiled sweetly at him. 'I've got a headache,' I lied, 'so I don't feel like watching the play. Is there anywhere I can go to lie down for a few minutes?'

He stared at me momentarily, sizing me up, and I stared back at him brazenly. I felt like having fun and stupid old Marlon was no fun at all at the moment.

'I can take you to a back room for a short while,' he said at last. 'Follow me.'

We went along some corridors into the back of the theatre reception area, and I watched his large arse wriggle in trousers that were too tight for him. My bare pussy decided it liked the look of this young man and began to get wet. He stopped at a door marked PRIVATE, reached into his pocket and brought out a bunch of keys. The room was disappointing. It was tiny and drab with only a small couch, a desk and a wash-basin in it.

'It's the usher's private area,' the young man said. 'There's only me on tonight, so we won't be interrupted.' He looked into my eyes with his big, brown ones. 'Are you sure this is what you want?'

I nodded, stepping into the room. He shut the door behind me. 'I haven't got long,' he said, glancing at his watch. 'The play will be over in about twenty minutes.'

'Long enough,' I said, undoing my blouse.

He grabbed me before I had finished, pushed me onto the couch and tried to pull my skirt up. It was too tight. 'Take it off,' he ordered.

I did as I was told and stood before him, my hands on my wet, open pussy, presenting it to him. I was so excited I could hardly breathe.

He was very young, no more than seventeen or eighteen, but he seemed to know what he wanted. He pushed me round, then down onto the floor on all fours.

Before I could even see his cock, he was thrusting it into me from behind. Lucky I was wet, because he was very well-endowed. He filled me up completely. It was just what I needed. I thrust my arse towards him, pulling his cock into me with my strong muscles, enjoying every minute of it. Nothing was said, and a few moments later he came, shooting a load of spunk into me and groaning very loudly. I didn't have an orgasm, but then I wasn't really expecting one. I felt empty when he pulled out of me, desperately wanting more, but there wasn't time for a second round.

Now that he had finished, he seemed embarrassed. It was probably the first time a complete stranger had offered it to him on a plate.

'Can I use your sink to clean myself up?' I asked. I wasn't at all embarrassed. I'd seen and done far too much in my short lifetime for that.

He nodded and rushed for the door. He couldn't get away quickly enough. 'You've got about five minutes before I come back and lock up.'

Five minutes later I was snuggling up to Marlon as we watched the climax of the play. I thought about another type of climax which I hoped to experience before the end of the evening. When the play finished I applauded as loudly and enthusiastically as everyone else.

'You were in the loo a long time. Are you all right?' Marlon said when we were in the car driving back to his place.

'I had a headache. I found an usher and asked him for some aspirins. He let me lie down in a back room for a short while.'

'That was nice of him.'

'Yes. He was very obliging.'

'Are you feeling better now?'

I smiled at Marlon. He was really rather sweet. 'Much

better, thanks.' I hadn't put my thong back on and I was feeling hornier than ever. The young usher had merely whetted my appetite.

Marlon lived on his own in a large penthouse flat. He wasn't short of a bob or two. I wandered around admiring the place while he watched me and smiled. When I reached the main bedroom, I gasped with surprise. The whole room from ceiling to floor was decorated with mirror tiles. The only item of furniture in the room was an old-fashioned kingsize bed with ornate, metal rungs around the top and elaborate drapes which were tied back with thick, gold cord. It was an incongruous blend of old and new and I wasn't sure I liked it.

'Where do you keep your clothes?' I asked

'The other bedroom. I've turned it into a dressing room. I've got lots of old theatre stuff in there too. Would you like to see it?'

'Of course.'

The room was amazing. Mirror tiles again, this time encompassing about six long, metal rungs with clothes hanging on them. It was like a huge, walk-in wardrobe. The rungs were full up with clothes of every description, from very old intricate items dating back to goodness knows when, to up-to-date everyday items such as jeans and sweatshirts. One whole rung was filled with women's clothing.

'Why have you got all these ladies' clothes?' I asked, fingering a beautiful long, red silk dress which looked Chinese.

'My ex-wife was an actress. You may have heard of her: Sasha Lee. That wasn't her real name, of course, just like Marlon isn't mine.'

'Oh!' I was surprised. 'What's your real name, then?'

'Michael Smith. Pretty boring, eh? Marlon King sounds much better. My wife's real name was Sandra Pratt, before she became Sasha Lee.'

I started to giggle as I walked along the row of ladies' clothes. Near the end there were some old-fashioned corsets with tie ups. Then a very short-skirted maid's uniform, and a bunnygirl's outfit, a gymslip with a white blouse and a nurse's uniform. I stopped in my tracks. Marlon was standing right behind me. 'Did your wife wear these as well?' I asked.

'Very rarely. She did enough dressing up in her acting jobs, so she wasn't very interested in doing it to liven up our sex life, which was almost non-existent anyway.'

'Who does wear them then, or have they been there for years, unused?'

Marlon observed me closely. 'Anybody who wants to wear them. Some of my girlfriends. I had one girl who loved dressing up.'

'What's your favourite outfit?'

'The maid's, I think. Worn with a suspender belt and black stockings and no knickers, it's really sexy. The bodice on the top pushes the boobs up so high that even small ones look good, and girls with big tits – like yourself – show most of their nipples.'

I ran my hands over the uniform.

'Would you like to wear it?' Marlon asked politely.

I bit my lips, and a rush of pleasure coursed through my body. 'OK.'

'I'll leave you to try it on, then. When you're ready I'll be waiting in the lounge where you can serve me up a drink.'

Marlon walked off stiffly, and I giggled again. This was going to be fun. The uniform was very tight. I had to leave the bodice half undone at the back in order to get it over my breasts, which were spilling out everywhere. The skirt hardly covered my bum. Without bending over, in the mirrors I could see the lower half of my plump, white cheeks, with the black suspenders down the middle, enticingly revealed. There was a little white, frilly cap and apron to go with the uniform. I thought the cap looked silly, but I put it on anyway. I found a pair of very high-heeled black patent shoes on a shoe-rack by the side of the rung and squashed my feet into them. They were far too small and hurt my toes badly, but I tottered to the door in them, ready to make my grand entrance.

Marlon eyed me up and down coldly. Whilst I was in the dressing room he had changed his hairstyle, so that it was now parted in the middle and greased down flat. He'd also put on a long-tailed dinner jacket and bow tie. He looked much older and very impressive.

'Do you realise, Miss Johnson, that you are showing half your arse,' he boomed when he saw me.

I stepped back in surprise, almost believing he was for real. 'Sorry,' I muttered, hanging my head and trying to play the part.

'Sorry, sir!' he shouted. 'Get me a drink. I need it after seeing how disgraceful you look.'

'Yes, sir. What would you like?' I even curtsied after I had spoken.

'Pour me a brandy, a large one.'

Marlon had placed a decanter of drink and some glasses on the coffee table in front of him. I knew from the smell that it wasn't really brandy; Marlon had told me that he only drank wine. It smelled more like apple juice. I bent over to pour it into a glass and, as I did so, my right breast popped out from the bodice. I started to giggle again.

'How dare you laugh like that, girl!' Marlon roared. 'You're a disgrace. Put that thing back in.'

Marlon watched me whilst I tried to squeeze my breast back into the bodice. I was taking my time – on purpose, of course – and he got impatient. 'Come here, let me do it.'

I stood in front of him, my errant breast with its excited nipple protuding close to his face. He grabbed hold of it, pulling at the nipple, squeezing it roughly, as he pushed the breast back into my bodice. When he'd finished he shoved me round and gave me a resounding smack on my bare buttocks, making me cry out in surprise. 'That'll teach you to be cheeky,' he said.

I burst out laughing at the pun, and his hand came down on my backside even harder, bringing tears to my eyes.

'Get me that drink,' he growled.

I finished pouring out the apple juice, and tottered back to him. The shoes were killing me. I was actually a bit shaky. Marlon was a good actor.

Marlon sat back on the sofa and sipped at the apple juice as if it was brandy. I stood a short distance away, unsure of the next act.

'Don't just stand there, girl,' Marlon roared. 'Come here and do something to keep me entertained.'

I noticed he was stroking the area around his crotch. I caught on quickly. I went over to him and reached down to undo his flies. He had no underpants on and his cock shot out like a jack-in-the-box. I took it into my hand, but he slapped it away and yanked my head down. So in my mouth it went, long and hard, thrusting against my tongue, reaching down to my throat, whilst he carried on drinking as if I wasn't there.

After a while he pushed me away. 'That's enough, girl. You can't even do that properly. I feel hungry. There's some bread and honey on the kitchen table. Go and get it for me.'

I stood up and hobbled towards the kitchen, aware that he was watching my bare arse, which was still stinging from his slaps. Sure enough, there was some bread and honey on the table. I took it in to him. He grabbed the jar of honey. 'Let's see if it's all right. You might be trying to poison me.' He unscrewed the lid, put the jar down to his crotch and dipped his cock in. Then he pulled it out, thick and dripping with honey. 'You try it first,' he said pointing the sticky rod at me.

This time I knelt in front of him, taking him full into my mouth, sucking him eagerly. It tasted good. When I had swallowed all the nectar I pulled my mouth away and looked up at him with wide, innocent eyes. 'It's perfectly all right, sir,' I said, trying hard not to giggle again.

Marlon almost smiled, but he pulled himself together. 'Get up,' he ordered.

As I stood up, the tight, flimsy shoes gave way. The right heel snapped and I lost my balance, falling headfirst into his lap, my boobs tumbling free of the bodice, my bare arse quivering in the air. I couldn't stop laughing, expecting at any moment to feel the full wrath of Sir Marlon's hand on my buttocks. But instead he yanked me up onto his lap with my back facing him, pushed my legs open and entered me from behind.

'Ride me,' he shouted into my ear. 'Ride me so hard it hurts.'

I placed my hands on his knees for support, leaned forward a little and started to pump up and down on his cock. After a while he reached round with his hand and started to rub my clit. I was more than ready for it. Usher boy at the theatre had put me in the mood and now my appetite was at breaking point. My pussy quivered with delight and within a few minutes I started to come. I didn't hold back. The best orgasms are those when you can yell out and wake the whole neighbourhood up. I screamed with pleasure, and Marlon came too.

Marlon drove me back to my flat. He was very happy. After he'd kissed me goodbye, he said, 'Perhaps you can be a bunnygirl next time. I'll call you in a few days' time.'

I stood on the pavement, watching him drive away,

feeling sad knowing that there would be no next time for Marlon and me. Which was a shame because I rather fancied being a bunnygirl. Never mind. Perhaps I could dream up a few games to play with Ryan.

Chapter Seven
Virgo: The Shy Sex-Pot

23 AUGUST

*M*y lifestyle has changed. I am not a lady of leisure any more. A few weeks ago my landlord threatened to throw me out of the flat if I didn't pay the rent pronto. Using all my feminine wiles – I was almost on my knees – I managed to persuade him to give me a few more weeks to come up with the money. It's a pity he's old, fat and ugly and totally unfanciable, otherwise I could have used him in my challenge.

A few hours after he called, I hot-footed it down to the local employment agency all dolled up in a smart, navy-blue office suit – the skirt just above the knee – and a freshly ironed white blouse. The agency fell for it, hook, line and sinker, so here I am, using my rusty office skills, working in a massive office block close to the City for a company called Junipers who manufacture spare parts for cars. Now is that boring, or what! At the moment I'm on my lunch break, sitting at my desk in the middle of a huge, open-plan office in the accounts department, munching my sandwiches whilst trying to write. I managed to pay off the backlog of rent last week, so I won't be thrown out yet, but the next lot is due at the end of the month.

In the evenings I've been struggling to do my write-up on Leo and keep Ryan happy at the same time. He's been very understanding. We haven't had sex for over a week and I'm bursting for it. That will change very soon, I hope, because I am proud to say I've already found my Virgo. I think I've been very clever actually. Before I started the job I'd already worked out that one of the best places to find a typical Virgo was in an accounts office. Virgos love figure-work and analysis. They can drool over bought and sales ledgers for ages without getting bored. So when the agency told me about this temporary position, I grabbed it.

I've been here nearly three weeks now and have met plenty of blokes who could be Virgos but I just happened to find out by chance that the assistant office manager, a youngish chap called Patrick, has a birthday on 5 September. How did I find out? Well, Carole, one of the girls in the office, keeps a list of everybody's birthdays so that she can buy them a card which she passes round the office to sign. When she was taking my details down, I happened to notice several September birthdates, and one was Patrick's.

Now Patrick seems like a really nice guy. Terribly shy like many Virgos, but good looking when he takes his glasses off. He's got thick dark hair and a little goatee beard. He'll be 29 in two weeks' time, just right for my quest. I've been trying to get to know him on a more intimate level, without much success, I might add. I think he likes me because he always gives me a nice smile and will speak to me if I approach him, but that's as far as it goes. Carole assures me he's not married and hasn't got a regular girlfriend. She doesn't think he's gay either, so I guess I've got to persevere. But now we've reached the first day of Virgo I'm going to have to push it a bit more. Why do I always have this struggle? Why couldn't I have had twelve men, one from each birth sign, lined up, eager and waiting? But then that would have been too easy.

At the moment Patrick is in his office with the door closed, as usual. I've got about half an hour of my lunch break left so I think I'll go and talk to him. Wish me luck. I'll need it!

Patrick was working on his computer when I strolled into his office without knocking. He looked up and smiled.

'Have you got a minute?' I asked.

'Shouldn't you be on your lunch break?'

'I am. But I'm bored. There's nobody to talk to, apart from you.' I made myself comfortable in the chair opposite his desk.

Patrick's eyes behind his large, thick-rimmed glasses bore into me. 'I'm very busy,' he said eventually.

I had the distinct feeling he didn't want me there, but I persisted. 'You're entitled to a lunch break too. You never seem to have one.'

'Managerial staff don't worry about lunch breaks,' he said stiffly, turning his attention back to the computer.

I sat watching him for a few minutes, crossing and uncrossing my legs in their silky black tights, trying to get his attention. I have to admit that office suits and blouses aren't the sexiest of outfits, but the skirt was fairly short and I thought he might find my legs attractive – most men did. When he didn't look up, I decided more drastic action was needed. I got up and walked round to his side of the desk.

'What's all that about?' I asked, staring at the mass of figures on the computer screen. I was standing very close to him, gently brushing the lower half of my left leg against his right leg.

He didn't seem at all pleased. 'Oh, just some work

figures. Nothing you'd know about.' He pulled his leg away from mine. So he had been aware of it, then.

I edged closer and touched his arm. 'I'm sorry if I've offended you,' I said, putting on my best hurt voice.

He jerked his arm away. 'You haven't offended me,' he said quietly, his words belying his actions.

I didn't know what to make of him. Short of taking all my clothes off and begging him to fuck me, what could I do?

'They're the figures for the last lot of parts delivered to Bristol Works,' Patrick said suddenly. 'I'm working on their accounts.'

'Oh.' As if I really cared. But at least he was talking. I turned a little, presenting Patrick with a nice view of my arse as I bent over and stared at the computer screen.

A moment or two later I felt the lightest of touches on the back of my leg just below the skirt. An exultant thrill burst through me. His hand started to inch upwards.

Without warning, the door burst open and Carole marched in. 'Excuse me, Patrick, I wondered –' She stopped, mouth wide open, surprised to see me there.

Patrick almost jolted out of his seat. He yanked his hand away from my leg. I stood up straight, watching him go red as a beetroot as he struggled for words, and felt very sorry for him. He was far too shy. I smiled at Carole. 'Patrick's just giving me some lessons on the computer.'

'Oh, I'll come back then, shall I?'

'No,' Patrick blurted out. 'Mariella's lunch break is over. She's got lots of work to do this afternoon.'

I was dismissed. But I wasn't unduly worried. At last I had made some progress. It was only a matter of time before he was putty in my hands.

At five o'clock there was a massive surge of people talking, laughing, anxious to get home. The office miraculously emptied. I sat at my desk and watched the action, wishing I could join them, but I had work to do. Patrick was still in his office, working late as usual.

Carole appeared at my desk, donning her cardigan. 'Not off yet, Ellie?'

'No. I need to finish this list.'

Carole eyed me speculatively before turning to glance at Patrick's office. 'If I were you, love, I wouldn't waste much time trying to get off with him. Several of the girls in here have tried. He's just not interested.'

I grinned at her. 'Perhaps they haven't used the right tactics.'

'Huh, who knows? He's far too young and intelligent for my tastes, anyway. Well, good luck. Let me know if you succeed. I'll give you a medal. And don't forget to tell us all the juicy gossip tomorrow.'

A few moments later there was only me and Patrick left in the office. I eyed his closed door. All was quiet within. In fact, the office was very eerie now it was devoid of people.

I took my time finishing the list in the hope that he would come out and see me and comment on my conscientious efforts. But he didn't. I don't think he realised I was there. Once again, I would have to make the first move. I stood up, undid the top three buttons of my blouse, and marched over to Patrick's office. This time I knocked on the door. I didn't want to frighten the poor fellow completely.

I heard a sudden movement, like the sound of drawers closing, then his muffled voice called me in. He didn't seem surprised to see me. Good sign.

'Haven't you got a home to go to,' he said wearily.

Not such a good sign. I suddenly felt a bit pissed off with the whole thing. Blast my father; he'd got me into all this. I glared at Patrick. 'Yes, I have got a home to go to – just about – but if I don't stay late and earn some extra dosh, I'm going to be thrown out on my ear.' I crossed my arms indignantly over my boobs which were spilling out of the open blouse.

Patrick was instantly humbled. 'I'm sorry. I didn't mean to be rude.'

I softened immediately. I can be quick to anger at times and have been known to frighten men off, but I couldn't afford to ruin my chances with Patrick. I needed him. The thought of a last-minute frantic search to find another Virgo guy left me cold. I decided to brazen it out.

'I thought we might be able to carry on where we left off at lunchtime, now that the office is empty,' I said, smiling seductively at him.

Patrick sighed. 'Look, Mariella. I'm very sorry. I didn't mean to touch you at lunchtime. Let's forget it happened, shall we?'

I was bristling again. 'You did mean to touch me. Your hand was halfway up my leg. If Carole hadn't come in, you'd have been stroking my pussy.'

He was flustered. 'OK, yes, I did want to, in a way. You're very sexy. But I didn't really mean to. I, I don't want to have sex with you.' He hung his head, afraid of my response.

I kept my cool. 'Are you gay?'

His head shot up. 'No, of course not.'

'Well then. What's the problem? You like girls, you think I'm sexy. We're all alone.'

'There's, there's a girl I like in the sales office.'

'So? Are you going out with her?'

'No. I don't know whether she likes me or not.'

'Ask her. Find out. Would you like to have sex with her?'

He winced. 'No. Yes. I don't know.'

Suddenly I understood. 'You've never been with a girl, have you?'

'Not fully, no.' He finally looked up at me, his eyes showing humiliation and sadness behind the glasses.

I wanted to laugh. I'd picked a right one here. A typical Virgo virgin! I remembered Daniel, the Virgo who had made out he was a Taurus in order to go out with me. But he had probably been a closet gay man. Patrick wasn't. I had to get through to him somehow.

'Patrick,' I said softly, 'don't be ashamed. I could teach you. Then you can go to this girl in the sales office and ask her out.' I undid the rest of the buttons on my blouse and reached round to undo my bra.

'Don't!' he cried, putting his hands to his eyes. 'I can't do it.'

Too late. The bra snapped open and my tits spilled out. I cupped them proudly, one in each hand. The nipples were already hard and protuding. 'Do you like them, Patrick?' I crooned. 'Take your hands away from your eyes and look at me.'

Slowly, he pulled his hands away and stared at my swollen breasts. I pulled at the nipples, making them stand out even more. 'You could do that to me, Patrick. You can suck them too, if you like.'

He gave an involuntary movement, his hand going to the area round his crotch.

It was hard work, but I was winning. 'Are you excited, Patrick? Is your cock hard. Would you like me to hold it?' I remained standing in front of his desk, jiggling my breasts.

He couldn't keep his eyes off me now. So I pulled up my skirt and began to peel down my tights and knickers. I stepped out of them using one hand, whilst holding my skirt up around my waist with the other. 'Come on, Patrick,' I cajoled. 'You can do it. I know you want to.'

His breathing was getting heavy as he stared at me. Shaking, he reached up and took his glasses off. At last I could see the lust in his eyes. His hand was on his crotch, rubbing himself. He hardly seemed to know what he was doing.

'You can come and get me, if you like,' I said, putting a hand to my pussy and parting the lips so he could see my swollen clit. I rubbed it invitingly.

He didn't move. He seemed rooted to the spot. I could almost see the shock waves going through him. So I went to him, still holding my skirt high, and began rubbing my bare pussy against his thigh. Still no movement.

I sighed. 'OK. Let's get your cock out and see what you can do.' I reached down to his flies.

Before I could get to the zip, his hand grabbed mine and held it in a steely grip. 'Stop it!' He was almost snarling.

Stunned, I dropped my skirt and stared at him, unsure what to do next.

He relaxed his grip on my hand, and I took it away. 'Why?' I asked, shaking my head with exasperation. 'You need me, you want me. Can't you just relax?'

He shook his head wildly. 'No. Can't. I'm no good.'

'How do you know, if you've never tried?'

'I'm –'

'You're what?'

'Too small.' He blurted it out and hung his head again.

I didn't know whether to laugh or cry. 'Who says you are?' I persisted.

'I know I am. When I look at other men – only in the toilets, of course – I can see.'

With a quick movement, whilst he was still wallowing in self-pity, I reached down, unzipped his trousers and pulled his cock free from his pants.

He gasped with shock and tried to shield it with his hands. The poor guy was almost in tears.

But I had a good grip on it. It wasn't that large, but it wasn't that small, either. In fact, it was rather nice. I began to pull on it gently, my thumb caressing the sticky nub. He was very excited.

'Patrick, oh Patrick, you silly man,' I said softly. 'You're lovely.'

He stared at me in disbelief.

'I mean it.' I let go of his cock with my hand, bent over, and took him into my mouth. He felt good. I was beginning to feel very horny.

At last he began to respond, pushing his cock deep into my mouth, panting excitedly. I was enjoying it, but I didn't want him to spill his load down my throat; I had to get him into my pussy in order to fulfil my pledge. I pulled away. 'Fuck me,' I ordered. 'Fuck me with your lovely cock, now.' I yanked my skirt up and leaned against the desk, opening my legs wide.

After a moment's hesitation, he finally took the plunge. With one urgent movement he thrust into me like a man demented, pushing me violently back across the desk. My head crashed into a paperweight, making me feel slightly dizzy, but I ignored it. I pulled my legs up around his waist, encouraging him, thrusting my bare tits against his chest.

Suddenly he stopped, and looked in horror towards the door. I twisted my head round to see a very shocked cleaner, bucket and mop in hand, standing in the open doorway.

'Get out,' Patrick hissed at her, 'and don't come back.'

I was stunned by Patrick's venom. But I forgave him. If ever there was a man in dire need, it was him.

The cleaner backed out of the room, mumbling her apologies.

I tried to laugh, but the sound got locked in my throat as Patrick bore down on me again, intent on shooting his load. As he pummelled into me, his fingers tore at my breasts, squeezing and scratching them so violently I cried out in pain. Then his back arched and he let out a huge groan of satisfaction. I didn't come, but I wasn't too disappointed. I was just happy that I'd won and he'd finally lost his virginity.

I broke away quickly, anxious to get going now that it was all over. Patrick didn't seem to notice. He was grinning from ear to ear, the most relaxed I'd ever seen him. 'That was fantastic,' he said, his eyes shining. 'Was it good for you?'

'Lovely,' I said, not wanting to spoil his pleasure by telling him that I had not had an orgasm. I was already buttoning up my blouse and looking for my knickers.

Patrick watched me, smiling inanely.

'What's so funny?' I asked as I found my knickers and put them on.

'I can't believe I've done it. I'm so happy. Can we do it again?'

I nodded, without thinking, anxious to be gone.

'How about tomorrow night? Stay late again.'

I suddenly realised I didn't want to. I had all the research I needed for my book, but he looked so eager. I hated the thought of letting him down, so I agreed. Half an hour later, lying in the bath at home, I wished I'd said no. But that would have been cruel. Whilst I carried on working in that office it looked like I was stuck with him.

Ryan pushed me face down onto the kitchen table and slammed his cock into me from behind. Doggy style was his favourite position. I yelled out with pleasure. It was fantastic to have him inside me again.

He thrust harder, pushing deeper and deeper into me, building up a rhythm, sending me crazy. Mindlessly I responded, pushing my arse against his crotch, and frantically rubbing my clit until I burst violently, my juices spilling onto his cock, making him come too. Together we heaved and shuddered until, finally spent, we collapsed giggling onto the floor.

It was then he noticed the scratch-marks on my breasts made by Patrick. He stiffened, pulling away from me. 'What did he do to you?' he asked gruffly.

'I told you. It was his first time. He lost it a bit and wouldn't let go of them.'

Ryan stroked my breasts gently, then stooped to kiss them. 'Bastard! Don't go with him again will you?'

'I'll try not to. But now that he's discovered he can do it, I'm worried he'll want it again.'

'You'll just have to be firm with him, won't you?'

I nodded, and put my arms round Ryan's chest, hugging him tightly to me. At moments like this I loved him very much. He was concerned about me. I made up my mind that I definitely would not let Patrick have his wicked way with me again.

Patrick pumped into me like a man obsessed. I hadn't had the heart to refuse him. All day he had been like a new man, smiling and confident, chatting to everybody in the office. Carole and the other girls couldn't believe it when I told them all about my passionate session with him the night before. But when Patrick kept making excuses to leave his office and strut around in front of my desk, they knew it was true. Patrick had been conquered. At lunchtime the girls bought me a huge cream cake by way of congratulations. I started to feel quite proud of myself. When five o'clock came, Patrick rushed out of his office to make sure I wasn't leaving. What could I do? One more time, I said to myself. Just to let him know it wasn't a freak accident and to make him confident enough to go to that girl in sales and ask her out.

He'd put a DO NOT DISTURB notice on the door this time. Not that it was necessary. I very much doubted whether the poor cleaner would burst in again. This time he had undressed me completely and ran his hands wondrously over my naked body, noting the scratch-marks on my breasts and apologising profusely. I was growing to like him more. The sex was better too. He had tentatively touched my pussy and I encouraged him by showing him where my clit was and how to rub it. He was a good learner.

We were on the desk again. It was a bit uncomfortable, but his constant pumping and inexpert fumbling was actually beginning to excite me. I tried not to move in response, though, in case he got overexcited and ejaculated too soon. So I lay still, with my eyes closed, fantasising that it was Ryan on top of me, quite enjoying myself. But just as I was getting into it, Patrick came and that was that.

When we were getting dressed, I mentioned the girl in sales. 'Have you asked her out yet?' I said.

'No. But I will do soon. You're helping me so much, Mariella. I'm really grateful.'

'I won't be here forever,' I said, hoping he would take the hint.

'I know. But while you are, I'd really love to carry on seeing you.'

'OK, one more session then.' The words came out before I realised what I was saying.

Patrick smiled at me confidently. 'Just a few more times, eh?'

By the end of the following week I was well and truly knackered. Patrick had fucked me every night for the last nine days. He was getting more and more bold in his self-expression. Last night we had done it on the floor. Somehow he'd managed to smuggle a duvet into the office. It certainly made it a lot more comfortable. But he was getting far too cosy with the whole set-up. He expected me to stay behind and have sex with him every night. A couple of times I'd tried to tell him I'd had enough, but he wouldn't listen and I felt obliged to satisfy him. After all, it was me who had turned him into a raging sex-pot in the first place.

Today it was Friday. I really needed to get home and do some writing. Trying to keep both Patrick and Ryan happy – Ryan asssumed I had stopped my sessions with Patrick – left little time for writing. In two weeks' time we would be entering the sign of Libra and I'd written nothing about Virgo.

At five o'clock Patrick appeared as usual, hovering around my desk, eyeing me lustily. I really should have told him to get lost, but I didn't. Meekly I followed him to his office and took my clothes off.

Patrick ran his eyes over me, studying me with his cool, analytical Virgo mind. He was highly sexed, yes, but never romantic. 'Turn round and bend over,' he said, his voice oozing with a confidence that wouldn't have seemed possible a week ago.

I did as he asked. He came up behind me and rubbed himself against my backside. 'Do you remember, you kept rubbing yourself against me when you came into my office looking for sex,' he said smugly.

I nodded. It was the truth, but I didn't like hearing it.

He put his hand down and grabbed my right cheek, squeezing it hard. 'I like your bottom,' he said.

I felt a thrill of pleasure. His hand continued to explore my arse until his fingers found the nub of my anus. Then he stopped.

I felt quite excited. 'Push a finger in,' I urged.

He waggled a finger about, unsure of himself. I could feel his heart pounding against my back. He was very close.

'Go on. I don't mind.'

He gave a little groan then thrust a finger into my tight, little hole. I've always enjoyed anal penetration – not too much of it, I might add – but fingers in particular make me feel very horny. It worked like magic. He was actually exciting me.

I leaned back against him, sighing. 'That's lovely, Patrick.'

Encouraged, he inserted another finger and I moaned in delight.

For a while we stood together, in harmony, enjoying the contact. Then he pulled his fingers out and spun me round to face him.

I was disappointed, but at least he was getting more adventurous. Given time and a girl who really liked him, he would be a good lover. This time he fucked me twice within the space of an hour. The second time I finally achieved a mediocre orgasm. He was so pleased with himself that I was truly happy for him. But I knew it had to be the last time.

The following Monday when I didn't turn up for work, Patrick rang me at home soon after nine o'clock. I was still in bed.

'I'm sorry, Patrick,' I said, yawning into the mouthpiece. 'I've had enough. You're so good at sex now, you don't need me.'

'I know I don't.' His voice was very excited. 'I was going to tell you myself on Friday that it was the last time, but you disappeared too quickly. On Friday morning I asked Michelle out – the girl in sales I told you about – and she said yes. We had our first date on Saturday. It was brilliant. I really like her. We didn't do the full thing – just snogged and groped a bit – but I'm sure it won't be long before we do. So I don't need you any more.'

I suddenly felt very deflated, used and unwanted. I had to pull myself together and remind myself that this was what I'd wanted, and I had used Patrick just as much as he'd used me. I wished him well and hung up. Tomorrow I would speak to the agency about another job, but right now I just wanted to sleep, and sleep.

Chapter Eight
Libra: The Cool Charmer

23 SEPTEMBER

I'm in a bit of a dilemma. Anna rang me up last week, very excited about a proposition which had been put to her. She has declined the offer, but wants me to take her place. She wouldn't tell me any more than that over the phone. We arranged to meet in town at our usual place so that she could explain it all to me. I was very intrigued.

After leaving Junipers I found another temporary job, here at this godawful women's magazine. It sounded exciting at the agency, but now that I'm here, I'm bored to tears. The place is full of women with not an ounce of talent in sight. The only male employee is a grouchy, bald-headed artist who looks about sixty. Next week I'm going to leave – thank goodness – and it's all down to Anna and her proposition.

When I met her, Anna looked great. I think it's really ironic that she could take her pick from dozens of hunks who want to go out with her but she chooses an old man who takes pleasure in dominating and humiliating her. I don't understand, but then 'each to his own' is my motto.

The proposition when she told me about it sounded too good to be true. An acquaintance of hers, a multimillionaire by the name of Edward De Vigny who is half-English, half-French, is celebrating his fortieth birthday on 12 October and is anxious to arrange a very special celebration at his chateau in the Dordogne region of France. He wants six young women, three French and three English, to go to stay for a week in his chateau, living in five-star luxury, all expenses paid. In return they would have to be willing to join in a variety of activities he has arranged. Sex wasn't mentioned but it was almost certain to be part of the theme, so Anna assured me. She had met De Vigny once, briefly, at a party and had thought him very attractive – a real charmer – irresistible and sexy. He's a Libran, of course, which is why Anna thought of me in the first place. When I asked Anna why she hadn't fallen for him she reminded me that she had been in love with my father at the time and wouldn't have contemplated being disloyal. Now, she said, she was committed to Lester so she would have to turn the invitation down. But she was sure De Vigny would not mind me taking her place.

The more I thought about it, the more I liked the idea. A week in France, living in the lap of luxury, was just what I needed. But what about my shaky financial status? I couldn't afford to lose my flat. Anna was so keen for me to accept the propostion that she said I could live with her and Lester until my money came through. No, thank you! Live with that creep? Not on your nelly. I politely told her that I didn't want to come between her and Lester, so she promptly offered to loan me a few thousand pounds to tide me over. I was gobsmacked. She really is a sweet person. At first I said, 'I couldn't possibly,' but she soon persuaded me it was the best thing to do if I wanted to go to France and finish my book. She was right, of course. I eventually agreed that she should phone Edward De Vigny to see if I could take her place.

I didn't bargain on Ryan getting all stroppy about it. He was totally against the idea, still is. He said it would be tantamount to 'prostitution' and that De Vigny was buying young girls' favours. He called him a 'spoilt rich despot' and begged me not to go. I explained it was nothing like that and I might not even have sex with De Vigny, to which he retorted, quite rightly I suppose, then what was the purpose of me going?

We argued about it for ages. I could see his point of view. I would be one of six beautiful women from whom De Vigny could take his pick and ask to do anything he wanted. I would have to sell myself to him so that he chose me in favour of the others. If he didn't find me immediately attractive, I would have to work even harder. If we didn't have sex I would have wasted my time and more than likely ruined my chances of claiming my father's inheritance. Was it a gamble I was willing to take? And if I did take it up, where would that leave me with Ryan?

Several days later Anna informed me that Edward De Vigny would be delighted to have me as a guest at his chateau. I was to arrive on 9 October and leave on 16 October. That would give me just under a week to find another Libran if things didn't work out. I accepted the invitation, handed in my notice at work and avoided Ryan for a few days.

Of course I couldn't keep quiet about it forever. When I eventually told Ryan he blew his top and walked out on me. He phoned me later from Gemma's flat just after they'd made love and pleaded with me to change my mind. He sounded a bit drunk. I could hear Gemma cooing at him in the background and felt sick with jealousy, so I said I would cancel the arrangements.

Hence the dilemma. One part of me desperately wants to go to France. I feel committed to Edward De

Vigny and confident I can succeed with him. Besides, I owe it to Anna after all the trouble she's gone to to make it work for me. On the other hand, I don't want to lose Ryan. We have just got back together again. I'm convinced he and I are made for one another: it's me he loves, not Gemma. Right now I feel like a Judas. He thinks I'm not going to France but I probably will. I didn't cancel the arrangements like I promised. Yesterday I received a card from Edward De Vigny saying he was very much looking forward to meeting me. I also received a cheque for £5,000 from Anna, making it doubly difficult for me to back down. I've got to make a decision soon because there's so much to do – book the Channel crossing, find out about trains – and I don't fancy driving there. And I must have some new outfits of course. If only Ryan would see sense.

I arrived at the Le Chateau Blanc, as arranged, on 9 October, feeling very nervous and inconsequential. True to its name, the chateau was a huge white fairytale castle built on the side of a hill overlooking the river, surrounded by beautiful scenery. It was pretty amazing. A sour-faced housekeeper showed me to my room and told me in stilted English to stay there until I was summoned to the drawing room by the master.

The room was large and very beautiful, with a four-poster bed and an ensuite bathroom. The views from the window were fantastic. I stood looking out in a daze for ages. Then I nudged myself into action, had a shower and tried to decide what to wear. I needed to look sexy, but I didn't want to overdo it. So I chose a simple, flowing strappy dress which came down to my knees but revealed plenty of cleavage. I kept my make-up simple too. When I was finished I was so nervous that I started biting my nails, something I hadn't done since I was a child.

Then came the wait. An hour passed and nothing

happened. I began to get impatient. Dare I leave the room? I opened the door and peeked out; there was nobody in sight. The corridor was long and dark, ornately decorated with paintings and murals. I crept forward and started to study them, intrigued by their history and brooding quality. One of the murals was a study of about thirty naked men and women involved in various sexual activities. It was a seething mass of arms, legs and bosoms. I was fascinated by it.

A voice suddenly boomed out behind me. 'What are you doing? Mr De Vigny will let you know when he wants you to leave the room.'

I spun round and came face to face with a midget. A tiny man with a huge face. Stunned, I started to blabber. 'I, I'm sorry. Who are you?'

'I'm Lobo, Mr De Vigny's valet. He doesn't want you girls roaming around the place yet. He's preparing a surprise for you. The bell in your room will ring when he's ready for you to come down. Follow the staircase to the left and you'll find him and the other girls in the banqueting room. Now go back to your room please.'

I did as I was told. I laid down on the huge bed and sunk my head into the pillow, heedless now of what I looked like. A few tears escaped. I felt lonely and apprehensive. Edward De Vigny could be a monster for all I knew, and I was trapped. Why on earth had I agreed to come?

I was asleep when the bell sounded, shrill and crisp, more like a whistle really. I sprang up. My hair was a mess and my eyeliner was smudged. I did a hasty tidy-up job with shaking hands before leaving the room. I followed Lobo's instructions and found the banqueting room easily. The massive doors were open. Inside was a long table filled to the brim with all kinds of food and decorations. Six pairs of eyes stared up at me. Everybody else was already there.

'And you must be Mariella.'

A man stood up from the table. I stared at him. It could only be Edward De Vigny. He was just as Anna had described him. Drop-dead gorgeous and utterly charming. His thick, mid-length brown hair fell in luxurious waves around his face and his large expressive eyes twinkled merrily at me. He wasn't a monster at all! I stood like a zombie, drooling at him.

'Last but not least, eh?' De Vigny drawled in an accent which sounded like a mixture of American and French. 'Do sit down, Mariella.' He pointed to an empty seat next to a beautiful Asian girl.

De Vigny eyed me up as I sat down. I smiled at him, anxious to make a good impression. I felt he had already made his mind up what he thought about me.

He was still standing. 'OK, girls. Now that we are all here, let me introduce you to one another. This is Jasmin.' He pointed to the girl next to me, and moved round in my direction. 'Mariella, Colette, Amy, Anne-Marie and Lisa. You all know why I've invited you here. In three days' time it will be my fortieth birthday. I am having a big party on that day and you girls are to be the star attraction. You'll be part of the cabaret later on in the evening, just a little play I want you to perform, nothing too difficult, I can assure you. During the next three days I'll be organising it all with you. I've also got one or two other things planned which I'll let you know about later. Now, I don't want any of you wandering off away from the chateau. You must remember that you are here at my request, and I want you to stay in the grounds. I'll do my best to give you a good time. If you don't like being here, or can't abide by my rules, you can leave. OK?'

We all nodded fervently, swept along by his pleasant voice and good looks. Of course we wanted to stay.

He continued. 'I want you all to be friends. No jealousy, no catty remarks. I want this to be a place of love, peace and harmony for one week – with a little bit of nooky thrown in for good measure.' He grinned seductively, eyeing us all in turn.

We were hooked. Jasmin looked at me and smiled, a sweet smile, full of eastern promise. De Vigny would love her. But all the others were beautiful too. I felt quite dowdy by comparison.

De Vigny sat down. 'It's time to eat,' he said, pointing to the feast before us. 'Dig in, as they say in English.' He looked pointedly at me before turning to Amy and Lisa, who were also English.

The food was glorious. Everything you could imagine. Servants waited on us with the hot courses to go with the cold buffet on the table. I tried not to eat too much – I was overweight as it was – but I couldn't resist it. The bourguignon was superb, the *tarte au poire* to finish was exquisite. If this was the sort of food we were going to get for the rest of the week, I would be a very happy bunny indeed.

De Vigny made sure we all drank lots of champagne, and kept making toasts to his 'girls'. By the end of the evening we were all more than a little bit tipsy. We retired to a large, comfortable lounge. De Vigny motioned Jasmin and Lisa to sit next to him on the sofa. He put his arms around them both and cuddled and fondled them. The rest of us sat round the room watching him, undoubtedly feeling a little jealous but desperate not to show it.

He asked us all in turn what we did for a living. Lisa and Colette were small-bit actresses, Amy was a model, Anne-Marie was an entrepeneur who owned several large businesses – she had known 'Teddy', as she called him, since they were children – and Jasmin was a high-class escort. When it came to me and I told them I was an astrologer, they were all immediately fascinated, of course. Most people are. They think I'm going to tell them their future.

De Vigny was very impressed. 'I'm a Libra,' he said.

As if I didn't know. I told him all the good things about Librans: charm, balance, diplomacy, popularity, poise and intelligence. But didn't mention the not-so-good qualities: indecision, coldness, self-seeking, to name but a few.

The evening wore on. De Vigny cuddled us all on the sofa in turn. Colette and I were last. As his arm came round me, his hand pressing against the side of my breast, I decided I liked the feeling. I wanted more. Trouble is, we all did.

De Vigny sent us off to bed at around 1 a.m. He kissed us all goodnight on the cheek as if we were his children. 'Get your beauty sleep, girls,' he said. 'You'll need it. We've got lots of work to do tomorrow.'

We spent the next two days working on the short play Teddy – he insisted we call him that after the first night – had written for us. It was a silly little sitcom, in which we played a group of housemates who discover a clown – played by Lobo, of course – hiding in their garden. I felt embarrassed to be part of it, but Teddy was obviously very proud of his work and wanted us to perform brilliantly on the night.

In the evenings we were treated to luscious food, good conversation and oodles of cuddles and kisses from Teddy, but no sex. At least not with me, anyway. None of the other girls mentioned anything, so I assume they weren't gettting it either. I began to wonder if the lovely Teddy was capable of producing the goods. If he wasn't, I was going to have a hard time of it when I got back to England.

By the third day, 12 October, De Vigny's birthday, we were all looking forward to the big social occasion, donning our party frocks and getting onto the stage in the ballroom to do our party piece. Teddy told us we were to make our way to the changing room at precisely eleven o'clock when the entertainment was due to start. Evidently a small troup of dancing girls had been commissioned to come along too.

The party was fantastic. Over two hundred guests had arrived. Some of the blokes were really fanciable – I recognised one or two from the television. Many of them were French, so the conversation was a bit limited. Luckily, I can speak a little French, just enough to get me by. The food was out of this world, as usual, and the band were excellent. De Vigny had thought of everything, no expense spared. After dinner we all sang 'Happy Birthday' to him, whilst he carefully cut the top tier of a massive, beautifully decorated, ten-tiered cake. The evening was shamelessly glitzy and way over the top, but everybody seemed to be thoroughly enjoying it.

At two minutes past eleven, I sauntered into the changing room to find everybody waiting for me.

'Ah, Mariella, last again. I think you need some lessons in punctuality.'

Teddy's voice was sharper than usual and I blushed with embarrassment. 'Sorry.' I was only two minutes late.

Teddy looked at his watch. 'Right, girls, you're on in just over ten minutes, after the dancers. But there's no need to get changed into your costumes. I've changed my mind. I want you all to perform in the nude.'

We all gasped in shock and stared at him in disbelief. Then I thought he was joking and started to laugh. 'Good one, Teddy. Let's get our costumes on, girls.'

'I'm serious.' De Vigny's voice was like ice.

Lisa shook her head angrily. 'No way. I'm not taking my clothes off to perform in front of that lot out there.'

The rest of us nodded in agreement.

Teddy changed his tactics. 'Please, girls,' he wheedled. 'It's my birthday. I asked you here especially to do this.' His tone was pleasant but his eyes glittered with warning.

'I don't mind,' Anne-Marie said quickly in her excellent English. 'It will be fun. Come on girls.' She took her dress off. She was naked underneath. Teddy smiled gratefully at her, his eyes raking over the dark thatch of hair covering her pussy, while the rest of us stared in stunned silence at her beautiful body.

It's all right for her, I thought. She's got a perfect figure. Not a patch of cellulite.

'And the rest of you,' Teddy said, looking at each of us in turn.

'No!' said Lisa.

'Then I think you had better go and pack immediately. Lobo will call for a taxi to take you to the station.'

Lisa's bottom lip fell in shock. The rest of us got the message and started to peel off our clothes.

I put my arm round Lisa's shoulders. 'Come on, Lise. It's not that bad. At least we'll all be the same.'

Teddy was smiling, benignly confident of victory. 'You've got five minutes to make up your mind, Lisa. I'd hate to lose you. You've a lovely girl.'

Lisa slowly took off her dress, followed by her bra, tights and knickers, then stood holding her hands to her crotch. I was surprised that she was so shy. After all, none of us were innocent maidens. Jasmin was a professional.

'Take your hands away and get out onto the stage,' Teddy ordered, his voice hard again. 'I want you lot to put on the performance of your life. Strut around, use your bodies. Do everything you can to get all those guys out there panting with lust. I want to hear their applause. OK?'

We all nodded. My nipples were hardening up and my pussy was damp. I was very nervous but excited at the same time. It felt very erotic to be standing in front of Edward De Vigny, ready to go on stage with nothing

113

on. I desperately wanted him to like my body. My breasts were certainly the biggest of all of us.

The dancers burst into the room, chatting and laughing. They were all topless, with huge painted nipples. Their lower halves were covered by a tiny pleated skirt, with G-strings underneath. They looked very raunchy, more than enough to get the guys in the audience in a state of arousal.

'Go, girls!' Edward ordered, smacking each one of our bottoms as we filed past him. Anne-Marie led the way.

The cheers as we walked onto the stage took our breath away. We stood like zombies for a moment, dazed, embarrassed and excited. Then we heard De Vigny on the side, ordering us to get going, and we shot into action. Anne-Marie had the opening line, thank goodness. She was the most confident of us all. Lobo didn't bat an eyelid when he saw our naked bodies. He obviously knew all along what was going to happen.

There was a lot of bending over in the play, and now I knew why. Goodness knows how many times I had to present my bare arse to the audience. How could we all have been so naive to get ourselves into this? Lisa was so nervous she kept fluffing her lines and we had to help her out. In the end, Amy did most of her work. After a while I forgot I had no clothes on. I proudly strutted around as Teddy had asked and jiggled my breasts at the men in the audience. I got a few cheers of my own, and so did Anne-Marie, who performed excellently.

At the end of the play the applause was deafening. When we came off the first time, Teddy pushed us back on again to take another bow, then we had to take a third one with our backs to the audience and wriggle our arses. It was great fun. All of us, except for Lisa, came off laughing and proud of our performance.

'Brilliant! Great work, girls! I knew you could do it.'

Teddy was over the moon. He looked across at Lisa who was already getting dressed. 'I'll speak to you later.'

She nodded unhappily. It looked like Teddy was going to give her the chop. I felt very sorry for her.

Teddy let us get dressed and go back to the party to mingle with the crowd, but he informed us that under no circumstances were we to indulge in sex with any of the men. Which, as it turned out, was very difficult. Most of the men were still on cloud nine and got erections the moment they saw us. I had great difficulty getting one drunken idiot's hand out of my knickers, partly because he was so insistent and partly because I was getting very horny. I was at that stage where I needed a good shag, but I certainly didn't want to face the wrath of Edward De Vigny by risking it with one of the partygoers. Teddy was a cool customer all right. Not so amenable as I had first thought, but I still wanted him, mainly to fulfil my quest, but also because he excited me.

An hour after the show had finished, the party was still going strong and I was getting all hot under the collar. Too many gorgeous guys trying to touch me up was doing my head in. I needed to cool down. I left the ballroom and walked down the corridor a short way until I came to the drawing room. From here I could get into the conservatory, which was cooler at this time of the night. As I approached the conservatory, I heard muffled sounds and, after slowly creeping towards the open, glass doors, I peeped inside. On the floor in front of me was a man's bare arse with his trousers at half mast, bobbing up and down as he hammered into the woman below him. There was not much moonlight in the room, so I found it difficult to see who they were at first, then as my eyes adjusted I realised that the illustrious backside belonged to none other than Edward De

Vigny himself. A few moments later, as she started to moan with pleasure, I also recognised Lisa.

So he could do it after all, and quite nicely by the look of it. Lisa was certainly enjoying it. I strained forward so that I could see them better. I managed to get a glimpse of Teddy's glistening cock as he surged in and out of Lisa's pussy. I held my breath, frightened to move, my open pussy throbbing with excitement at the glorious sight.

Teddy started to thrust into Lisa with violent, jerky movements. Lisa was delirious. 'Please, please, oh yes, please, fuck me, fuck me, harder, harder,' she kept moaning, until eventually she uttered a small scream and started shuddering. Teddy came too, swiftly and sharply, groaning loudly. I stood in silence watching them, my hand rubbing wildly at my clit. I needed an orgasm too.

Then Teddy suddenly heaved himself off Lisa and I shot back behind the curtain on the conservatory door. I was trembling. If Teddy saw me I'd be dead meat.

I heard Lisa mumble something, and then Teddy's voice telling her quite sharply to get up. I had to get out of here quickly. I crept back into the drawing room and ran to the door. As I opened it, De Vigny's voice sounded in my ear and his hand gripped my arm. 'Mariella. What are you doing here?'

I turned round. He was glaring at me. Lisa stood behind him, putting her fingers to her lips and shaking her head. She didn't want me to say anything.

'I, I needed some fresh air. I heard a noise in here.' It was the truth, but with a huge chunk missed out.

I could tell Teddy didn't believe me, but he let go of my arm and smiled his usual, disarming smile, the one that melted hearts. 'Did you see anything you shouldn't see?' he queried craftily, staring me straight in the eyes.

I shook my head. 'No. Nothing.'

'All right then. Go back to the party, and don't mention a word about me being in here with Lisa, OK?'

He opened the door and I shot out, thankful to be let off so lightly. I didn't go back to the party. Instead I went to my room. I wanted to think things over, decide if it was worth staying or not. But when I flopped down onto the bed, I fell asleep.

The next morning the big news was that Lisa had gone, taken in a taxi to the station before breakfast. Teddy would not say any more than that. I felt uneasy and wondered why, when they had obviously enjoyed each other's company last night. But I put it out of my mind.

Teddy was back to his charming self. Full of smiles and compliments and affectionate cuddles. Who could resist him when he was like this? We all went for a long walk in the morning, trudging up and down hills, until we were exhausted, except for Edward that is. He pushed us along, slapping our bottoms as if we were naughty children if we lagged behind. It would have been funny if it wasn't so gruelling. In the afternoon he laid on a quiz. We were taken to an old school room where the five of us were made to sit at desks and answer mountains of general knowledge questions. Teddy said there would be a wonderful prize for the winner so we all tried very hard. When we had finished, he sent us off for an afternoon coffee break whilst he went through our answers.

We sat in the drawing room, chatting excitedly, wondering what the prize was going to be and who would win it. None of us mentioned Lisa, though I am sure we were all thinking about her and worried that the same fate would happen to us. The housekeeper brought us some coffee and home-made biscuits, which we munched greedily. All that physical and mental exercise had made us hungry.

Jasmin was nearly in tears. 'I know I not win,' she said in her broken English. 'I not very clever.'

We all laughed. None of us were the brains of Britain, or should I say France?

Teddy made a grand entrance an hour later, Lobo, as usual, hot on his heels. 'I have a winner,' he announced, waving the questionnaire papers in front of us.

We all turned to him expectantly.

'It is an English lady.'

Amy and I looked at one another in surprise. There were only two of us left now that Lisa had gone. Colette, Anne-Marie and Jasmin smiled delightedly at us but I could tell they were bitterly disappointed.

Teddy kept looking from me to Amy and back again, teasing us, making us wait.

'The winner is – Mariella,' he finally announced triumphantly.

Everybody cheered. I was delighted. I hadn't realised I was such a brain-box. And my prize? Was it a session in his bed? I hoped so. Then I could go home happy.

'And your prize is a trip over the Dordogne in my helicopter, tomorrow.'

I gasped with surprise and pleasure. How wonderful! Teddy eyed me speculatively. 'You like your prize then?'

'It's great, fantastic! I love flying. I've never been in a helicopter before. Thank you, Teddy.'

The rest of the day I was on cloud nine. I forgot about seducing Teddy and writing my book, and everything else come to that. All I could think about was getting up in that helicopter.

It was a small, four-seater helicopter. The pilot sat in the front, with Teddy and myself in the back. It was lovely warm day so I wore a skirt and T-shirt without a bra. Teddy eyed my breasts lasciviously and spanked my bottom playfully as I got inside. I hadn't seen the pilot before. I smiled pleasantly at him and said hello, but he ignored me.

'Don't say anything to Jacques,' Teddy warned. 'He hates being interrupted whilst he's flying.'

We soared into the air and I felt my heart lurch with excitement as it always does when an aircraft takes off.

Teddy took my hand and smiled warmly at me. Then he brought it to his lips and kissed it. 'You are a very beautiful woman, Mariella.'

I lapped up the flattery. I didn't doubt he said it to most women, but my ego still responded and my heart missed a beat. 'And you are a very attractive man, Edward De Vigny,' I heard myself reply, shifting my body slightly towards him and focussing my eyes steadily onto his. We were flirting with one another and loving every minute of it. For a few moments we sat in silence, watching the river snaking its way along the valley below us.

'You like it here?' Teddy asked eventually, his hand still clasped in mine.

'Yes, I do. It's beautiful.' I looked at him beguilingly, my lips slightly parted. I was longing for him to touch me.

He leaned over, cupped my chin in his hand and kissed me softly on the mouth. My lips tingled with pleasure. He made no move to push his tongue into my mouth, just continued nudging his lips gently against mine. When he pulled away, he put his hand to the back of my neck and started stroking it.

'Tell me,' he said suddenly. 'What did you really see in the conservatory the other night?'

'You and Lisa on the floor. Everything.'

He nodded slowly, his thumb coming round to fondle my throat. 'Did you find it exciting?'

'Yes.'

'Would you like me to fuck you, here, now?

'Yes.'

119

'Yes what?'

'Please.' My voice got stuck in my throat.

His fingers pressed more tightly around my neck whilst his other hand started moving slowly up my skirt, brushing my thighs with featherlight strokes. Then he kissed me again, passionately this time, crushing his lips against mine, opening his mouth, but still no tongue. Impatient as ever, I thrust my tongue into his mouth, but he instantly pulled away.

'Make love, not war,' he murmured into my ear, nibbling at it gently. 'We have all the time in the world.'

This was a very different man to the one I had seen humping Lisa in the conservatory. I felt very flattered and very excited that he wanted to make love to me.

His hand reached out and started to rub my pussy gently over my knickers. I opened my legs, inviting him to pull my knickers aside, but he didn't. After a while the slow, rhythmic rubbing of his fingers over my wet knickers started to drive me crazy. I reached down and tried to pull them off but he slapped my hand away. 'When I'm ready,' he said sternly, and pulled his hand away completely.

I was dismayed, thinking I'd blown it, but he started to kiss my neck and then his lips slowly moved down towards my breasts.

There wasn't much room in the helicopter and we both had our seatbelts on so it wasn't easy to move about. As Teddy nuzzled into my boobs I looked at Jacques, the pilot. He hadn't said a word. It was as if a robot was flying the machine.

Teddy caught me looking over his shoulder. 'Don't worry about Jacques. He's well trained.'

My heart plummeted. 'Has he done this often, then?' I said sharply.

Teddy grinned. 'I don't bring my women up here just to look at the scenery,' he said.

My ego instantly deflated. Edward De Vigny was a lecher. I wanted to hate him, but I couldn't.

'I only bring very beautiful women up here, though. I'm very choosy.'

'Not Lisa, though,' I couldn't help adding.

Teddy bristled. 'Lisa was a mistake. I don't like women who let me down, and she did, big time. She was awful in the play. I told her to leave, and the next minute I know she's on her hands and knees begging for it. What could I do?'

Poor Lisa. Things hadn't turned out well for her. But I was glad Teddy hadn't wanted her the way he wanted me. His hand was moving up my skirt again. This time I let him take it at his own pace.

Half an hour later, just as Jacques brought the helicopter down to land, Teddy penetrated me for the first time – with his fingers. I was at fever pitch, naked now, but still strapped into my seatbelt. The helicopter bumped down and Teddy pulled away, leaving me with my legs gaping open and my aching pussy soaked with desire.

I lay back in the seat, my eyes closed, moaning softly to myself, my hand automatically reaching down to finish the job off.

I vaguely heard Teddy's voice say, 'Get her out, Jacques, and bring her over to the sauna,' before my seatbelt was unclipped and two strong arms pulled me out of the helicopter. I opened my eyes to find myself naked in Jacques's arms as he strode across the lawn.

'Put me down,' I cried, kicking out at him.

'*Non!*' Jacques's steely arms gripped me tightly. He was a huge man, too strong for me. I saw Teddy hurrying along a little way ahead of us, and relaxed a little.

He looked back and grinned. 'That's a good girl, Mariella. You're too big for me to carry. Won't be long now.'

We headed towards the outskirts of the chateau to a small wooden hut.

Teddy opened the door. 'This is the sauna, Mariella. Lobo should have got it prepared for us.'

Once again I marvelled at Teddy's organisation. This whole outing had been planned. It looked like Teddy was finally going to shag me in the sauna. The hot air hit us. Jacques put me down when Teddy's back was turned, his large hands raking over my body as he did so. I glared at him, but said nothing, and he turned on his heels and left.

Teddy took my hand, drew me into a small room and sat me on top of a towel on the bench. Sweat was already pouring out of me. He quickly undressed himself and sat next to me.

Slowly he began to make love to me again, reaching out to touch every part of my body as I sat there trembling, waiting for him to penetrate me with his huge cock. I reached out to touch it and this time he didn't push me away. We were both very wet, our sweat mingling as we stroked each other.

Teddy leaned over and licked my nipples. 'Mmm, nice and salty,' he murmured.

I responded by licking his neck just below his ears and running my hands through his damp hair. He tasted lovely. We began to sway together, our bodies building up to a crescendo of desire. I couldn't go on much longer. My clit was swollen and ready to burst.

At last Edward De Vigny reached out and opened my legs as wide as he could so that he could enter me. His movements were deliberate, his eyes watching me all the time. When he bent down in front of me and slowly pushed his cock into my throbbing pussy, I swooned with ecstasy. Nobody had ever made me wait as long as this man. I was nearly there. Gradually he stepped up the pace, each thrust getting quicker and stronger. When his hand came down and touched my clit, I

122

started to spasm and then I was lost to the world. He came too, and I knew no more until I opened my eyes and found myself locked in his arms as he rocked me to and fro. I was deliriously happy. 'I love you,' I blurted out, my eyes shining up at his.

He looked at me sadly, and I wished I hadn't said anything. I don't really know why I did anyway. I loved Ryan, not Teddy – didn't I?

'Sorry,' I said, tears coming to my eyes. 'I shouldn't have said that, but it was so wonderful.'

Teddy hung on to me as if he was frightened to let me go. 'Thank you, sweet Mariella. I won't forget you in a hurry.'

I came back down to earth with a bang. I struggled out of Teddy's arms. I didn't love him, of course I didn't, and he certainly didn't love me. I was just the latest in an endless line of women whom he would have forgotten about this time next week.

I looked round for my clothes, but they weren't there. They were still in the helicopter.

Teddy saw my distress. 'There's a bathrobe hanging outside,' he said flatly. 'Put it on and go back to the house. I'll get your clothes later.'

I ran out of the room, anxious that De Vigny wouldn't see my tears. The heavy towelling bathrobe and the cool air soaked up the moisture on my body as I sped across the lawn towards the brooding presence of Le Chateau Blanc.

That evening I packed my bags and crept out of the chateau without saying goodbye to anybody. I left a brief note of apology for Edward in the drawing room. I couldn't face him again. My emotions were in utter chaos. If I stayed I might be tempted to stay forever, permanently waiting for him to throw me scraps of love along with all his other women. Did he intend to do the same to Colette, Anne-Marie, Jasmin and Amy, or had he already ensnared them into his love nest? Was this how Lisa felt when she left?

I stood alone on the station platform, tears tumbling down my face. Something brushed against the top of my leg. I looked down to see Lobo staring up at me, his eyes sad and knowing. 'Master Edward asked me to give you this,' he said, handing me a little box. I opened it up to find a small, gold, heart-shaped locket on a chain. Written on the outside in tiny italic letters were the words *JE T'AIME*.

Chapter Nine

Scorpio: The Sex Magnate

23 OCTOBER

I'm in the doldrums. For two weeks I have been moping around the flat, sleeping, eating and getting fat. I've got no man, no job, no money and, worst of all, no sex. I wish I'd stayed in France. When I arrived back in England I found a note from Ryan saying he was finished with me. Sharing Edward De Vigny with lots of other women doesn't seem such a bad proposition now. Every time I ring Ryan I either get his answer service or he hangs up on me. I've been round to his flat several times but he won't answer the door. I even swallowed my pride and rang Gemma to ask if he was with her, but she was very non-committal and when I lost my temper and called her a 'selfish cow' she hung up on me. Surprisingly I've still got a few friends: Anna and Zoe have been ringing me constantly, trying to cheer me up. Anna wants me to go and stay for a few days but I really don't feel up to facing Lester. In my state anything could happen. I might even fall for his dubious charms. Ugh!

Today is the first day of Scorpio and I've done nothing to find a suitable contender for my book. Truth is, I don't feel like it anymore. Without Ryan's support I'm tempted to give the whole thing up. What's money after all? Will it make me happy? And why am I still writing this stupid diary? Habit, I suppose. I've had enough. I've got a foul headache, so I'm going to take a few aspirins and go back to bed. I just want to sleep and forget about everything.

The phone kept ringing, but I didn't answer it. I was too busy watching Richard and Judy on the box. I hadn't moved from the flat for a whole week since writing my diary. Supplies were running low. I was living on frozen meals. And to compound all my problems, I looked a sight. An eruption of zits on my chin was just about the last straw. I couldn't imagine anyone wanting to shag me now.

An hour later somebody was banging on the door. I ignored it.

Then I heard Zoe's voice yelling through the letterbox. 'Ellie! Ellie! Are you all right? Open the door.'

I sprang up from the couch and tiptoed to the hall-way. Why wasn't Zoe at work? I couldn't let her see me like this. Panicking, I shouted at her to go away.

'No, I won't,' she yelled back. 'I'm going to stay here 'til you let me in.'

I stood in silence in the hallway, willing her to go away.

'Ellie, please,' she begged. 'I've been trying to ring you all morning. Why won't you answer the phone? I'm worried about you. Look, it's my lunch break. I drove like a maniac to get here. I've only got forty minutes left, but I'm not going back 'til you open the door.'

I began to feel ashamed of myself. Zoe was a really good mate. She was willing to risk the wrath of her boss in order to make sure that I was all right. I shuffled forward, hugging my dirty dressing gown around my chest, and slowly opened the door.

She shot in, then stopped in her tracks, staring at me. Tears came to her eyes. 'Oh, Ellie! What are you doing to yourself?'

Suddenly she was in my arms and we were hugging one another. I couldn't let her go. 'I'm sorry, Zo, didn't mean to be such a bitch,' I sobbed into her shoulder.

Zoe let me cry, every so often patting my back as if I was a baby. Finally she managed to extricate herself and lead me into the lounge. Then she took charge. Out came her mobile phone. 'I'm going to ring up my boss and tell him I won't be back this afternoon.'

I shook my head wildly. 'No, no. He won't like it. You've got to go back. I'll be all right now.'

'No way. I'm not leaving you like this. I'll tell him my mother's been taken ill. Then you, my dear Ellie, are going to clean yourself up, have a shower, wash your hair and put that wretched dressing gown in the wash. It stinks.'

I smiled and she smiled back. I was on the road to recovery.

Two hours later, a different person stared back at me in the mirror. With plenty of concealer on my chin and full make-up on, my zits were hardly noticeable. Zoe had blow-dried my hair so that it hung round my shoulders in soft waves and made me dress in one of my most expensive outfits – a matching black suede jacket and trouser suit with a tight, low-cut pink top. I looked good and, for the first time in ages, I felt good too.

'Where are we going?' I asked as she herded me out of the door.

'First of all, we're going shopping. You've got no coffee, no milk, no nothing, in fact. Then we can go into town and have a sitdown over a cup of tea whilst we decide what we're doing tonight.'

I held onto Zoe's arm tightly, feeling nervous at

leaving the flat for the first time in a week. I was so lucky to have her. I loved her to bits.

By the time I'd guzzled down two cups of tea and stuffed my face with cake, I was beginning to feel more like my old self, except I was about half a stone heavier.

'I'll diet tomorrow,' I said, and licked the cream off the top of a strawberry tart.

Zoe laughed. She was stuffing her face as usual but wouldn't put on an ounce of weight. Life could be so unfair at times.

'So, what would you like to do tonight, Ellie? A film, a meal, a club?'

'I don't know. You decide. What about Tony? He won't want to come with us, will he?' Zoe was still seeing the incorrigible Tony from the Ibiza trip back in June. I couldn't believe she had stuck with him for so long.

'Of course not. We aren't joined at the hip, you know. Talking about Tony the Gemini, what have you done about finding a Scorpio?'

My face clouded over. I began to feel depressed again. 'Nothing. I've given up on it.'

'Oh, Ellie! You can't. All that hard work you've put in. And what about the money and your father's house? You'll be losing out on such a lot.'

I shrugged my shoulders. 'Money isn't everything.'

'I know. But it helps when you haven't got a penny to your name. This is all because of that rich bloke who owns the chateau, isn't it? De Vey, or whatever his name is?'

'Partly, yes. I fell for him badly, Zo. I can't face the thought of it happening again. Then there's Ryan.'

'Ryan. Huh! You're not seeing him anymore, so what does it matter? He's a bastard to let you down like he has, anyway.'

'Be fair, Zoe. I let him down too. He thought I wasn't

going to France. Up until then he had supported me in everything. Besides, there are other things he doesn't know about.'

Zoe's eyes opened wide. 'Like what? Tell me.'

'You know, my little fling with the theatre usher who wasn't a Leo, and not being able to say "no" to Patrick at the office.'

'Oh! I assumed you told Ryan about them.'

I shook my head unhappily. 'No. And I'll never get him back if I tell him now.'

'You want him back then, even though he's probably shacked up with Gemma?'

'Yes, I do. I know I fell for Edward De Vigny, but I think it was the way he made love to me more than anything else. It was as if I really mattered to him. With Ryan, it's different. He's not romantic but the sex is brilliant. We know each other so well, warts and all. I love Ryan for who he is, whereas Edward was just a dream.'

Zoe nodded knowingly. 'I understand, but sitting around moping about it isn't going to get you your father's money. You've got to carry on, Ellie. You're over half way through. We'll go out tonight and find a Scorpio together.'

I laughed. 'What, you'll have him too?'

Zoe pondered a moment. 'I suppose I could. In fact, if you really don't feel up to it, I could find a willing Scorpio, shag him, and then tell you all about it so you could write it up as if you'd had him.'

'That's cheating.'

'I know. But it would be worth it to you.'

'No, I can't do it. I might be good at telling little white lies or omitting to tell Ryan what I'm doing, but I couldn't cheat like that. I want to be able to look that snooty solicitor in the eye at the end of March and tell him I've done it, knowing it's the truth.'

'Good on you, Ellie. But you will let me help you,

won't you? Where are we most likely to find a Scorpio? They're supposed to be highly-sexed, aren't they?'

I laughed. 'That's an understatement. Even the quiet ones are closet sex maniacs.'

'A porn cinema, then? Or perhaps a strip-show, or a sleazy lap-dancing club?'

'Mmm, there'd probably be lots of Scorpios at those places but I don't fancy going somewhere like that at the moment, even if we are together. Besides, I might get one who was into SM, or something peculiar.'

'What's wrong with that? I've had some good fun doing kinky things. Did I ever tell you about the guy who covered me in clingfilm so that I looked like an alien and then made me whip his bare arse whilst we watched *Star Trek*?'

I laughed. 'No, you didn't. I don't think I'd like anything like that. I want to get some satisfaction too, you know.'

'Get him to whip you, then.'

'Ouch! I'm too much of a coward. A good spanking is about my limit.'

'OK, chicken. But there is somewhere else I've just thought of: a new club in town. Lots of girls go there and they attract the blokes, so it's always packed. Tony and I went a few weeks ago. Every time he vanished to the loo I was beseiged with guys trying to chat me up. I could have got it on dozens of times.'

'Did you?'

'Of course not. I was with Tony.' She grinned. 'But I was sorely tempted.'

'If we go, do you promise that you'll find out the sign of anybody I fancy and if he's a Scorpio you'll pass him on to me?'

'Yep. No problem.'

'OK. You're on.'

We went back to my flat, unloaded the shopping, ate a pizza and re-vamped our make-up. I changed into a sexy little number, a short, halterneck red dress with no bra. Underneath I wore a pair of brief red panties. Zoe borrowed one of my dresses – a white one with gold trimmings – but because I was a size fourteen (going on sixteen at the moment) to her ten, it looked like a boat on her.

'It doesn't matter,' she said cheerfully, tying a belt round the middle to make it fit better. 'I look sweet and innocent, just like a virgin. Lucky I'm not out to catch a man.'

We giggled as she performed in front of the mirror, putting on a demure little-girl act. We both knew she would attract the blokes whatever she was dressed in.

As we left the flat I realised that I was actually enjoying myself. I'd hardly thought of Edward De Vigny or Ryan since Zoe had turned up. She had got me firing on all four cylinders again. I was more deter-mined than ever to fulfil my task.

The music thumped loudly. Crowds of trendy people in designer gear thronged round us. Zoe and I stood close to the bar, leaning against the railing which divided the bar from the dancefloor. I felt light-headed and happy. I had already danced with several men, none of whom were Scorpios, unfortunately. I wondered if it was all a bit too hip or shallow for a typical Scorpio. Zoe had not had any luck either.

'There's a small room over there, with another bar.' Zoe pointed to the other side of the hall. 'It's darker in there, great for a crafty snog. You might find a Scorpio hanging out.'

I nodded and we dodged across the dancefloor to reach the archway which led into the smaller room. It was packed. Couples were seated everywhere, crushed against one another, lips on lips, hands groping naked flesh. Zoe and I stared in fascination.

'Let's get another drink,' she whispered.

We squeezed through the mass of blokes who were standing around, pints in hand, trying to look nonchalant as they watched the antics of the seated couples. Just as we reached the bar, a hand reached down and grabbed my right buttock. I spun round to face a very attractive, dark-haired youth. He looked Italian or Spanish. I grinned at him encouragingly.

Zoe saw what was happening. 'What sign are you?' she asked the lad sharply.

'Eh? What?' he asked, raising his eyebrows and looking at Zoe as if she was mad.

'Sign of the zodiac, you idiot. Aries, Taurus or what?'

'Oh, er, Leo, I think. I was born on August the seventeenth.'

'Yep. You're a Leo all right. You can piss off then.' Zoe pulled my arm and dragged me away. 'You can't just have it off with anybody,' she said seriously. 'I know you're gagging for it, but remember, you only want a Scorpio.'

She was right, of course. Lucky she was with me.

We bought ourselves another outrageously expensive glass of wine and managed to squeeze on the end of a seat beside a couple whose tongues seemed permanently wedged in one another's throats. We looked around and surveyed the talent.

Zoe suddenly nudged me. 'Don't look now, Ellie, but there's a guy on his own in the corner, opposite the gents', who keeps looking at you. He could easily be a Scorpio. He's really sexy – lovely, deep-set eyes.'

I took my time. I didn't want to make it obvious. But when I finally looked at him, he was staring at me full on. My heart missed a beat. He did look rather Scorpio-like. I turned to Zoe. 'Yes,' I said quietly. 'He looks OK. Find out what sign he is, Zo.'

Full of confidence, Zoe stood up and walked straight over to the man. They talked for a few moments. He kept nodding, and then he looked over at me again. Zoe came back to me, looking quite excited. 'You're on,' she said. 'He's a Scorpio all right, but you can check him out for sure. He says he fancies you.'

Suddenly I felt embarrassed. 'What did you say to him, Zoe?'

'Never mind that. Get your arse off that seat and come and say hello. His name is Brad, by the way. He looks a bit like Brad Pitt, don't you think?'

I followed Zoe over to Brad. His eyes raked into me. Leaning against the bar he had looked much shorter than he really was. Standing next to him I only came up to his chest.

'This is my friend Ellie,' Zoe was saying. 'She's an astrologer. That's why I asked what sign you were.'

I blushed. Zoe was so direct at times. Brad's eyes pierced into mine. 'Does the fact that I'm a Scorpio make me more interesting?' he said in a deep, sexy voice.

I didn't know what to say. For some reason I was dumbstruck.

'Of course it does,' Zoe piped in. 'Scorpios are very nice people.'

'Are they?'

Again he looked at me and I nodded stupidly. This was a great start. I was beginning to lose confidence.

'Well, sometimes.' Even Zoe was finding him hard work. 'Nice and sexy anyway. Not that I know much about astrology. Ellie's the expert.'

'Is she now?' His eyes looked deep into my soul. My stomach started churning and my pussy gave a little flutter. He was already turning me on and we'd hardly said a word to each other.

'Why don't you and Ellie have a dance?' Zoe suggested brightly.

'I don't dance. Not to this sort of music anyway. Ask me again when it slows down. Oh, here's my mate.'

Another man approached, with an attractive black girl on his arm.

Brad introduced us all. His friend was called John. The girl – his latest pick-up – called herself Suki. The five of us stood chatting for a while. I gradually relaxed and found my tongue, thanks to John, who was remarkably easy to talk to – a Gemini as it turned out. But all the time, I was aware of Brad standing next to me, his powerful aura blending into mine, making me want to touch him, find out about him, see if he fulfilled all of his sexual promise.

John asked Zoe to dance, leaving Brad and I to cope with Suki. She immediately turned her attention to Brad, rolling her lovely brown eyes seductively at him, and thrusting her large breasts towards his chest, totally confident of her sexuality. I felt very jealous.

Brad seemed amused. Between the flirts and thrusts he looked at me and smiled apologetically, and I realised with great relief that he was humouring the sultry Suki. Eventually he put his arm around my waist, politely said 'Excuse us' to Suki and pulled me towards the dancefloor. Goodness knows what had happened to John and Zoe, but I could hazard a guess. Zoe might think she loved Tony, but she loved sex more. An open, chatty guy like John was just her type.

The music had slowed down at last. Brad pulled me into his arms and we smooched on the crowded dancefloor.

When Brad's hand started to reach up my dress and move towards my bum, I took no notice. His hand felt lovely on my bare cheek, and I was trembling all over. But when he reached down with his other hand and pulled the back of my dress right up to reveal my half-naked arse, I felt a bit exposed. 'Don't,' I whispered. 'Everybody can see me.'

His hands gripped my buttocks tightly. 'Don't worry. Just go with it. If you don't make a fuss, nobody will notice.'

I had no option. His hands continued to squeeze my

buttocks and every so often he pulled my cheeks slightly apart so that I could feel a brush of warm air against my anus. I felt a peculiar mixture of extreme embarrassment and great excitement. I didn't dare look round in case anybody was watching but I didn't want him to stop. Eventually, he slipped a finger inside my panties and rubbed it along the crease between my pussy and my arse, making me wet all over. My breathing was heavy, my head buried deep against his chest. Occasionally he reached down and kissed the top of my head, usually before he went on to the next step. But soon the slow music stopped and the techno started up again. He pulled away and pushed me back towards the small room. I was flushed with excitement.

John and Zoe were back. They had found a place to sit right in the corner of the room, and were locked in one another's arms. The pristine white dress was crumpled up around Zoe's thighs, and John's hand was casually stroking the top of her legs.

'Move up a bit so that Ellie and I can sit down,' Brad said to John.

'No room,' John said, 'unless Zoe sits on my lap.'

Zoe giggled. She had a double vodka in her hand and was already half cut. She twisted herself onto John's lap where she sat facing us with her legs apart, showing most of her knickers. They started snogging again, and John's hand went back to Zoe's crotch. Brad and I watched in fascination as John slipped his hand inside Zoe's knickers. Zoe started moaning. She seemed oblivious to the world.

'Nice show,' Brad whispered to me. 'Are you as uninhibited as your friend?'

'No way. I'm much shyer than Zoe.'

'Now, why don't I believe you? Let's sit down.'

He squashed himself next to John and Zoe and tried to pull me onto his lap, but I resisted. 'I need a pee,' I said, turning away and making a beeline for the ladies'.

The ladies' was at the other end of the hall. When I came out Brad was leaning against the wall outside the door waiting for me. Without a word, he grabbed my hand and pulled me along the narrow hallway, past the doorway to the dancefloor towards a double swing door and into another corridor. Then a little way further on he turned right into a small, empty alcove, where he pushed me against the wall and pulled my dress up.

It all happened so quickly I was powerless to stop it, even if I'd wanted to.

'I want to fuck you,' Brad said throatily, tugging at my panties and ripping them off.

He looked at my bare pussy and gave a little groan. 'Beautiful,' he murmured, undoing his flies and pulling out his cock.

'Just a quickie, for now,' he said grabbing my buttocks and pulling me up so that my legs were round his waist. His cock rammed into me sharply. I was still a little tight and I gave a short gasp of pain, but it soon gave way to pleasure as his thrusts built up and I started to get wet. His hands gripped onto my buttocks as he pulled me up and down on his rock-hard cock. It was fantastic. I felt like putty in his hands, soft and pliable and ready to burst. He came suddenly, shuddering inside me, moaning loudly, biting into my neck.

When he put me down I felt deflated.

'Don't worry,' he said, smiling broadly as he chucked me under the chin. 'There's loads more where that came from. Let's get out of here. I know a great place we can go.'

'What sort of place?' I asked, feeling a bit apprehensive as I bent down to pick up my panties.

'Wait and see. You'll love it.' He grabbed the panties from my hand, stuffed them into his pocket and pushed me out into the corridor. He was in full control and I wasn't sure whether I liked it or not.

'I need to tell Zoe where we're going,' I said.

'OK. She and John might like to come too.'

Back in the small room John and Zoe were almost shagging one another. Zoe was against the wall in the corner of the room, partially shielded by John's body. She was caressing his cock with both hands whilst most of John's right hand seemed to have disappeared inside her knickers.

'Zoe!' I hissed. 'Pack it in. Brad's going to take us somewhere else.'

John looked up, dazed and tipsy. 'Hi, Brad. I'm just about to get my end up.'

'Not here, John. You'll get thrown out. The guy at the bar has already got his eye on you. We're moving on to my place.'

John's eyes lit up. 'You mean, your place. Great! OK.' He pulled his hand out of Zoe's knickers, gave it a quick sniff and then tucked his cock back into his trousers.

Zoe was in a state, as usual. If it hadn't happened so many times before I would have been worried. But Zoe could look after herself. Come tomorrow morning she would be as bright as a button, eating a big breakfast, drinking coffee with no sign of a hangover or any regrets about her excesses of the night before. She gazed at me with bleary eyes. I pulled her dress down and helped her up. She staggered a bit, but was OK when she got her balance. John took over and they followed Brad and I out to the car park.

Brad hadn't had much to drink, thank goodness. I sat in the front next to him, whilst Zoe cuddled up to John in the back. When I looked round a few moments later, her head was in his lap and she was sucking him greedily.

'Jealous,' said Brad, eyeing my thighs. 'If you're in a bad way, open up the glove compartment. There's something in there which might keep you happy.'

I opened it up to find a huge vibrator. I stared at it in wonder.

'Go on,' said Brad. 'It'll fill you up for a while.' He chuckled to himself.

'No, thank you,' I said starchily. 'I don't need it.'

'Oh yes, you do.' Brad pulled the car to a sudden stop in a small layby, pulled the vibrator out, pushed my legs open and tried to insert it into my pussy.

At first I resisted. I was angry with him. I felt I was losing my sense of identity, but when he persisted and turned the vibrator on so that it gently reverberated inside me, creating huge waves of desire, I sank back into my seat and gave way.

'Don't take it out until I say so,' Brad ordered, starting the car engine up again.

John's voice came out from the back seat. 'Hey, Brad, did I hear the word vibrator?'

'Piss off, Johnny. You take care of your bit of pussy and I'll take care of mine.'

I looked at Brad in shock, but he grinned back at me and I relaxed again. The vibrator was really making me horny.

At the next set of traffic lights, Brad reached down and pulled my dress up around my hips so that he could see the vibrator inside me. I held it there tightly, unwilling to relinquish it now that it was doing its job. By the time the car arrived at Brad's place, I was on the verge of an orgasm.

Brad watched me, his eyes wrinkled up in amusement. 'That's a good girl. Give it all you've got.'

I arched my back and lifted my arse from the seat, pushing urgently at the vibrator, needing to feel its hardness deep inside me; needy to fill the tickle that reverberated all the way to my clit. Then I came, screaming with desire, everything forgotten. I was in a world of my own.

Brad pulled the vibrator out of me before I had finished shuddering. 'No,' I wailed, hitting out at him. 'Want more!'

Brad took no notice. He pushed me out of the car onto the pavement where John and Zoe were waiting, huddled together in the cold night air.

Brad put a jacket round my shoulders and led the four of us up some steps. I was in no fit state to work out where we were and what sort of building we were entering. Inside it was lovely and warm, and I melted against Brad's shoulders contentedly.

A girl at a reception desk smiled at Brad. 'Hello, Mr Endersbeigh. What room would you like today?'

John suddenly lurched forward. 'Can I have the Fountain Room, please?'

The receptionist looked at Brad. 'Is that all right with you, Mr Endersbeigh? It is vacant at the moment.'

'Fine. Let him have it. I'd like the Dungeon Room.'

'I'm sorry. It's occupied until one a.m.'

'Get them out, then, now. And let them use one of the other rooms free of charge.'

'Yes, Mr Endersbeigh. I'll call Andy to move them immediately.'

I stood close to Brad, watching and listening to the interaction between him and the receptionist. It sounded like he was in charge in some way. I was intrigued.

Zoe came up behind me and nudged me in the ribs. 'Get a load of this place, Ellie. I've heard about it, but never been here.' She sounded almost sober.

'Come on, Zoe,' John said, pulling at her arm. 'We're off to the Fountain Room.'

Zoe grinned and started to follow John. 'See you later, Ellie. Have fun.'

Brad and I were alone. 'How are you feeling?' he asked, suddenly full of concern.

'OK. What is this place and why are you taking me to the Dungeon Room?'

'It's a kind of leisure centre. I –' The phone on the reception desk rang, interrupting him.

The receptionist picked it up, and nodded at Brad. 'Andy says you can go down now, Mr Endersbeigh.'

Brad took my hand and smiled encouragingly at me. I held back.

'Come on, Ellie. You don't have to do anything you don't want to do. You'll have a great time, I promise you.'

Reluctantly I let him lead me down a flight of stairs into a large, dark room. When he turned on the lights, I gasped with shock. I couldn't carry on playing the innocent anymore. I think I had known all along which road I was being taken down. The very thing I had avoided all my life, which Zoe kept telling me was good fun, was staring me in the face: every kind of S & M equipment imaginable. Stocks, whips, a huge bed with chains and handcuffs and dozens of other pieces of apparatus that I'd never seen in my life.

'No!' I said, shaking my head. 'I don't want this.'

Brad put his arm round my shoulders. 'I think you do. If you've never experienced it before, it'll blow your mind.'

'Not mine. I don't enjoy this sort of thing.'

'How do you know if you've never tried?'

'I just do. It doesn't turn me on.'

'I think you're wrong. You're a natural. Believe me, I know what women like. The first moment I saw you, I knew you'd fit in here.'

I started shaking. Deep down I knew that he was right, but I was too frightened to acknowledge it.

Brad led me to the bed. 'Let's take this silly dress off first and get you into something more appropriate,' he said gently, pulling my dress up.

I let him do it. He found me a black leather catsuit. The top had holes for the nipples, and the bottom half had front and back openings. Brad pulled my nipples through the small holes in the tight material, making them elongated. Gently he sucked them to make them erect. I tried not to respond, but I couldn't help it. My body always has a mind of its own. He lifted me up to a standing position and thrust two fingers in my pussy and two fingers up my arse. I trembled with delight.

'I want to explore every part of your body,' Brad said, reaching down to suckle my tits whilst his fingers probed deep inside me. 'But first I want to stimulate you, make you feel on fire.' He took his fingers out and led me over to the stocks.

'Get down on all fours and put your head through the hole,' he ordered.

I backed away. 'I don't want to,' I said.

'OK. I'll do it then.'

I stood watching in amazement as he ripped all his clothes off and knelt down. 'Go and get the whip on the wall,' he said, putting his head through the hole and sticking his arse in the air.

I got the whip and stood with it dangling by my side, waiting for him to tell me what to do. 'Give it to me, then,' he shouted.

I tried to bring the whip down onto his backside but I couldn't. I tried again and managed a light flick.

Brad laughed. 'You'll need to do it much harder than that.'

'I, I can't.' To my horror, I started to cry.

Brad extricated himself from the stocks and took me into his arms. The scent of his naked body against mine made me want him all over again. I nuzzled against him. 'I want you, just you,' I murmured.

'OK. You can have me, after you've tried out the stocks.' He pushed me away from his chest and stared deeply into my eyes. They were totally mesmerising. I wanted to swoon, to lay myself at his feet, give myself to him totally.

Sensing the change in me, Brad gently pushed me to the floor on all fours. I put my head through the hole and stuck my arse out, just as he had done. His hand caressed me, his fingers running up and down the crease. He reached downwards, to my pussy. It was soaking wet. Then he took his hand away and brought it down with a resounding smack on my cheeks. No problem. I was used to this and I loved a good spanking. I wiggled my arse and he smacked me again, harder, and a third time harder still, so that it was tingling. Then he brought down the whip and I yelled out in pain. And again, even harder. My buttocks started to smart and tears came to my eyes, but my pussy had gone into overdrive. When the pain subsided, I realised I was extremely excited. After the next lashing, Brad pushed my legs open wider and thrust four fingers into me. I lost my mind, and thrust my arse at him for more lashings. A few minutes later, when I was sobbing deliriously with pain and passion, he pulled me out of the stocks, picked me up and threw me on the bed, face down. Before I realised what he was doing, he had handcuffed my hands and feet to the chains on each corner of the bed. He pushed several cushions under my stomach so that my backside was raised in the air, and down came the whip again, cutting into my tender cheeks once more. By now I was loving it. Not once did I tell him to stop. Both my openings were gaping wide and aching with pleasure. I wanted him so much that I would have done anything.

He stopped whipping me. 'Do you want me to fuck you, whore?' he whispered in my ear.

'Yes. Yes, please.'

He whipped me again, and I screamed out loud. 'Do it to me, now.'

'Master! Call me Master.'

'Fuck me, Master.' I sobbed into the pillow as the whip came down again.

Then his hands were on my tingling cheeks, pulling the leather away, and his cock was nudging against my most private hole. I raised my arse in welcome and a hand found my clit. Before I knew what was happening, I was heaving with an almighty orgasm that tore me apart. Time stood still once again and I was totally immersed as countless waves of lust ripped through my body. I wasn't even aware of Brad coming, so lost was I in my own kingdom of pleasure.

I shall never forget that night when I finally lost my last shred of inhibition (or so I thought) and relinquished myself to the wondrous pleasure of S & M. Brad was right: I had been in denial. When I told Zoe all about it the next day, she wasn't surprised. She suggested we go to the 'Treasure Trove' again one day and try out different rooms. Evidently the Fountain Room was full of water apparatus, including a waterbed, with a real fountain in the middle in which Zoe and John had spent most of the night shagging. There were other rooms to explore: a games room, a nature room, and many more. Brad turned out to be a big-shot in the porn industry. Surprise, surprise. Not only did he own the Treasure Trove, but he owned several other companies, including a soft-porn film company. When Zoe told me, I was a bit miffed that he hadn't asked me to be in one of his films, but he obviously knew I would have refused. He seemed to know me inside out after just a few hours. All I know is that Sagittarius is probably going to be a huge disappointment after experiencing the delights of a Scorpio.

Chapter Ten

Sagittarius: The Amorous Adventurer

22 NOVEMBER

I'm on cloud nine. The wanderer has returned. Ryan turned up out of the blue on my doorstep last week and begged me to go back with him. I couldn't believe it. He looked terrible, all haggard and bleary-eyed and in desperate need of a shave. He told me he had hardly slept a wink since we'd broken up. I was over the moon to see him. When he finally stopped blubbing about how sorry he was, I opened my arms and he collapsed into them, declaring undying love. It was so romantic. We made love that night like never before. Any remaining thoughts I might have harboured about loving Edward De Vigny disappeared from my mind for ever.

I can't believe there are only six weeks to go before the end of the year and I've successfully completed eight months of my challenge. Today the Sun moves into Sagittarius and this time my work should be a doddle, now that I've got my very own Sagittarian back. Writing about Ryan shouldn't be a problem. He's complex, he likes women, loves sex and is very adventurous in bed. He hates routine and being tied down, and because I'm a Saggie too, I understand where he's coming from. We're both the same, except that I like men, of course.

I returned to work after my session with Brad. I need the money to help pay off my debts. This time I'm in an office full of men who I can flirt with to my heart's content, but now that Ryan's back, there'll be no nooky with any of them – yet. I say that because one of them is a Capricorn and he's rather nice, so I'm nurturing him with next month in mind. I've found out he belongs to a rambling club, so I've half a mind to join it too. Hang on, I'm going ahead of myself here. I've no need to write about Mr Capricorn yet. I can relax for a while. I've got Ryan, my Sagittarian, to keep me happy for the next few weeks.

Ryan rubbed the soapy bubbles into my breasts, giving my nipples playful pinches now and then. We were in the bath together, cleaning ourselves up after a glorious shagging session which had started on the kitchen floor and ended up in the bathroom. It was gone midnight and we were both exhausted, but my nipples were hardening with desire, and below the water I could see Ryan's cock rising to attention again.

'I think he needs cleaning,' I said, reaching for his penis.

'You've already done him twice.'

'I know, but he needs a bit more.' I ran my hand round the head of his cock, getting a great deal of satisfaction from feeling it grow hard.

Ryan sighed with pleasure and leaned back in the bath. His swollen cock rose out of the water.

I bent over on all fours and took him into my mouth. He tasted clean and soapy. I sucked on him as if he were a lollipop, opening my mouth wide and taking in as much as I could. Since he's been back we can't get enough of each other. We fuck every night, sometimes two or three times. We've tried out a few new positions too, but the old favourites die hard. I love being on top with my boobs dangling in Ryan's face, and my arse in the air with his fingers pushing into my anus. Ryan likes me on all fours – anywhere but the bed – where he can really push into me hard and make me feel like a whore. Because we're both Sagittarians, we can't bear to be in a rut. We're both constantly seeking new excitement.

Ryan pushed me away from him in the bath. 'Your turn,' he said.

I leaned back on my elbows, my head just above the water, and thrust my pelvis at him. He held my legs up with his hands and thrust his tongue into my pussy. The feel of it dipping inside me and lightly sucking on my clit made me horny all over again. I closed my eyes and started to moan with pleasure. We were building up to another shag.

Ryan stopped. 'We've both got work in the morning,' he said half-heartedly.

'Fuck work.'

'I'd sooner fuck you.' He pushed me over onto my knees, splashing water everywhere, and plunged into me from behind. The wetness of our bodies made it doubly exciting. The water was getting cold, and my pussy was sore, but I hardly noticed. Having Ryan's cock inside me was the only thing that mattered.

Half an hour later we lay curled up together in bed, fast asleep. Ryan was staying over more and more now. Our relationship had never been better. That's why I was so stunned when, the following day, Ryan asked me to do something which I really did not want to do.

We had just finished dinner – lasagne, served with salad – lovingly prepared by my own hands.

Ryan sat back in his chair, patting his stomach contentedly. 'Lovely meal, Ellie. Your cooking's getting better.'

I smiled. 'Thanks. But don't expect it too often.'

He looked into my eyes. 'As long as I have you.'

I savoured the romantic moment and leaned forward to kiss him, but he backed away, suddenly seeming a bit agitated. 'I met an interesting guy at work today,' he said, not looking at me as he tapped his fingers on the table.

I was instantly suspicious, but kept my tone neutral. 'Oh? Who's that?'

'Duncan Middlemass. He's an engineer.'

'What's so interesting about him?'

'Well, apart from being quite rich and a Sagittarian – his birthday is today, by the way – he's been married for ten years and for five of them he and his wife have been swingers.'

'You mean they do a bit of wife-swapping?'

'Yeah. But they belong to special swinging clubs too.'

I grinned at Ryan. 'Did he tell you all the juicy details?'

'Some of them. He said it's great fun, and it's kept him and his wife together. He swears they love one another more than they ever did.'

Ryan was looking at me so intently, I think I knew then what he wanted, but I played the innocent. 'I don't think I'd like it,' I said.

'That's a shame, because I told him we would probably enjoy it, so he's invited us to his place next weekend.'

I stared at Ryan in shock. We'd only just got back together. We were happy.

'If you said yes because he's a Sagittarian, then there was no need. I've got you.'

'I agreed to it because it sounds exciting, something different for us to experience, but the fact that he's a Saggie does seem ideal. I think you should find out what other Sagittarians are like. You'll be prejudiced writing about me.'

'So you don't mind the idea of me being shagged by somebody else, possibly with you there watching, then?'

He gave a wry smile. 'I've got used to it, Ellie. How many guys have you had this year, apart from me? Eight up to Scorpio, isn't it, with Capricorn, Aquarius and Pisces to come.' He waved my immediate protestations aside. 'And don't start saying it's only work, because I know you've enjoyed it. Now I'm asking you to do something for me. Just one night swinging with another couple. Is that too much too ask?'

'And what about you? Do you want to fuck somebody else's wife, somebody you've never met?' My voice was frosty and I was almost in tears.

Ryan shrugged. 'Maybe. I'd like to try it – just once.'

I stared morosely at Ryan. I couldn't believe he was asking me to do this when we were so settled, but I could see his point. I decided to make one last stand.

'Ryan, please, I don't want to do it. I'm happy the way we are.'

'I know you are, and I'm really chuffed to be back here with you. We belong together. But you know how much I like change and variety – we both do – and it would only be the once, I promise. Unless of course, we get a taste for it.' He grinned wickedly.

What could I say? How could I refuse him, when everything he'd said was true?

'OK,' I said reluctantly. 'But don't expect me to enjoy it.'

Ryan gave a loud guffaw of derision and grabbed me by the waist. 'The day you don't enjoy sex will be the day I stop living.'

We did a little jig on the kitchen floor. Then we took our clothes off and fell in a laughing heap onto the kitchen table.

* * *

Duncan and Sheryl Middlemass lived in a big detached house in Sussex with an acre of garden, a swimming pool, and a menagerie of animals, including four horses which used to be racers. Evidently Sheryl had inherited a lot of money from her parents and didn't need to work. She spent most of her time mucking out stables, seeing to the horses and riding around the countryside, according to Ryan.

When they opened the door to greet us on the Saturday morning I couldn't believe how normal they looked. Duncan was dressed in a tracksuit and trainers and wore glasses, whilst Sheryl looked a mess. Her long, dark hair was pulled back into an untidy bun at the nape of her neck and her sloppy jumper and baggy trousers looked well past their best.

Duncan put his grubby hand out to me and smiled warmly. 'Hi, Ellie. Please excuse us. We've been doing a bit of work in the garden.'

I shook his hand, feeling uncomfortable and over-dressed in my smart jacket and skirt and my three-inch high-heeled shoes. Ryan hadn't mentioned that the Middlemasses were the outdoor types. At that moment two Great Danes came bounding up and started nudging at me. Neither Duncan or Sheryl made any attempt to restrain them.

'What are they called?' Ryan asked. He loved dogs, whereas I was more of a cat person.

'Tilly and Toby,' Sheryl said proudly, rubbing their necks. 'Tilly's having pups in a few weeks' time. She's getting really fat.'

'Oh, how nice,' I said, putting on a brave smile but wishing the ground would open up and swallow me when I remembered what Ryan and I were really here for.

'Well, don't just stand there, come in,' Duncan said, waving us through the door.

Sheryl took us straight to the kitchen and put the

kettle on. The room was huge and very untidy. Sheryl obviously didn't do much housework. Two more dogs, small ones this time, came hurtling towards us and started sniffing round our ankles.

Duncan threw a pile of magazines which were cluttering up the table onto the floor and sat looking at us. 'Good journey, Ryan?' he asked.

'Fine. Didn't take too long.'

Duncan smiled benignly and nodded his head several times. I wondered how on earth we were all going to pass the time until we started 'swinging'. I kept looking at Duncan to try and find something about him I liked, but I could only see a plain, dull man who was doing his best to be friendly. I wondered if Ryan fancied Sheryl. She didn't look his type at all.

We sat sipping tea, eating biscuits and making inane conversation for quite a while, until Sheryl said, 'I thought we might all go for a ride this afternoon to help us get to know one another.'

'That's very nice of you,' I said quickly, 'but we've just driven nearly thirty miles to get here. Couldn't we do something else?'

Duncan and Ryan burst out laughing, whilst Sheryl gave me a funny look. 'I meant on the horses,' she said drily.

I was horrified, not at my gaffe, but by the fact I'd never been on a horse in my life and I had no intention of doing so. 'I don't ride,' I said smugly.

'You don't really have to. You can go on Jasper. He's so well trained, he'll lead you along.'

My heart started quaking. Ryan gave me a warning look, but I ignored it. 'I don't want to,' I said sulkily. 'Besides, I don't have anything suitable to wear.'

Sheryl looked from Duncan to Ryan and then back at me. 'Please yourself,' she said coldly, and walked out of the room.

Ryan took my hand. 'Why don't you give it a try, Ellie? You might like it.'

Duncan leaned forward and took my other hand. 'I promise that if you really don't like it we'll bring you back here.'

I couldn't stand my ground any longer. I felt like the meat between two slices of bread ready to be eaten up. 'All right, I'll give it a go,' I said reluctantly, pulling my hands away from both men. I decided then and there that this was going to be a horrible weekend. I didn't like Sheryl or Duncan and I was fast going off Ryan for bringing me here in the first place.

The horses were saddled up and ready. Sheryl had lent me a clean pair of jodhpurs which were so tight I was frightened they were going to split. Ryan was in a pair of old jeans he had brought with him. Sheryl found us both a riding helmet. Mine didn't fit properly so I handed it back to her. 'No, thank you,' I said. 'I don't need it.'

'You must. It's against the law not to wear one.'

She placed it back on my head and did the strap up underneath my chin. I felt so stupid, I was nearly in tears.

'Don't worry, you look great,' Duncan said affectionately and I suddenly warmed to him.

Duncan helped me up onto Jasper. I had to admit he was a handsome horse, almost jet black with a white flare on his face. He didn't move as I sat there, terrified, looking down at the ground which suddenly seemed very far away. I desperately wanted to get down and go home.

Ryan had no such problem. He steered his horse, Whisper, next to me. 'This is fantastic,' he said, eyes shining happily.

I realised with a sinking heart that there was no way I could let him down now.

151

'Right. Are we all ready?' Sheryl shouted in her brusque voice. 'Ryan, you come alongside me. Duncan, you stay with Mariella.'

Sheryl pulled at her reins and off she trotted on her beautiful young horse, the biggest of the four, called Canon. Ryan copied Sheryl's actions and Whisper immediately went into a slow trot, leaving Ryan looking very unsteady, but with a huge grin on his face.

Duncan peered at me kindly. 'Are you OK, Mariella?' He wasn't wearing his glasses. Without them he looked different; much nicer in fact. I noted that his large, brown eyes were actually quite attractive.

'Yes. I'm fine,' I lied. 'And please, call me Ellie.'

'OK, Ellie. Let's go.'

Duncan's horse, Millie, moved off and Jasper meekly followed. I held onto the reins tightly, terrified I was going to fall off.

'Don't look so worried,' Duncan said, glancing behind at me. 'We won't do any trotting until you are ready.'

Sheryl and Ryan were already way ahead.

'Ryan's taken to it like a duck to water,' Duncan chuckled. 'Sherrie will like that.'

'Pity I'm not more like Ryan,' I said and sniffed in the cold, damp air. 'I haven't taken to it at all.'

'You will, Ellie. Jasper likes you, I can tell. He only likes people who like him and know how to sit in the saddle.'

I laughed. 'You're having me on.'

'Would I do that?' He brought Millie to a halt and waited for me to draw up beside him. His eyes were twinkling and his nose was red. 'You're doing really well, Ellie.'

I suddenly felt proud of myself. I didn't feel frightened any more. Wary, yes, but much more relaxed. 'I'm beginning to get used to being up here,' I said cheerfully.

'Great. Just keep it up and we'll have you trotting in no time.'

An hour later, Jasper and Millie were trotting side by side and I was thoroughly enjoying myself. It was exhilarating to be jogging up and down in the saddle, in control of a creature much bigger than myself. I had no idea where Sheryl and Ryan had got to and I didn't really care. Duncan was looking after me very well. I was beginning to like him.

Duncan brought Millie to a standstill and Jasper followed suit almost without me doing anything. Duncan pointed in the distance to a small building. 'See that hut over there? It belongs to us. That's where we're heading. Sherrie and Ryan should be there already. Ah, yes, they are. There's smoke coming out of the chimney. That means they've got the fire going.'

I stared at the hut. I could just about see Canon and Whisper tethered up outside. 'Are you saying this was all arranged?' I asked incredulously.

'Yes. We're staying the night in the hut. Don't worry, it's really quite comfortable. All mod cons and two small bedrooms.'

'But I haven't got anything to change into,' I said in a wailing tone.

'Doesn't matter. Everything you need is there. If you want it, that is.'

I wasn't quite sure what he was implying but I had a good idea. I still felt very nervous and apprehensive about the whole set-up. I began to wonder what Sheryl and Ryan were getting up to.

Duncan smiled at me. 'Let's get a move on. Sherrie will be wondering where we are.'

When we arrived at the hut, I didn't want to get down from Jasper. I felt so good sitting there, like a queen on her throne. Eventually, Duncan placed a hand firmly on my thigh and helped me down with his other hand. My legs gave way and he reached out to catch me and held me tight against him. I had never ached so much in my whole life.

'You'll soon feel better,' Duncan said, helping me along.

Inside, the hut was gloriously warm. A huge log-fire was made up and the tantalising aroma of bacon filled the air. Sheryl emerged from the kitchen. I gasped in surprise. She was totally transformed. Her long, dark hair was loose and wet around her cleanly scrubbed face and all she was wearing was a knee-length pink silk wrapover, loosely tied round the waist. When she moved, her breasts wobbled seductively beneath the sheer material and her nipples and crotch were clearly visible.

'Where's Ryan?' I asked, glaring at her with open hostility.

'Still in the shower. You and Duncan can have one next.' She disappeared back into the kitchen.

I looked at Duncan, but he was staring after Sheryl, his eyes glazed with longing. For some inexplicable reason, I felt jealous.

Ryan burst into the room. He too was dressed only in a dressing gown, his dark, hairy chest glistening with moisture.

'Hi. You made it then, Ellie?' He came over and put his arm round me. I wondered for the first time if he had already shagged Sheryl, but unless it had been a five-minute quickie, they probably wouldn't have had the time.

'She thoroughly enjoyed it,' Duncan said, beaming all over his face.

'Really? Oh Ellie, that's great. We'll have to do it again.'

I nodded, catching his enthusiasm.

Sheryl came back into the room with two plates of egg and bacon. 'Sit down and eat, Ryan,' she ordered.

'Duncan and Mariella will have to clean themselves up before they eat.'

Ryan sat down at the small dining table obediently, but I was getting pissed off with being told what to do by Miss High and Mighty Sheryl Middlemass. 'I'll have a shower later,' I said. 'Is there anything decent for me to change into?'

'There's a wrapover similar to mine, or you can wear Duncan's thick woolly one. He probably won't want it. He prefers to be in the altogether when we're here, don't you, darling?'

Duncan nodded and smiled apologetically at me. 'Well, if you don't want your shower yet, Ellie, I'll have mine.' He dashed off, leaving me watching Sheryl and Ryan eating their eggs and bacon. It smelled good. I began to feel out of place again; hungry, dirty and unattractive, but worse still, deep down I knew it was all my own fault. Ryan tried to draw me into the conversation he and Sheryl were having, but I wasn't interested. I sat in the corner of the room, glaring at them as they laughed and teased one another, wishing I was somewhere else.

Duncan emerged from the shower with his thick, woollen dressing gown on.

Sheryl looked at him in surprise. 'You'll fry in that.' She got up and went into the kitchen, her breasts bouncing merrily. A few minutes later she came back with a huge plateful of bacon and eggs for her husband.

Ryan looked over at me as I skulked in the corner, concern in his eyes. 'Why don't you have your shower now, Ellie?'

I desperately wanted one, but I felt like a naughty schoolgirl being told what to do, and I'd had more than enough of that at school. Forever the rebel, I shook my head and ran out of the room into one of the bedrooms, where I flung myself down onto the bed and started bawling my eyes out.

Ryan came in and tried to comfort me.

'Get out!' I shouted. 'I didn't want to come here in the first place, but you made me. It's all your fault I'm so miserable.'

'Ellie, please. Keep your voice down. You'll upset Duncan and Sheryl.'

'What about me? Don't I deserve some consideration too?'

'Yes, of course you do. But now that you're here, can't you try and enjoy yourself?'

'No, I hate it here.'

Ryan sighed. 'You're acting like a spoilt baby.'

'Piss off.'

Ryan lost his temper. His hand came down on my backside with a stinging slap.

I cried out in surprise. 'That hurt!'

'It was meant to. Now get off that bed and go and have a shower.'

'No.'

This time his hand yanked my jodhpurs down then came slicing onto my backside. 'Get up, Ellie, otherwise I'll fuck you now.'

I was furious still, but my senses were starting to betray me. 'You've probably shagged Miss Horseface already,' I raged into the pillow.

Ryan's hand came down again, and he started to peel my jodhpurs off. He was really angry. 'That was very unkind, Ellie. You can be a real bitch, at times. And for your information I have not shagged Sheryl yet. She's worth more than a quickie. Though now that you mention it, I am quite looking forward to making love to her.'

His words tore into my troubled heart. I started to struggle as Ryan triumphantly released me from my jodhpurs and knickers. 'Go to her, then,' I yelled. 'She won't be any better than me. I hate you, I hate you.' I started to sob loudly. So loudly, in fact, that I didn't hear him leave the room.

Moments later I felt a hand gently stroking my buttocks. At first I thought it was Ryan and stopped crying to allow myself the pleasure of his touch, but then I realised, with mounting horror, that the hand didn't feel right. The contact was too soft. I pulled myself up and looked round to see Sheryl and Duncan sitting on the bed, facing one another on each side. It was Sheryl's hand which was caressing my flaming cheeks.

My instant reaction was to recoil in disgust. 'Get your hand off my arse,' I shouted.

Sheryl moved her hand. 'I'm sorry,' she said. 'I've not been very nice to you, have I? I really am very sorry.'

My anger instantly evaporated. She had admitted she was in the wrong. I was exonerated from my wilful outburst. 'I'm sorry too,' I heard myself saying magnanimously. 'I've behaved very badly.'

Sheryl smiled. 'Perhaps we could start again? Would you like your eggs and bacon now?'

'That would be lovely. Thank you.'

I watched her leave the room, cool, calm and in control of herself. And so was I now. I realised that Sheryl and I were no different emotionally. We'd both been frightened of losing our man. But there was no way that was going to happen. Duncan loved Sheryl and Ryan loved me. End of story. I turned to face Duncan.

'You've got a lovely arse,' he said, grinning happily.

'I know. The rest of me is pretty good, too. But I suppose you'll see that later. In the meantime, I'd better find that wrapover and go and have my lunch. I'm starving. After that, I think I'll have, er, a shower.'

Duncan laughed. And I did too.

Late that afternoon the four of us sat by the fire drinking champagne, Duncan and Sheryl in two big armchairs, Ryan and I on the sofa. The evening was drawing in and it felt cold enough for snow outside, even though it was only the beginning of December. Sheryl's wrapover had come loose and her breasts were virtually exposed. Ryan and I sat admiring them, small yet full, with lovely pert nipples. Every so often she would lift her arms up over her head and pull her hair back in a very sexy way. I could see that Duncan and Ryan were getting turned on by her, but I wasn't jealous anymore, just thankful that she was doing her best to make the evening a success.

Duncan stood up. 'I think it's about time I took this thing off. I'll roast if I don't.' He undid the cord, slipped the bulky dressing gown away from his body and stood in front of us naked. The three of us sat and admired him. For a man of 33, he was in remarkably good shape. Unlike Ryan, there was no sign of a pot-belly. His muscles were taut and his skin a golden brown. I felt my libido rising. Sheryl was staring at her husband, openly horny by now, her nipples hardening and extending. I wondered why she was so keen to swing when she was obviously very much turned on by her husband. Then I realised I was the same. I loved Ryan, but the excitement of experiencing sex with another man was irresistible. I couldn't draw my eyes away from Duncan's physique and his rising shaft. We were all mesmerised, lulled into a soft sensuality by the warmth, the drink and the fire. Duncan sat down and Sheryl stood up to take her wrapover off. Ryan began to stroke my leg. I knew he was excited, and so was I. Sheryl had a lovely body, smooth and golden, with a thick, dark thatch down below. She stood there, touching her breasts and her crotch invitingly. Ryan shot up from the sofa, his cock already pushing out from the gap in his dressing gown. Sheryl sat down and allowed Ryan to take centre stage. Slowly he peeled his dressing gown off and stood there for a few moments, one hand proudly presenting his huge cock to the audience before he sat down again. That only left me. Trembling with a potent mixture of nervousness and excitement, I stood up and slipped off my wrapover. My skin was whiter than Duncan's and Sheryl's, and I must have been at least a stone heavier than Sheryl, but I was proud of my body. My firm, large breasts with their cherry-red nipples and my large, shapely arse excited most men. I turned round and bent over a little so that Duncan and Sheryl could see how beautiful I was before I too sat down. After that, the four of us endeavoured to carry on talking as normal, but it was almost impossible. My pussy was leaking onto the sofa, Sheryl's eyes kept dipping down to Ryan's cock, and Duncan couldn't keep his eyes off my breasts. It was very erotic.

Sheryl was the first to make a move; she had been the leader throughout the day. She stood up, came over to Ryan, took his hand and pulled him gently down onto the floor in front of the fire. 'Are you all right here, or do you want to go into the bedroom?' she murmured.

Ryan looked at me. I nodded my assent. I had no inhibitions or fears now. We were all in the same boat.

Ryan relaxed and his hands began to explore Sheryl's lithesome body, touching her everywhere. When he reached down and opened up her pussy to find her clit, I held my breath. I knew what it felt like. I knew how good Ryan was at pleasuring a woman. Sheryl moaned loudly. I looked at Duncan, but his eyes were glued to Sheryl. I could see that her pleasure was his pleasure.

Eventually, Sheryl reached out and took Ryan's cock into her hand. I could almost feel it in my hand. At that moment I wanted Ryan more than I'd ever wanted him. Sheryl moved round so that her cunt was underneath Ryan's face. He lunged forward and probed her moist, open hole with his tongue. I could see him dipping into her, sucking out her juices. My pussy started to throb with desire. Duncan was leaning forward in his chair, his hand on his cock.

When Sheryl took Ryan's cock into her mouth and

the two of them became locked into a glorious show of mutual sucking, I could hardly contain myself. I wanted to join in, go to him, touch him, lick him, kiss him. I wanted him to know that I loved him enough to allow him the pleasure of exploring another woman. When Sheryl started moaning loudly, Ryan pushed her onto her back and finally took her in the missionary position. She arched towards him, clasping her legs around him as his cock surged in and out. Ryan was in full control and Sheryl loved it. He took his time and, when she cried out for more, raised the level of his thrusting and pumped into her mercilessly. I began to masturbate myself, but when I glanced across at Duncan, he shook his head and motioned to me to pull my hand away. So I did. I knew our turn was soon to come and I was looking forward to it.

Sheryl's climax was long and explosive. Ryan came quickly afterwards. Then he collapsed on top of her and they lay together, their juices mingling, their bodies hot and sticky. They seemed totally oblivious to their audience.

I was in a state of extreme heightened awareness. I had not thought it could be so wonderful to watch two people make love, especially when one of them was my boyfriend. I was learning new things about myself all the time.

Ryan and Sheryl gradually came round. Silently they stood up. Ryan sat down in Sheryl's armchair and pulled her onto his lap. She didn't object.

In a trancelike state, Duncan came over and pulled me to my feet. Then we were on the floor together and Duncan's hands were all over my body, stroking my face and neck, squeezing my breasts and buttocks, and pushing into my pussy. He was so horny he couldn't wait. Before I was totally ready, he pushed me onto my back and thrust his cock into me. I welcomed him, moaning and arching my back, but he came too soon. I lay beneath him squirming, desperately wanting more. The silence of my disappointment was deafening. I opened my eyes slowly to see Ryan pulling Duncan off my body. Then he sank down on top of me and started pushing his semi-erect penis inside me, reaching down for my clit and sucking my breasts tenderly. I was hardly aware of what was happening but I felt horny again. My aching pussy sucked Ryan's cock deep inside, making him expand, making him want me. My finger-nails scourged down his back; my tongue pushed deep into his mouth. Minutes later, I exploded onto his cock. When I came to, Ryan was sitting up watching me affectionately, and Sheryl and Duncan were back in their armchairs.

Remarkably, Duncan seemed embarrassed. 'I'm sorry, Ellie. I couldn't hold on to it. You're so sexy.'

'That's all right. Don't worry about it.'

Sheryl sprang up and put her wrapover back on. 'Anyone for dinner?' she chirped.

That night we slept in our own beds with our own partners.

'I thought you were fantastic tonight,' Ryan whispered, hugging me tightly. 'Thanks for being so understanding.'

'Thank you for finishing me off,' I said, and giggled. 'You did a grand job: first Sheryl, then me. Poor Duncan. He looks so manly. Do you think he suffers from premature ejaculation and that's the reason why Sheryl is so keen on swinging?'

'Possibly. Or it could be just as he says: you're far too sexy.'

'You always manage to satisfy me.'

'Yeah. But we've been doing it for over a year now. It was very difficult to hold on the first time. You nearly blew my mind.'

'Don't I always? Besides, it was the first time with Sheryl and you held on for her.'

Ryan chucked me under the chin playfully. 'Mmm, but she's not as sexy as you, is she? Give me your tits and arse any day.'

I snuggled up to him happily. 'What are we doing tomorrow? Do you know?'

'I've no idea. But I'm sure Sheryl's got something interesting planned.'

As it was, we were disappointed. After breakfast we all donned our riding gear and set off back towards the house. Duncan and Sheryl were very quiet. I thought they might have had an argument.

Duncan rode with me again, and I felt that same wonderful feeling of freedom and power I had discovered yesterday.

'Is everything all right between you and Sheryl?' I asked when he pulled Millie in alongside me.

'Not really.'

'Do you want to talk about it?'

'No. Yes. It's this swinging lark. I only do it to make Sheryl happy. As you might have gathered, I'm not very good in the sex department, and she gets very frustrated. She loves me, I know that, otherwise she wouldn't stay with me, but after last night with Ryan, she's feeling very dissatisfied with me.'

I felt sorry for him. 'You're not that bad. There's plenty worse than you.'

'Thanks,' he said sarcastically, and I knew I'd offended rather than helped him. He would have preferred to be lied to and told how marvellous he was.

We finished the journey in silence.

Back at the house, Ryan appeared in a very agitated state at the front door with my bag in his hand and told me we were leaving straight away. There was no sight of Sheryl.

Duncan eyed us testily. 'Why are you going? Sheryl's got a special little party arranged with a load of other swingers this afternoon.'

'I know. She told me. But we're not interested, are we, Ellie?'

Ryan looked at me warningly. I knew, for some reason, I had to agree with him. I nodded. 'I think we've had enough, Duncan.'

'Enough of me, more like,' Duncan grouched. 'OK. Go then. Thanks for yesterday, anyway.'

Ryan couldn't get me out of there quick enough. Five minutes later, he stopped the car in a small layby and took me into his arms.

'What's the matter, hon?' I was mystified.

'Oh, Ellie, I'm so sorry. I didn't mean anything like this to happen.'

'What?'

'It's Sheryl, she's gone mad. She's got the hots for me. When we were riding back she told me she was fed up with Duncan, and that she's fallen in love with me. After one night! She asked me to run away with her. I refused, of course, so when we got back to the house she tried to seduce me in the kitchen.'

'And did you? Shag her again I mean?'

'No. Of course not. I managed to get free and run off. I didn't ask for any of it, I promise you.'

I laughed. 'That'll teach you to go swinging. Trouble is, you're too good at it. That rampant cock of yours is enough to drive any woman wild with passion.'

Ryan grinned with relief. 'I thought you'd be mad at me and say it was all my fault. You seemed to be getting into it last night.'

'I suppose I was. But as I said before, I'd rather have you.' I pulled his head to my breasts and ran my fingers through his hair.

Ryan looked up at me. 'You're great, Ellie, do you know that?'

'Of course I know it. Now stop blubbing and give me a kiss.'

'When this is all over – your challenge, I mean – what do you say about you and me living together and possibly creating a little Ryan, or even a little Ellie?'

Tears sprang to my eyes. 'Oh, yes. I'd like that.'

Ryan pushed his hand up my jumper and found a nipple. 'We could have a little practice now. Get those awful clothes off. It's a long time since we did it in the car.'

I hadn't had time to change after we rode back. Laughing, Ryan helped me out of the jodhpurs and pulled off the jumper. The heater was on in the car but it was still cold. I shivered in his arms.

'I'll soon make you warm, Ellie.' He started to lick and kiss me all over. Gradually my body turned to fire. His tongue reached into all my private parts: my mouth, my navel, my pussy, my arse. I felt deliriously happy. The windows steamed up and cars drove by, but we didn't care. We belonged to one another. When he lifted me into the back seat, laid me on my front and raised my buttocks in the air, I felt that old familiar thrill, knowing I was special and that this was his favourite position. As his cock thrust into me, it felt like the first time. I swooned and fell head over heels in love with him all over again.

Chapter Eleven
Capricorn: The Eternal Grinder

22 DECEMBER

I'm writing this in a hurry. Tomorrow Ryan and I are off to Shere to spend Christmas with Anna and Lester and I've got a mountain of work to do before we leave.

Anna is pregnant. The baby is due at the beginning of August. She took a test last week and rang me immediately with the good news. I'm pleased for her because she seems so happy, but I'm still a bit apprehensive about Lester and his roving eye. I hope he behaves himself over Christmas. With Ryan around, he'd be a fool to try anything on with me.

The only problem with going away is it cuts out a week of my valuable time, and I've got to corner my Capricorn. On the other hand, I'm getting on so well with Ryan that I really don't feel like making the effort to ensnare another man. Ironically, even Ryan is saying it would be foolish of me to give up now and blow all my father's money. Luckily, I've found my ideal Capricorn and made a start, but it's proving to be a hard slog. Like Virgo, this man is hard to net. He's the guy at work

I briefly wrote about last month, the rambling enthusiast. His name is Arthur. Awful name, I know: sounds like he's decrepit. But he's only 24, and quite hunky by Capricorn standards. He's tall and slim – a bit too slim really – with fine brown hair and small, even features and a nice smile when he makes the effort, which unfortunately isn't very often. He's also quite shy and I do find shy men difficult to handle. Luckily I got off to a good start by chatting to him at work and drawing him out of himself. As soon as I found out about the rambling I told him how much I enjoyed walking (another little white lie) and that I would love to join him on one of his weekend outings. He was obviously very chuffed and invited me along to a walk that weekend near Woking on the outskirts of London. That was two weeks ago, not long after the 'swinging' weekend in Sussex. Fortunately, the weather held out, but the walk was a nightmare. I struggled for several hours, trudging through the mud in my trainers, jeans and leather jacket, trying to keep up with a group of twenty ardent ramblers who I knew were privately mocking my bad choice of attire. They were comfortably dressed in walking boots, warm but light walking trousers, and anorak-type jackets. When he saw me, Arthur stared at me in dismay, but to his credit he said nothing until the end of the walk, when he said very quietly that if I were to go on another walk with the group, I would be better off wearing walking boots and more comfortable clothing. I agreed with him and promptly rushed out to spend some of my hard-earned dosh on an expensive pair of ladies' walking boots and some waterproofs.

Last weekend I went out with Arthur's group again, all decked out in my new gear. I was treated with much more respect this time – some of the people even chose to walk and chat with me – and I had to admit the walking seemed much easier. Unfortunately, my seduction techniques were a bit difficult to employ whilst

walking at breakneck speed through swampy under-
growths. Even when we stopped for lunch, it was a
quickie: a couple of sandwiches and a chocolate bar.
There we sat, all twenty of us squashed up like sardines,
elbows bashing, on a couple of benches by a pond,
chatting about – you guessed it – the merits of walking.
Later on, Arthur did put his arm around me once, but
that was only because I nearly tripped over. So I have
to admit I've failed dismally in the charm-school stakes
and am no further ahead in my challenge than I was a
few weeks ago. Arthur just doesn't seem to see me as a
desirable woman. I have hinted several times that I
would be open to a date. I've told him I love going to
the cinema, the theatre, ten-pin bowling, nightclubs and
eating out in restaurants, but he doesn't seem interested.
The only things he likes are walking and trains. He told
me he's got a massive model railway set worth
thousands of pounds in his bedroom, a converted loft
room in a small, three-bedroomed terraced house in
Morden. When he's not out walking, he plays with it
for hours on end. Lucky me! He still lives with his
parents and two brothers, otherwise I would have suggested he take me to see this eighth wonder of the
world. I still might have to resort to it if I don't get
anywhere soon. Who knows, he might get turned on by
me if I get turned on by his trains. I'm meeting him for
another walk just before New Year and keeping my
fingers crossed that somehow I'll be able to entice him
into action. I'm sure he's not another virgin because he's
mentioned several ex-girlfriends, so it's just a question
of getting him more interested in my body than his
bloody model railway set and striding about the
countryside in the mud. It's a tough task, but I'm going
to have to do it. I haven't got the time or the inclination
to go looking for another Capricorn. When he gets
going, I'm sure he'll be as randy as hell – most Capricorns are – but for the time being I'm going to forget all

about him and enjoy my Christmas with Ryan, Anna and Lester.

It was a cold, bright day, and the ground had hardened up a little, making it ideal for walking. Only eight of us had turned up for the walk. Most people were still working off their Christmas dinner or looking forward to New Year's Eve, which was the next day. But Arthur wasn't daunted in his enthusiasm. He strode on ahead of the rest of us, his lanky body loping along as he read the map.

My mind turned back to the lovely time Ryan and I had spent in Shere. Apart from one attempted grope under the dinner table, Lester had just about managed to contain himself. Ryan had been in top form, both in and out of bed. We had tried hard not to make too much noise when we shagged, but Anna commented wryly on Boxing Day that Ryan seemed to have the stamina of a horse, judging by the sounds coming out of our bedroom every night. I think she was a bit jealous because Lester had been treating her like a Dresden doll ever since her pregnancy was confirmed.

I trudged along behind the rest of the group, feeling very dejected. The constant effort of trying to get Arthur to notice me as a sexual human being was beginning to take its toll on my good humour.

At the end of the walk, Arthur said goodbye to me and rushed to his car.

I ran after him. 'Hang on a minute, Arthur. Have you got time to go for a coffee?'

He turned round in surprise. He was already turning the key in the car door. 'Not really. I want to get home and try out a few new bits on the railway.'

'Oh, that's nice. I'd love to see it.' I looked at him hopefully. It was 'make or break' time. I needed to wrangle an invitation to see this blessed model railway.

He didn't take the hint. 'See you at the office on Monday,' he said quickly, and got into his car.

I almost cried with frustration. What on earth was I going to do? I got in my car and drove home. For New Year's Eve, Ryan and I were going to a party with Zoe and Tony. Perhaps I would meet a Capricorn there.

The party was in full swing. After heralding in the New Year with the usual linking of hands and singing 'Auld Lang Syne' everybody got down to the real business of consuming great quantities of alcohol and getting merry.

Ryan was nowhere to be seen. I found Zoe in the corner of the kitchen wrapped around a bloke who was definitely not Tony.

I tapped her on the shoulder. 'Zoe, have you seen Ryan?'

'Nope.' She shook her head wildly, and grinned up at the man she was holding on to. As usual she was very tanked up.

'Where's Tony?' I asked pointedly.

'Don't know and don't care. This is Ross. It's his party.' She swung her body aside and gesticulated at the man. He hung on to her arm tightly so that she wouldn't fall. 'He's no good to you at the moment, Ellie. He's an Aquarian. But he might come in handy next month, eh?' She burst into peals of laughter.

I glanced at Ross. He was certainly very tall and sexy. He winked at me and I felt an immediate attraction. Pity I was looking for a Capricorn.

I wandered off and continued my search for Ryan. I found him eventually zonked out in the corner of the dining-room floor. He'd had a lot to drink. I tutted loudly. It looked like I was stuck on my own for the time being.

I went back to the kitchen, but Zoe and Ross had disappeared. Sighing, I started to pour myself another drink. A hand appeared and made a grab for my right breast. I spun round to find Tony grinning lecherously at me. That was all I needed.

'Get your hands off me,' I said, yanking his hand away.

'You don't fancy it, then?'

'No, Tony, I don't. Not with you anyway. Why don't you start behaving yourself? Go and find Zoe.'

'I saw her just now heading for the bedroom with Ross.'

'Oh, sorry. You know what she's like. But then you're not as clean as the driven snow either, are you?'

He grinned again. 'Do you remember Ibiza? You fancied me then.'

'Only because you were a Gemini. I'm onto Capricorn now.'

'So, who's in for a good shag this time? Anyone I know?'

I didn't like his attitude. The sneer on his face was really pissing me off. 'Get lost, Tony.' I walked away into the crowded lounge and sat down in an empty chair by the window. I was no nearer to finding another Capricorn, so it looked like I would have to pursue Arthur a bit more. Invite myself round to his house to see the railway and try to seduce him. It should be a lot easier without the waterproofs and the walking boots!

Some time later I was woken up by someone shaking my arm. 'Wake up, sleeping beauty.'

It was Ross. I shook myself awake and smiled up at him. 'What's the time?' I noticed the room was very quiet.

'Five o'clock. Everybody else has gone.'

'Oh. Even Zoe?'

'She left a short while ago with Tony. She didn't want to disturb you.'

'And Ryan?'

Ross didn't look too pleased. 'If you mean the guy who was sick on the dining-room floor, then collapsed in a heap on top of it, I'm making him clear it up now.'

I was embarrassed. 'I'm sorry. He's not usually so inconsiderate.'

'I know. He's mortified now. But what about you? Do you feel all right?'

'I'm fine.' He was staring at me and I felt myself getting hot and bothered.

His hand was lingering on my arm, his fingers slightly caressing. I shivered slightly. He moved his hand across and lightly touched my breast.

I opened my mouth in surprise and tried to say 'no', but the word got stuck in my throat. His thumb and forefinger found my nipple and gently teased it. Then he moved to the other breast and did the same thing. My nipples shot into action and pressed urgently against the thin material of my dress. Ross continued staring straight into my eyes. He was immensely attractive. His hand left my breasts and wandered down to the hemline of my short dress. I had no knickers on. Ryan had insisted, because he'd wanted to give me a New Year fuck in the car after the party. When Ross's hand reached my pussy, I gasped with pleasure.

'Do you fancy a quickie?' he asked huskily, his fingers probing into my wetness.

I came to my senses and I remembered that a few hours ago he'd been with Zoe and that Ryan was somewhere in the house. 'No, I can't,' I said, pushing his hand away. 'Ryan's here.'

'He told me you had an open relationship,' Ross replied calmly, pushing me back into the chair and stroking the tops of my thighs gently.

I was stunned and more than a little hurt by Ryan's words. 'We do not!'

Ross's hand was at my pussy again, stroking, probing, making me feel deliciously sensual and wanton. 'Why did he say so, then? I was speaking to him just before midnight and he told me that you were writing a book about men and sex and needed to experiment with different men, but he didn't mind because you had an open relationship and he could do what he wanted too.'

I felt the betrayal of Ryan's drunken revelations as a sharp pain deep in my chest. At the same time, I was very much aware of the pleasure Ross was arousing in me. I closed my eyes and relaxed back into the chair again, giving myself up to the delights of Ross's fingers as they deftly fondled and probed into my secret parts.

'Zoe said you might want me for your experiments next month,' he said slyly.

I opened my eyes and stared back into his own clear, cool blue ones. He was gorgeous. He looked as if he had stepped straight out of a boy band, with his styled blond hair, square-set face, large sensuous mouth and great body.

'Yes,' I murmured, as his thumb nudged against my clit and created a swift spasm of pleasure. 'I might. Providing you really are an Aquarian.'

'I sure am, ma'am.'

He saluted and I laughed.

'Born on the fifteenth of February 1973. Will that do you?'

As he said the word 'do', he thrust several fingers deep into my pussy and made me gasp. Then I heard Ryan's voice calling from the hallway.

Ross calmly pulled his hand away and stood up, so that by the time Ryan came into the room, I was sitting alone in the chair.

'Hi, Ryan. All cleaned up now?' Ross said.

Ryan grinned woefully. 'Yeah. Sorry about that, mate. I've scrubbed the floor in the dining room.'

He looked at me and I suddenly felt very guilty about my relapse with Ross. But then I reminded myself of what Ryan had said and the guilt vanished. He had changed into different clothes – no doubt belonging to Ross – and at least he looked clean.

'Mariella was asleep in the chair,' Ross said in an amused tone.

Ryan came over and bent down and kissed me briefly on the lips. 'Sorry, babe. I crashed out soon after midnight. I don't remember a thing.'

I smiled. 'Never mind. You're OK now.'

Ryan ruffled my hair affectionately. Ross looked on closely. I could see that he didn't miss a trick. Suddenly I was desperate to leave.

I got up. 'We'd better go,' I said, taking Ryan's hand. 'Thanks for a great party, Ross.'

'Glad you could make it. I'll invite you to the next one.'

When we got to the front door, Ryan broke away. 'Hang on a minute, Ellie. I've left my dirty clothes in the kitchen. I'll go and get them.'

He ran off. Ross smiled knowingly at me. 'Give me a call when you're ready,' he said. He slipped a piece of paper with his phone number on it into my handbag.

I nodded unhappily. It felt very clandestine, but I was in fact only making arrangements for the penultimate stage of my quest, so I had nothing to feel guilty about, did I? I wasn't very convinced.

Ross reached down and chucked me under the chin. 'Cheer up. I promise I'll give you a good time.'

'I know you will,' I said dreamily. And that was what I was worried about. I didn't want to resurrect any of the feelings I'd had for Edward De Vigny with any other man but Ryan, but I really fancied Ross and could already feel my emotions swaying in the breeze. It was going to be hard.

Ryan returned and I grabbed his hand. This was the man I loved.

On the way home in the car we had an argument. I confronted Ryan with what he had told Ross. Ryan said he had been drunk and couldn't remember saying any such thing, and that he certainly did not consider himself a free agent. I accepted his protestations as the truth, but deep down I was still a little miffed. After all, there's no smoke without fire, is there?

I didn't manage to wrangle an invitation to see Arthur's model railway until ten days later. He finally got the message when I said I'd really love to see his railway. When could I go? And then I forced him to name a day. I hoped and prayed he would be a bit quicker off the mark when it came to getting his trousers off.

As it so happened, I was in luck. His parents were away for a few days and only one of his brothers was around, a young lad of eighteen called Jack. Arthur quickly introduced us before dragging me upstairs to his beloved room. The model railway took up most of the space. In the corner there was a single bed and a small wardrobe, nothing else. Without the railway, the room would have been extremely spartan.

Arthur eyed his railway lovingly and began to switch on lots of gadgets. Gradually it came alive. Trains began to move, level crossings began to operate, lights came on. It really was fascinating. Nothing had been forgotten. Little people, some with prams and dogs and even bags of shopping, were walking along or waiting at the station, and there was a small housing estate in the corner. I stood there watching, totally enthralled for a long while, my quest forgotten in the magic of the scene before me.

Arthur smiled proudly. I could see he was getting excited, but it certainly wasn't because I was there. Eventually I got restless and remembered what I was supposed to be doing. I inched closer to Arthur and put my arm round him. He didn't seem to notice. When he bent forward to move a train, my arm fell away abruptly.

I tried again, but he seemed unaware of my existence. I'd worn a short skirt and was showing plenty of cleavage – which made a nice change, I thought, from the clothes he normally saw me in at work or out walking – but I might as well have been wearing a sack for all he seemed to notice. I began to lose patience. I would have to do something more drastic.

I made a little groan and put a hand to my chest, immediately below my breasts.

He finally looked at me. 'What's the matter?' he asked gruffly.

'I've got a pain in my chest,' I said rubbing at the lower half of my boobs and pushing them up a little.

He stared at me, his eyes eventually dropping to my breasts, and he blushed a bright red that suffused his whole face.

I was pleased. At last he had noticed that I was a woman. I smiled at him seductively, but he turned away embarrassed.

I moved closer to him again. 'Have you got any Alka Seltzers, or better still, some Rennies? I think it might be indigestion.'

He seemed cross. 'You might find some in the bath-room. Go and have a look. It's the last door on the right.'

I had hoped he would be a bit more attentive, but no such luck. He was a tough nut to crack all right. I found the bathroom and some Rennies in a small bathroom cabinet.

'Ah, caught you.' A voice came from behind me.

I turned round to face Jack. 'I've got indigestion,' I said feebly, holding out the Rennies as proof of my intent.

He laughed. 'Is that so? More likely to be sexual frustration, I'd say.' He eyed me up and down, his cheeky gaze finally resting on my breasts.

I was surprised, to say the least. He was only a young

lad, but he seemed to know more of the ways of the world than his older brother did. I smiled weakly. 'Have you got a glass for some water, please?' I asked.

'Sure. I'll get you one. But you don't really need those. You know it and I know it. I saw your little act in the bedroom. Poor old Arthur. You've embarrassed him now. He doesn't know one end of a woman's body from the other, unlike me, I hasten to add.'

This was the last thing I wanted to hear. 'But he's had girlfriends before,' I said indignantly.

'Oh yeah. Several. They all want to see what's in his trousers but all he shows them is his train set.' He burst into loud laughter.

I felt sorry for Arthur. I tried to support him. 'But the railway is fascinating. I'm glad I've seen it.'

'Mm. I saw your face. I have to admit you showed more appreciation than his other birds.'

I smiled. It seemed funny to be called Arthur's 'bird'.

'Jesus!' said Jack. 'You're beautiful when you smile. Arthur doesn't realise what he's missing. It'll take you forever to get him into bed, you know. Would I do instead?'

I suddenly felt very dejected. 'Only if you're a Capricorn,' I snapped.

He opened his eyes wide in mock amazement. 'Funny you should say that. I am a Capricorn.'

I stared at him, convinced he was lying. 'No you're not. You just want to shag me. Well, I'm not up for it, thank you. Now get me that glass of water. Arthur will be wondering where I am.'

Jack's face fell. 'I am a Capricorn. Promise. My birthday was on Christmas Day.'

'Liar.' I moved forward and tried to push him out of the way.

He caught my arm and shook me roughly. 'Don't call me a liar. Do you want me to get my birth certificate to prove it?'

His voice was no longer friendly or teasing. I realised he was speaking the truth. Our eyes met. His were cold and angry. I lowered mine. 'Sorry,' I mumbled. 'Now can you please let me go. You're hurting my arm.'

He dropped my arm, but in the next instant he pushed me back against the bath. I teetered a little before falling backwards into the bath and landed heavily on my backside. My legs flew in the air and my head banged against the wall on the other side. For a moment I was stunned, then seeing Jack's shocked, apologetic face above me, I started to laugh.

Then he was in the bath with me, pulling up my skirt, plunging his hand inside my knickers. I felt the usual jolt of pleasure as his hand cupped my crotch but instinct made me struggle. Jack was strong and wiry. He pushed me back and pinned me down with one hand as he ripped off my knickers with his other hand. He yanked my legs open and began to pull at his flies.

In that instant I knew I was going to let him have me. I was fed up with waiting for Arthur. Jack was a Capricorn too. I would fulfil my quest and get out of this place as quickly as possible.

Jack released his cock. It was big and hard. I hardly had time to admire it before he was plunging it into me. I wasn't ready. The shock of his aggressive thrusts into my tight pussy made me cry out. He pushed harder, and I began to feel myself getting moist and the discomfort subsiding. He started building up a rhythm. Almost out of habit, I locked my legs around his waist and pulled him close to me.

'Jack! What on earth are you doing?'

I looked up from underneath Jack, straight into Arthur's shocked eyes. I felt like crawling into a hole. Any desire I had for Jack disappeared completely.

Jack, however, continued pumping into me, determination etched on his face. A moment or two later, he came violently, shuddering, and collapsed onto my chest. I pushed him off, helped by Arthur, who was yanking at him from behind.

'You silly fool, Jack! What have you done?' Arthur cried.

Once out of the bath, Jack had the grace to look very ashamed of himself. He looked down at me as I tried to rearrange my clothes. 'Sorry,' he muttered. Then he turned to his brother. 'She wanted you, but she got me instead.'

Arthur stared at him. 'If you've hurt her, I'll take you to the police station myself.'

I started to clamber out of the bath, amazed by Arthur's protective reaction.

Jack looked at his brother in horror. 'Hang on a minute, bruv'. It wasn't rape. She wanted it, didn't you?' He turned to me for verification.

I nodded miserably at him and scooped up my torn knickers from the floor.

Arthur saw them and turned on Jack again. 'It looks like rape from where I'm standing. Get out! Get out of this house, Jack. I don't want to see your face for a long while.'

Arthur's hand came crashing down onto his back and Jack flew out of the room. Arthur turned to me and put his arm around my shoulders. 'Are you all right, Mariella?'

I burst into tears. Arthur's unexpected kindness was too much to bear and very unwarranted. I had encouraged Jack and, if Arthur had not interrupted us, I probably would have ended up enjoying it.

Arthur pulled me against his chest and stroked my hair. 'It's all right, Mariella. You're safe now.'

I let him comfort me, feeling a sham, but enjoying the attention.

When I stopped crying, Arthur led me out of the bathroom and downstairs into the lounge. He sat me on the sofa and pulled my feet up onto it. 'You lie there and relax whilst I make you a cup of tea,' he said.

He came back a few minutes later. The tea was horrible – far too weak and milky – but I drank it to please him.

'Are you going to report Jack to the police?' he asked eventually.

I looked up in surprise. 'Of course not. He's young and horny, that's all.'

'Thank you, Mariella.' He gave a little embarrassed cough. 'Did, did you really want me?'

I took his hand. 'Yes,' I said softly. 'But you've been too wrapped up in your walking and model railway to notice me.'

'That's not true. I've liked you since the first moment you walked into the office. I was building up to asking you out properly. I wouldn't dream of touching you until you agreed to be my girlfriend.'

I felt awful. He was so sincere. All he needed was time. But it was time I didn't have. 'I thought I was your girlfriend,' I lied, reaching out to stroke his face.

His eyes lit up. 'Really? I've been an idiot, haven't I? I put off showing you my railway because I thought you would go off me.'

I smiled at him. 'Your railway is fantastic. But I think it's time you forgot about it for a while, don't you?'

He looked at me in amazement. 'You mean, you mean you still want me after what happened with Jack?'

'Of course I do.' I started opening the buttons on his shirt.

He reached out and gingerly touched my breasts, first one, then the other.

'Don't be frightened of them, they are real,' I said, laughing.

He got a bit bolder and started to pull my jumper up. I helped him to take it off. Then I undid my bra. My breasts fell free.

179

Arthur gave a gasp of delight. 'They're beautiful,' he said, reaching out to cup them in his hands.

'Get the nipples between your thumb and finger and roll them around a bit,' I ordered.

Arthur did as he was told and quickly got quite good at it. My nipples rose to attention. After a while I took one of his hands away from my breasts and placed it on my bare pussy.

He sighed with pleasure. 'That feels nice.'

Encouraged by his reactions, I reached out and undid his flies. 'Get up and take your clothes off,' I said huskily.

He did as he was told. His naked body was lean and hairless, not really my cup of tea at all. But I wanted him. I couldn't really count Jack's quickie as a true guide to a Capricorn man. I had set out to seduce Arthur and it looked like I was finally going to get him. I stood up and took the rest of my clothes off whilst he watched, his desire clearly growing stronger by the second.

He looked at me with wonder in his eyes. 'You are so beautiful. I've been blind. I really do want you, Mariella.' He pulled me into his arms and started to kiss me.

I was pleasantly surprised. His tongue dipped into my mouth and his lips were firm and strong. He pushed his naked body against mine and we swayed together, his highly aroused cock crushing against my abdomen. He stooped down and placed his hand on my buttocks. He squeezed them tightly and lifted me up a little so that our mouths could meet more easily.

Gradually he took over. No longer was I telling him what to do; he was telling me. 'Take my cock into your mouth,' he ordered. And I did, willingly, bending over so that my dangling breasts rubbed against his legs. As I sucked on him greedily, I gently cupped his balls in my hands. Everything was in slow motion. Arthur

180

wasn't in a hurry like Jack had been. I was being made to wait and was thoroughly enjoying it.

After a while Arthur pushed me down onto the carpet and started stroking my body all over. When his hands reached my pussy and found the nub of my swollen clit, I lost control. 'Fuck me, Arthur,' I cried out.

He smiled enigmatically and continued to rub my clit gently. I was so close to coming. I wanted him inside me.

'Please,' I moaned, reaching out for his cock and trying to thrust it into my sopping wet pussy.

He resisted, and I could hold on no longer. My pussy started to throb in his hand.

Seconds later, Arthur took his hand away and thrust his cock up and into my aching hole. I was in seventh heaven. The last few waves of excruciating pleasure racked my body and I lay back on the carpet, satiated. Or so I thought.

Arthur had his hands on my arse and was sliding himself in and out of my wet pussy with rhythmic ease. I opened my eyes and looked at him. He smiled sexily at me. 'You wanted to be fucked, didn't you?'

I nodded. I was in a daze, amazed at the unexpected pleasure Arthur was giving me. On and on he went, eternally grinding into me, making me more and more excited. I could feel myself building up into another crescendo. Only Ryan had ever made me come twice in such a short time.

When I started to moan and beg for more, Arthur reached down for my clit. Shortly afterwards I exploded again. This time Arthur came with me and, for a few precious moments, we clung together in a glorious world of our own, our bodies in mutual harmony. It was at times like this I felt sex was the most important thing in my life. I was amazed that I could reach orgasm with so many different types of men. The pleasure I was receiving from them was certainly making my father's challenge worthwhile. The money coming to me at the end of March would be nothing compared to the thrill of my experiences. It was true what Ryan said: the day I stopped enjoying sex would be the day I stopped living.

Chapter Twelve
Aquarius: The Intellectual Explorer

20 JANUARY

*T*oday's the big day. I'm going to ring Ross to tell him I'm ready. Goodness knows how it will develop, but one thing's for sure, I won't have any problem getting him to make a move like I did with Arthur. Poor Arthur! I felt really mean when I told him I didn't want to go out with him. He was so upset he didn't appear at work for the next two days. When he did return, he looked awful. He made a determined beeline for my desk to ask me what he'd done wrong. I tried to soothe him, tell him it was all my fault, but it didn't work. In the end, I had to tell him about Ryan. The look on his face was heartbreaking. He hasn't spoken to me since. I've been so miserable at work that I'm thinking of quitting. The agency won't like it. They keep finding me these wonderful jobs only for me to decide I want to go somewhere else. But I really don't think I can face seeing Arthur every day for much longer.

I'm looking forward to meeting up with Ross again,

but I'm also apprehensive about it. Ryan and I are getting on like a house on fire. I'd hate to upset the status quo. Ryan knows that Ross is my Aquarian and he's accepted it readily enough, but I noted the fleeting glimpse of dawning comprehension and the deep, troubled frown when I told him exactly who my Aquarian was. I don't think Ryan can take much more and I'm not sure I can, either. I don't mean the sex – that's great – it's the emotional pressure of trying to keep Ryan happy that's proving to be so difficult. Still, never mind. My challenge will soon be over and maybe then Ryan and I can get on with our lives. I'm not sure whether I'll be pleased or sorry when the end of March comes, but one thing's for sure, I will have learned a great deal about men, and myself.

Ross answered the phone immediately.

'Hi, Mariella. Lovely to hear from you.'

The rich tones of his deep voice set my pulse racing. 'I'd like to take you up on your offer, if it's still open.' I tried to sound matter-of-fact, but inside I was quaking. Supposing he had changed his mind?

I heard a short intake of breath before he replied. 'Yes. Of course. When? I'm free tonight if you can make it.'

It was a bit soon, I thought. But why not? A decent, quick shag would get it over and done with. 'OK. What time shall I make it?'

'About 7.30. I'll order us a take away if you like. I can't ask you to dinner because I don't cook. It's against my principles.'

'Take away would be lovely. I prefer Chinese, by the way.'

'Fine. See you later then.'

I put the phone down and gave a little whoop of joy. It looked like this one was in the bag already.

* * *

I dressed very carefully for Ross. He was an intelligent man so I didn't think he would appreciate anything too brassy. I put on a smart, black cocktail dress which revealed only a little of cleavage but showed off my long legs to great advantage. I also swept my hair back into a little spiky bun and went easy on the make-up. When I looked into the mirror I liked the new, sophisticated image that stared back.

Ross eyed me appreciatively. 'You look very nice, Mariella.' He was wearing a black, open-necked shirt with white trousers. Very sexy.

I handed him a bottle of wine. 'To help our Chinese go down,' I said.

He led me into the kitchen where our meal was set out on the table. I stood there awkwardly, surveying the scene. For some reason I felt very nervous, not my usual confident self at all.

Ross gave me a lovely smile. 'Don't be shy, Mariella. It doesn't become you. Sit down and tuck in.'

As the evening progressed, I gradually relaxed. Ross was very good company. He seemed more interested in making conversation than making love. He could talk about anything.

'You're very clever,' I said, my eyes shining with admiration as I sipped my wine.

He grinned. 'I know. I have a Masters in chemistry.'

He wasn't short in the modesty stakes either! 'So, what do you do for a living?'

'I'm a lab technician, working my way up the field fast, though. I hope –' He was interrupted by the phone ringing. He picked it up. 'Oh, hi. Lovely to hear from you.' He put his hand to the mouthpiece and motioned to me. 'Excuse me, Mariella. Why don't you go into the lounge and wait for me? I won't be long.'

I left the kitchen reluctantly. I wanted to hear what he had to say to the person on the other end of the line. Was it a girlfriend?

Ross's lounge was very spacious and tastefully furnished. The right-hand side of the room was covered wall to wall with bookcases, filled to the brim with books. I started to read some of the titles. Most of them were scientific or technical books, but in the middle bookcase there were several shelves of erotica. All the famous names and titles were there: *The Kama Sutra*, Henry Miller, D.H. Lawrence, Anaïs Nin to name but a few, plus many more rows of modern erotic paperbacks. I pulled one out, flipped the pages to the middle and started to read. I was immediately drawn into a bizarre sexual scene involving four men and a woman. The woman was on all fours being fucked by three of the men – a cock in each orifice – whilst the other man was underneath her sucking her tits. I felt myself getting excited. I flipped on a chapter or two and found another scene describing in lurid detail the pleasure of two men and two women who were lying on the floor in a kind of square licking each other's arses. I felt myself go hot all over. Did Ross practise this type of thing? My pussy was damp and pulsing with pleasure as I avidly read a few more scenes. Some of the actual set-ups and positions were almost impossible to imagine. I found myself in various contortions as I tried to visualise how they were doing it.

I was so absorbed in what I was reading that I did not hear Ross enter the room.

'Good book?' he enquired, peering over my shoulder.

I jumped and the book dropped to the floor.

Ross picked it up and looked at the cover. 'Ah yes. I remember this one. I read it over and over again. A lot of water's gone under the bridge since then. Nowadays I get more practice doing the real thing.' He handed the book back to me. 'You can borrow it if you want.'

So he did go in for group sex. I didn't know whether to be pleased or sorry. I found it exciting to read, but to actually participate? I wasn't sure.

'Don't look so righteous, Mariella. Take the book. Have some more if you like. You did say you were experimenting with sex.'

'They were Zoe's words, not mine,' I said primly. 'I'm not sure I'd do this sort of thing.' I thrust the book back into the bookcase and sat down on the sofa. I was shaking a little.

Ross came to sit next to me. I edged away a little. He suddenly seemed very intense.

'I think we need to get one or two things straight, Mariella, don't you?'

I turned on him. 'My name is Ellie. Why does everyone want to call me "Mariella"?'

'Because it's a lovely name. It's Italian, isn't it?'

I fiddled nervously with my hands. 'Yes. My mother was Italian.'

I was very much aware of his close proximity. He had a definite, masculine smell about him which was turning me on. My pussy was still pulsating a little and my thong was wet. I wanted him badly and he hadn't even touched me. What was even more disturbing was that all my usual seduction techniques seemed to have flown out of the window.

'OK then, Ellie,' he continued. 'You came here for sex with me as some kind of experiment for a book you are writing. Right? What sort of book?'

'Astrology,' I said weakly. 'How men relate sexually to their star signs.'

'Ah, how interesting. So you need an Aquarian and hey presto, here you are with me.'

I nodded. 'That's about it. Have I disappointed you?'

'Not at all. I'm impressed and proud that you have chosen me to be part of your book. But I think I ought to warn you. I don't go in for quick, routine shags. They rarely turn me on. Nowadays I enjoy different things –'

'Like group sex,' I interrupted.

'Yes, a lot of the time, but not always. Anything that's

unusual, unique or exciting makes me horny. I was rather hoping you had something in mind.'

'Me? No way.'

Ross sighed with disappointment. 'You would be quite happy to use me for a quick fuck on the sofa, wouldn't you?'

'No. Of course not,' I protested.

He suddenly changed the subject. 'Are you still going out with Ryan?'

'Yes. We're very happy,' I said defensively.

'Well, I suggest you go home to him then.'

I was stunned, not only by the coldness of Ross's tone, but the fact he wanted me to leave without having sex. I sat there rigid, staring at him, tears coming to my eyes.

Ross seemed unperturbed. 'Tears don't work on me, Mariella. I like my women to be uninhibited and bolshie. I thought you were like that.'

'I am,' I said, but even to my own ears, my voice sounded like a miserable whine. All my normal spunk seemed to have disappeared.

He became irritated. 'I am not going to be used for a quick fuck in my own house just so that you can get your book finished. You'd better go.' With that he stood up and strode out of the room, leaving me sitting there like a silly schoolgirl who had been chastised for being naughty. I sat there smarting, my anger suddenly mounting. I remembered my schooldays when the teachers had ignored me and dismissed me in the same callous manner.

I stood up, straightened my dress, and stomped into the kitchen, where Ross was calmly making himself a cup of coffee.

'You selfish bastard,' I cried, lunging at him with my fists flying.

He was caught off guard. 'What on earth –' He stopped in his tracks as I slapped his face. He grabbed my arms, but there was no stopping me. Using all my strength I broke free and hit him again, this time in the stomach. He doubled over and cursed. But he quickly recovered. He straightened himself up, reached out and grasped me by the waist. Then he spun me round, found one of my flaying arms and held me in an armlock. I struggled and swore at him, but this time he was stronger than me.

'Well! I am surprised at you, Ellie,' he said in my ear when I had calmed down a little. 'I was beginning to think I'd been mistaken about you. But I wasn't after all. I'm normally a pretty good judge of character.'

'Arrogant pig,' I hissed at him. 'I despise you.'

He laughed. 'No, you don't.' He pulled at my arm harder so that I winced with pain. 'You still want me.'

'Don't flatter yourself.' I turned my head round and spat at him. A large wadge of spit landed on his chest. I stared at it in horror. Then, for some reason I burst out laughing.

He was incensed. He pulled my arm harder and my laughter turned to cries of pain. Then with his free hand he yanked my dress up from behind, pulled out the strip of my thong and thrust his hand in the crease of my arse. 'This is what you're after, isn't it? Will a quick shag on the kitchen table do you?'

At that moment I really did hate him. I didn't know what to do. Anger would only incite him to violence and weakness would make him despise me more, but what really disturbed me was that for some dark, unknown reason, I still wanted him to fuck me. But not now, not like this. We stood in silence for a few moments. Then I suddenly relaxed my whole body.

'OK. You win,' I said. 'I'll do whatever you want.'

He seemed unsure. His grip on my arm relented a little. 'What do you mean?'

'I agree with you. A quick shag is boring. I'm willing to join in one of your group sessions if that's what you want, or if you prefer to experiment with something else, that's fine by me too.'

He let go of my arm. 'Why the change of heart?' he asked.

I looked at him openly and steadily for the first time. I finally felt in control. 'Because I'm writing a book about men's sexuality and I need you to be yourself. If you enjoy weird and wonderful sex, that's your choice. I shouldn't try to make you do something you don't enjoy. When it comes to it, at the end of the day all I need to do is experience your pleasure, and hopefully enjoy myself in the process.'

He nodded slowly, a smile coming to his face. 'I did underestimate you, Ellie. Not only are you high-spirited but you're intelligent too.' He rubbed his face ruefully. 'I'm going to have a lovely red mark here tomorrow.'

I smiled cheekily. 'Serves you right.'

We looked at each other with a new understanding.

'Can you get here this weekend?' Ross asked.

'Yes. I think so.'

'Good. Be here by midday Saturday, and I'll have something planned.'

I left feeling remarkably happy. For a moment back there it had looked like it was all falling to pieces, but now everything was on track again. Soon I would be going through yet another very different experience whilst making yet another conquest, but at least it would make my book worth reading.

The following night Ryan was due for dinner. He didn't turn up. At nine o'clock I threw the congealed food into the bin and rang his mobile. No reply, not even an answering message. At eleven o'clock, after having rung him about ten times, I went to bed, disappointed and puzzled. Something must have happened to him. I prayed he was all right, and fell into a deep sleep.

The next morning, on the front doormat, I found a letter marked MARIELLA in Ryan's large scrawl. I tore it open and read it, my heart thumping nervously:

Dear Mariella,

I won't be seeing you any more. I'm sorry I haven't got the courage to tell you to your face but I'm so angry I'm not sure I could control myself. Last night, whilst you were with Ross, I was in the pub with some friends and one of them happened to mention his older sister, a woman called Carole Maddingham, who works in the accounts office for a company called Junipers. Do you remember her? I'm sure it's coming back to you. Carole told him that during September of last year a randy office temp shagged their boss in his office every night for about four weeks. This girl was so brazen she didn't care if they were seen. She boasted about it to all the office girls and related the story of how one night the cleaner interrupted them on the job and got the shock of her life. Of course, we all had a good laugh about this in the pub – me included – until certain things you'd said came back to me and I realised it was you we were talking about.

How could you have lied to me like that, Mariella? I trusted you when you said it was only the once with him. But every night!! How many more lies have you told me? How many men have you fucked without me knowing? I can't take any more. I know I'm not perfect, but at least I've told you the truth. Have fun with Ross. I've decided to make a go of it with Gemma. I don't love her but I know where I stand with her. Don't try contacting me. I never want to see you again.

Ryan.

The letter fluttered from my hands and fell to the floor. I was in shock. I didn't go to work that day. I rang in with a sickie and took to my bed.

Somehow I managed to drag myself out of bed, have a shower and prepare myself for Ross on Saturday morning.

'You don't look very happy,' Ross said, ushering me into the house.

'Ryan's dumped me.'

'Oh. Well, look on the bright side. At least it makes you a free agent for the weekend.'

I scowled at him. 'Cut the crap, Ross. Just tell me what you want me to do.'

'Don't sound so enthusiastic. We can give it a miss if you want.'

I came to my senses and forced myself to smile. I ought to look happy even if I didn't feel it. 'No. Of course not. I've been looking forward to it.'

'Right then, come with me.'

He led me to the bedroom. 'Take your clothes off,' he ordered.

I was surprised. Surely he wasn't going to give me a quickie after all. I took off the new skirt and top I had carefully selected to wear this morning, followed by my underwear, and stood naked in front of him.

He inspected me thoroughly, walking around to view me at all angles. 'Very nice,' he said approvingly. On the bed was a large fur coat. He picked it up. 'Now put this on,' he said.

I did as I was told. The coat felt very soft and warm against my naked body. It reached to my knees. There were only three strategically placed buttons on it. I did them up. 'I hope this isn't real fur,' I said dubiously as I fingered the lovely material.

'Of course not. Do you think I could afford a real one?

Besides, I'm just as much against killing animals for fur as you are.'

I nodded. 'It's a lovely coat though.'

Ross grabbed his jacket. 'OK then, let's be off.'

I started to laugh. 'Like this? I'll freeze to death.'

'No you won't. You'll be warmer than I am in that coat.'

I stared at him in amazement. 'Where are we going?'

'First port of call is the local library.'

I burst into peals of laughter. He laughed too, and grabbed my hand. 'Come on, elegant Ellie, let's parade you around town a bit.'

We passed both our cars in the driveway. 'Aren't we taking the car?' I asked.

'No. We're going by bus. The town-centre car parks get packed out on a Saturday.'

He took my hand and pulled me close to him as we walked along. I felt the sharp, wintry air blow round my naked thighs. It wasn't an unpleasant experience, quite enjoyable in fact. At last I was beginning to shake Ryan's image from my mind.

We waited at the bus stop with around a dozen other hopefuls for what seemed like ages. Everybody kept looking at me oddly, as if they knew I had nothing on underneath. Every chance he got Ross would slip a cold hand between one of the buttons on my coat and stroke my bare flesh, making me shiver with delight.

The bus, when it came, was a big, old-fashioned double decker. Ross pushed me up the stairs in front of him, putting his hands up my coat and caressing the tops of my legs as he did so. We sat in the back seat, me in the corner huddled up against the window. Ross put his hand up my coat and touched my pussy. I jumped with pleasure but pushed him away urgently when the conductor came round for the ticket. The conductor eyed us suspiciously but said nothing. When he'd gone we both burst out laughing, making everybody in front turn round and stare. But we didn't care. Ross put his hand up my coat again and carefully opened my excited pussy with his fingers. Then he finger-fucked me until it was time to get off the bus.

The library in the centre of town was a brand new one on three floors. We waited until we had the lift to ourselves, then hopped in. Ross told me to hold my coat up while he massaged my buttocks and quickly slipped a finger in and out of my my arsehole. When the lift stopped I hurriedly dropped my coat down, but it wasn't until the door opened and we saw the people waiting to go down that Ross calmly pulled his hand away from my arse. I was shaking with pleasure at his audacity.

The top floor of the library was very peaceful. It was mainly the reference section. Students occupied desks as they quietly studied, whilst others – mainly men – sat around reading newspapers, oblivious to what was going on around them. Ross led me to a secluded and deserted corner and came to stand close behind me. My heart was thudding. What was he going to do next? He pulled up my coat and pressed his naked cock against my bare buttocks. I trembled with pleasure as he crushed it against my cool skin and I felt his hardness. The next moment he took it away and dropped my coat.

I looked round. An elderly woman standing close by smiled politely and I smiled back at her. Ross was on the other side of the lady, seemingly engrossed in a book. A huge bubble of laughter rose in my throat. I could hardly contain myself. Ross looked at me seriously, put his fingers to his lips and shook his head. I felt hysterically happy, very close to a fit of giggles.

When the old lady had gone, Ross drew me away. 'Naughty girl,' he said mockingly. 'You must keep quiet in the library.'

He led me towards the exit. 'I need a slash,' he said, heading for the gents.

I clung onto him. 'Can I come in with you?' I asked throatily.

'Hang on. I'll see if anybody's in there.'

A few seconds later he poked his head round the door and beckoned me in. It was very small, with only one cubicle toilet. Ross pulled me in quickly and locked the door. Then he pulled his cock out and thrust my head down to it.

I rolled my tongue round the head of his penis and pleasured him for a few minutes. He stood there in silence, only the expression on his face showing how much he was enjoying it. Eventually he pushed me away. 'I don't want a quickie in here,' he whispered. 'And I'm still dying for a pee.'

I watched him urinate into the toilet, fascinated.

When he'd finished we crept out again, holding hands and laughing.

We headed for the shops. 'I think it's about time you bought yourself something, Ellie,' he said. 'How about a nice dress? You'll need to try it on, of course.'

I got his drift immediately. We went into a large department store, where I picked up a few dresses at random and took them to the changing rooms. Ross casually followed me in, pulling the curtain across with a sharp swish as the assistant watched with a disapproving glare.

I took my coat off. Ross stared at me. I could see he was highly aroused again. He reached out and cupped my breasts in his hands before reaching down to suck and bite on my nipples.

'Try the dresses on,' he said huskily.

I did. But neither of us was really interested in what they looked like. After each one, Ross caressed a different part of my body. When I took the fourth dress off, he released his rigid cock again, pushed me against the wall and slammed it into me.

I gasped with surprise. He put his hand to my mouth and continued thrusting.

'Are you all right in there, madam?' the assistant called from just outside the curtain.

Ross took his hand away from my mouth.

'Yes. I'm fine,' I called out, trying not to giggle.

The curtain swished open and there she stood, a huge 'oh' of shock etched upon her face.

Ross reached out and pulled the curtain back, and we both burst out laughing.

'If you don't stop that this instant, I'm going to call the management,' the reedy voice of the assistant called out.

Ross and I looked at each other. 'Time to make a getaway,' he said, pulling his cock out of me, and hastily putting it away.

I threw on my coat and held it close to my body as we fled out of the changing room, almost knocking the assistant over. She stormed after us, shouting that the management were on their way.

We stopped running when we reached the main doors, and calmly walked out. I finally did my coat up and we strolled on, hand in hand, laughing at our little escapade.

We had a coffee in a crowded coffee bar. I was disappointed that Ross made no more effort to touch me, but I had to admit it was almost impossible for him to do anything without being seen. Besides, there were lots of children around.

Where to now?' I asked when we came out refreshed.

'There's a museum of erotic art up the road. Do you fancy going there?'

I grinned at him. 'Ooh, yes please.'

The museum was small and very quiet, but it was filled to the brim with paintings, old and new, of the naked form in all sorts of erotic poses, some of which were making me feel very horny. As we strolled along, studying the paintings, Ross kept slipping his hand inside my coat and fondling my breasts, even when there were other people in the room. Nobody seemed to notice: they were too intent on studying the paintings. We came to a very old oil painting of an enigmatic, naked young girl, her hairy crotch and rounded bottom very pronounced as two naked men with huge penises stood by her, one in front, one behind, smiling and pointing.

'It's obvious what they want to do, isn't it?' Ross said. 'Why they just couldn't paint her being fucked at both ends I don't know. But then if they did, it would be regarded as porn and not exhibited in this museum.'

'Silly, isn't it?' I agreed, and we walked on.

We came to a very small, empty room. 'Ah ha, just what I've been waiting for,' said Ross. He reached into his pocket and brought out a very small camera. 'Stand over there and open your coat wide, Ellie. I want to take a picture of you with these paintings.'

I stood close to the paintings and opened my coat to reveal my naked body, one eye on the door in case anybody should walk in.

'Stand with your legs open and your hands on your hips,' Ross said excitedly.

I did as he said and the flash went off.

'Turn round, hold your coat up and bend over. Quickly,' Ross urged, glancing at the door. 'I want to take a picture of one of the finest arses I've seen in a long while.'

I bent over with my coat scrunched up in my hands at the front and displayed my arse to the camera.

I heard the flash go. Somebody was clapping loudly.

'Bravo, bravo,' a voice shouted.

I dropped my coat and spun round to see a small, middle-aged, dapper man standing in front of Ross.

'That was wonderful, my dear,' the man said, beaming.

'You are an extremely beautiful young girl. Your boy-friend is very lucky.'

Ross pulled a comical face at me behind the man and shrugged his shoulders. He didn't know who the man was either.

I felt very embarrassed, but the man came up to me and took my hand in his. 'If ever you want some professional shots taken, come to me, my dear. I'll give you my card.' He thrust a small card in my hand and walked out of the room.

Ross came over and looked at the card. 'Henry Coppler,' he read out excitedly. 'He's really famous, Ellie. The best photographer of nude women in the business. You'll be made up for life if you go to him.'

I snatched the card away and thrust it into my coat pocket. 'I don't want to be a nude model, I want to be an astrologer,' I said stiffly, and strode out of the room.

We calmed down a bit after that. Ross took me back to his place, where he made me take off my coat and I cooked us a snack of beans on toast. The telephone kept ringing. Ross made every effort to stop me from hearing what was being said.

The third time it rang, he answered and said brightly, 'Gina, darling, how are you? I've missed you.'

I padded over to him in my bare feet, my breasts swinging, and rubbed myself against him. I could hear a woman's voice gushing away at the other end, and I felt jealous. Ross grabbed me by the waist and pulled me down onto his lap, face down, as he continued speaking.

'Wonderful,' he said into the phone as he probed the nub of my anus. 'I look forward to it. Make sure Josh brings his gear, won't you? Love you too. Bye.'

'Who was that?' I asked, sitting up on his lap.

'Gina. One of our groupies. She's going tonight.'

'Oh. So we're having a group session tonight then?'

'Of course. What did you expect? We haven't had a proper shag yet.'

'And Josh? He's going too, is he?

'Yep.'

'How many people will there be altogether?'

Ross put his fingers to my lips. 'Wait and see.' He pushed me off his lap and slapped my bottom. 'Go and do the washing up.'

I felt a bit peeved. I wasn't here to do his housework, but I didn't want to upset him, so I meekly went to the sink and did as I was told.

Later that night Ross drove us to a large house in North London. I was wearing the fur coat again, with nothing underneath. I was getting used to it by now and quite enjoying the sensuous feeling of the soft material against my skin and the constant shafts of air on my pussy. I was in a state of permanent excitement and so hot for sex that I desperately wanted Ross to keep touching me. I was disappointed when he didn't.

Ross let us into the house with a key, and then down a dim hallway into a large room, lit only by candles.

There were about a dozen people in the room, most of whom were naked. Some of the women were decked out in jewellery, though. The middle of the floor was covered by a king-size duvet on which a group of men and women – I couldn't really make out how many – were fucking each other in various positions.

I stared in fascination, my heart thumping.

One of the men who was watching the exhibition on the duvet sprung up from his chair to greet us. I couldn't keep my eyes off his erect penis which he was lovingly stroking as he spoke to us.

'Hi, Ross. Hi, Ellie. Take your clothes off and make yourself comfortable.'

'That's Justin,' Ross whispered to me, after he'd gone. 'He's the main organiser of our meetings.'

Ross whipped his clothes off and I followed suit. One of the watching girls came over to us. 'Lovely coat,' she said, stroking the material enviously and rubbing her small breasts against it.

Ross reached out and pinched the girl's nipples. 'Stop pretending you're a cat and come and sit with us, Bella.'

In a trance-like state I followed Ross and Bella to the other side of the room, where Ross sat in a big armchair and pulled us both onto his lap.

Bella immediately put her hand to Ross's cock and started masturbating him.

My feelings were in a turmoil. Half of me was finding the whole thing very atmospheric and exciting, but the other half felt threatened by all these naked men and women doing what they liked to one another.

The group on the floor were still at it, emitting quite a lot of grunts and groans. The observers were entranced by it all. Most of them were touching themselves, or someone else, as they waited for their turn on the floor.

Ross parted my buttocks and slipped a finger into my anus. It felt good. I wriggled my arse appreciatively.

Bella smiled at me encouragingly as she continued to fondle Ross's cock. I smiled back at her.

'Don't worry, we'll get our turn eventually,' Ross said. 'Then after that, it's a free-for-all. See that girl on the floor, underneath the tall, dark guy? Well, that's Gina, the girl on the phone. Gorgeous, isn't she?'

I stared at Gina as she writhed beneath the tall man. Another man had his penis in her mouth. From what little I could see of her face, she did look rather attractive. My confidence took a nose-dive and I began to wish I hadn't come.

Ross nudged me and placed something in my hand. I looked down at the joint distastefully. 'No thanks,' I whispered. 'I don't do drugs.'

He looked at me meaningfully. 'You do tonight.

Besides, it's not like the hard stuff.' He pushed the joint between my lips with his free hand and thrust another finger up my arse. My pussy gave a little jolt of excitement and I found myself opening my legs as well as my mouth. Bella leaned forward and started stroking the tops of my thighs. I looked down at her small hand with its delicate fingers as she began to explore. Apart from Anna, and her lovely shaved pussy, I'd never had any desire to experience another woman in my life, and I was stunned by her action, but I didn't stop her. Instead I lay back in Ross's arms, puffed on the joint and gave myself up to being fondled by Ross and Bella at the same time.

Ross gave me a look of admiration. 'That's my girl,' he said proudly, and suddenly I felt very happy.

Bella's little fingers found my clit and I squirmed with pleasure.

After several more puffs on the joint, I gave it back to Ross. 'I don't need anymore,' I said. I was already at the stage of no return.

Half an hour later, Justin came over and pulled me away from Ross onto the duvet. He lay me down, pushed me onto my side and held my leg up high. Ross came over with a bowl of white froth which looked like cream, and spread it with his fingers all over my pussy and down the crease of my arse. Then he put his head between my legs and dipped his tongue into the creamy mixture. Another man who I did not know came and licked my arse. I was trembling with desire. When I opened my eyes I could see the faces around me eagerly watching, desire etched on their faces, but I was beyond caring. In fact, I rather liked it; I felt very important. Another man came over and rubbed something into my breasts which smelt like it had cannabis in it. Justin started licking it off me, his teeth taking little bites at my nipples, making me groan with pleasure. Then I was yanked up on all fours and the man who had licked the cream from my arse entered my anus at the same time as Justin thrust his cock into my mouth. I wanted to cry out with pleasure but Justin's cock had filled my mouth up, so I bit on him lightly instead. He yelped but continued to push his shaft deep into my throat. Somebody was licking me, but I didn't know who. I opened my eyes briefly to see Bella below me and assumed it was her. I was at the stage where I didn't really care if it was a man or a woman who was turning me on. My whole body was gyrating with ecstasy. I was on fire; I wanted everybody to fuck me. With each thrust I wanted more and more. Finally I exploded, spilling my juices all over Bella's face. Justin and the unknown man shot into me, and I devoured Justin's spunk greedily.

A few moments later I was alone on the duvet, my body sore and empty. Ross picked me up and carried me to a sofa.

'You were wonderful, Ellie. Fantastic to watch. Do you want a shower?'

I looked up at his smiling face and realised for the first time that he hadn't entered me.

'You didn't stay,' I muttered. 'Why?'

'I wanted to watch you with the others. I know what you feel like inside. We've been at it all day. Justin thinks you're the tops. He'll want you back again.'

I sank back into the sofa. I was worried that I had not been properly shagged by Ross. I suddenly felt very tired. Did I have the energy to pursue him, yet again? 'I need you to fuck me,' I said weakly.

Ross reached out and stroked my belly. His eyes were full of affection. 'Oh, I will, don't you worry. In the meantime, you go and have a shower.'

I returned to the room a while later, clean and refreshed. I'd had to share the large shower with a couple of strangers but nobody touched me. It seemed that once we were out of the 'groupie' room, sex was taboo. The whole set-up was very strange.

By now, everybody had sectioned off into separate groups. All I could see was a mass of heaving bodies everywhere. I looked for Ross and eventually saw him in the corner of the room with Gina and another man whom I assumed was Josh. Gina was sitting astride Ross's prick with her back to him, whilst Josh was licking her clit.

A shaft of jealousy drove through me when I saw the pleasure on Gina's face. I strolled over, trying to appear calm. I needed Ross inside me, not Gina. They didn't seem to notice me as I stood beside them. A man came up to me from behind and squeezed my buttocks. 'Come and join our group,' he said.

I shook my head and smiled regretfully, not wanting to offend him. 'I'm with this group,' I said, pointing at Ross.

The man gave me a strange look and walked off. Gina and Ross finally noticed me and smiled.

Ross reached out and grabbed one of my breasts, and put it to his mouth. Gina continued to pump herself up and down on him, with Josh attached to her like a limpet. Part of me was suddenly repulsed by it all, but another part of me still wanted Ross.

I started stroking his chest and teasing his nipples. I'd found out long ago that some men had very sensitive nipples. I bent down and whispered in his ear, 'I want you to fuck me, Ross.'

Ross grinned. 'Now?'

'Yes.'

'I can't fuck two of you at once.'

I stroked his neck and nibbled at his ear seductively. 'Get her off.'

Ross gave me a lewd look then suddenly pushed Gina off his cock. It stood out in front of him magnificently, glistening with Gina's juices in the candlelight. Gina gave a moue of disappointment and glared at me. I ignored her and quickly straddled Ross face-to-face. The feel of him sharply entering me was exquisite. I pressed down on him and leaned forward. He kissed me, not with great passion, but with calculated slowness, his tongue probing around my mouth, his lips pressing softly against mine. I started moving up and down, slowly at first, then building up speed. Then I felt Josh's hands (I think) on my buttocks, helping me move, pulling me vigorously up and down on Ross's cock. I closed my eyes and let myself go. This was what I had been waiting for. Finally, Ross came inside me and I erupted a few moments later. I had completed my task.

The orgy went on all night, but I decided to opt out after my session with Ryan. I found my coat and tiptoed from the room, glancing over my shoulder as I left. Ross was already back with Gina but this time it was Josh who was thrusting inside her and Ross who was bending over to delight her with his tongue. I found an empty bedroom and collapsed onto the bed. I was asleep in seconds.

Ross found me the next morning and ushered me out of the room quickly. Evidently Justin was very fussy about people using his bedrooms.

We didn't linger in the house. Ross took me back to his place where I hurriedly got dressed.

'Would you like some breakfast?' Ross asked, although it was closer to lunchtime. He seemed very deflated.

'No thank you.' I just wanted to get home.

Ross seemed disappointed.

I hurried to the front door. At the last minute he grabbed my arm. 'Ellie –'

'Yes? What's the matter?' I asked impatiently.

'I get the feeling I'm not going to see you again.'

'I doubt it.' I felt very distant.

He nodded sadly. 'That's a shame. You were good, Ellie. If you ever change your mind, give me a ring.'

I nodded, anxious to be gone. A few weeks ago I had been worried that this man would upset the status quo and make me question my feelings for Ryan. It seemed ironic that now I had lost Ryan, my feelings for Ross had done a U-turn. He was great fun and exciting to be with, but now that the sex was over, he left me cold.

We said our goodbyes and I thankfully got into my car and drove home. Back at the flat I listened to the answerphone, hoping to hear some news from Ryan, but the only message was from Zoe telling me that her and Tony were going on a backpacking tour of Asia and were leaving that night.

I suddenly felt very lonely. The yearning inside me to hear Ryan's voice was too much to bear. I made myself a cup of tea and went to bed.

Chapter Thirteen
Pisces: The Saintly Sinner

19 FEBRUARY

I'm forcing myself to write this because it's going to be the final entry. It has also become a ritual which I can't ignore, even though I feel dead to the world. The last few weeks have been hell. I haven't worked, haven't slept and have hardly eaten. Worst of all, I have not heard a word from Ryan. I miss him like crazy. Every morning I'm full of good intentions to do something positive for a change, but by midday I feel so depressed I take to my bed again. I'm not proud to say that hiding myself away from the world under my duvet is my way of seeking oblivion. I know it sucks, but I can't help it.

The good news is I have managed to get my book up to date, with only the chapter on Pisces to finish. The bad news is I haven't found a Piscean. Not that I've been looking much. I can't use Ryan's list because I haven't got any contact numbers or addresses. Also, news travels fast. It would no doubt get back to Ryan that I was exploiting him yet again and it doesn't seem right.

Zoe is still backpacking her way round Asia with Tony, so she can't help me. I had a phonecall from her when she arrived in Hong Kong a few days ago. She sounded so excited it brought tears to my eyes. I'm not sure whether they were tears of happiness for her, or tears of self-pity for me.

Poor old Anna is in hospital. I rang her at home last week to see if she had any bright ideas on how to find a Pisces man, only to be told by a very worried Lester that she had been admitted to the maternity ward with a threatened miscarriage the day before and was being forced to rest. Lester contacted me yesterday, however, to say that things were looking up. The baby is still intact, thank goodness, and Anna is being allowed to do a little exercise. I feel awful: she has been in hospital for over a week and I've made no effort to go and see her, although I have sent her a 'get well' card. I've made up my mind. Today I'm going to drag my fat arse out of bed, get that car out of the garage where it's been sitting, untouched, for weeks, and drive to the hospital to see her. It's about time I put my make-up on, glammed myself up a bit and thought of somebody else for a change. Then after I've seen Anna, I'm going to return to the estate agents I visited at the end of June when I was looking for Mr Cancer to seek out that very nice Mr Pisces I met instead. I hope he's still around. I'll keep my fingers crossed, just in case.

Anna was sitting up in bed looking very cheerful. She hugged me delightedly. 'It's lovely to see you, Ellie.'

'You too,' I said, my eyes brimming with tears. Anna was such a sweet person.

She patted her stomach. 'Baby's fine. I had another scan today and the nurse asked us if we wanted to know what sex it is, but we said "no". Lester and I want it to be a surprise.'

'Mmm. I think I would feel the same if I was expecting. It spoils it if you know beforehand. How much longer will you be in here?'

'I've no idea. Not too long, I hope. My blood pressure's still a little high. It needs to come down a bit more before they'll let me out.'

'You could rest at home.'

'That's what I told them. Lester said he would take care of me. But I suppose the doctors want to be sure everything's OK. I'm surprised they don't need the bed for somebody else.'

'Where's Lester?' Has he gone home?'

'No. He went down to the hospital shop about half an hour ago. He should be back soon. Ah, here he is.'

I looked round. Lester was approaching the bed, a big grin on his face and a huge bunch of flowers in his hand. He thrust them proudly into Anna's arms.

'Oh Lester, they're beautiful,' she crooned, looking up at him, her eyes shining with adoration. 'Aren't they lovely, Ellie?' She pushed the flowers towards me.

'Yes. Beautiful,' I said, trying to sound enthusiastic as I leaned over to smell them. For some reason I found Lester's presence annoying. I still didn't trust him even though he was behaving like a perfect gentleman.

Lester smiled at me. 'So you finally made it then, Ellie.'

There was no sarcasm in his voice, but I felt he was trying to put me down.

'Ellie's not been well,' Anna said quickly. 'Ryan has left her.'

'Oh?' Lester's eyes pierced into mine keenly. 'Never mind, Ellie. I always thought he was a bit of a loud-mouth anyway. I'm sure you'll find somebody else more worthy of your, er, talents soon.'

'I don't want anybody else,' I muttered, choosing to ignore his derogatory comments about Ryan.

Anna took my hand. 'Don't upset yourself, Ellie. Lester's right. There are plenty of other fish in the sea.'

I had to smile at Anna's words. I wished there were

208

plenty of fish in the sea, Piscean fishes, of course, so that I could take my pick and get my challenge finished.

The three of us chatted companionably for a while. When I stood up to leave, Lester stood up too, saying it was about time he made a move.

'I'll walk to the car park with you, Ellie,' he said, smiling magnanimously at me.

He gave Anna a lingering, tongue-probing kiss good-bye and told her he loved her.

I hugged her tightly and promised to visit again soon.

As soon as we were out of the ward, Lester put his arm around my shoulders. I let him do it, hoping it was just the action of a solicitous friend.

What he said a few moments later shattered that illusion. 'If you're missing the sex with Ryan, I could console you, Ellie.'

I was stunned by his duplicity. 'No thank you,' I said coldly, shaking his arm away from my shoulders. 'If – and when – I need some sex, I'll be on the lookout for a young, virile Piscean, not an old man like you.' The words slipped out unintentionally. As far as I was aware, Lester knew nothing about my quest and I didn't want him to. I hadn't meant to be rude to him either. The last thing I wanted was for him to tell Anna what I had said and risk upsetting her.

Lester gave a snide laugh. 'Why on earth are you looking for a Piscean?'

'Oh, no particular reason.' I really wished I hadn't opened my big mouth.

Lester stopped in his tracks and grabbed my arm. 'Hang on. I think I'm a Pisces. Or is it Aquarius? I've never paid much attention to the stars.'

'When's your birthday?' I asked.

'The twenty-seventh of February – a week's time.'

'You're a Pisces all right.'

Lester grinned at me lewdly, showing the slightly stained teeth I found so unattractive. 'So, my dear Ellie, do I fit the bill? I might not be young, but I'm a very horny Pisces.'

'In your dreams, Lester,' I spat at him, and stormed off towards the main exit. Lester ran after me, reaching the door before I did, and held it open for me. I glared at him as I marched out into the cold, damp February air. Despite my anger, I couldn't help noticing that when he kept his mouth closed, he didn't look too bad. Either his wrinkles were disappearing or I was getting used to him.

Lester stopped in front of his car and turned to me anxiously. 'Why don't you get in for a moment and have a chat,' he said.

'What about?'

'Me, you, Anna, Ryan. Anything you like. I feel you need to talk to somebody. I'm here, and I'm willing to listen.'

I hung back, unsure. I didn't really want to encourage him, but the thought of a sympathetic ear after three lonely weeks without Ryan was hard to resist.

'Please, Ellie. I promise I won't come on to you again, if you don't want me to.'

'OK,' I said reluctantly. 'Just for a few minutes.'

He opened the passenger door for me and I slipped in.

'Now, tell me why you are looking for a Piscean,' Lester said once we were settled in the car.

'I'd rather not,' I said coldly.

'OK. Please yourself. I thought you might have wanted to confide in me. Does Anna know why?'

'Yes. But don't you dare bully her into telling you.'

'As if I would bully my darling girl. You seem to think I'm a big, bad ogre. I do love her, you know.'

'Do you?' I looked at him closely. 'Sometimes you don't act as if you do.'

He laughed. 'Do you mean when I'm making a pass at you?'

'Yes. If you really loved her, you wouldn't do it.'

He shook his head, protesting. 'I really do love her, Ellie. But I'm a man – an ageing one at that – as you've noticed. I need to get as much sex as I can before I become incapable of getting a hard-on. It's all a matter of pride, you know.'

'No. I don't know. Anna trusts you. If she knew you were trying it on with me, she'd be devastated.'

'I know. And that's why we won't tell her, will we?'

He put his hand on my knee and when I didn't rebuff him, he confidently slid his hand upwards along the inside of my thighs, pushing my legs slightly apart, until he reached the rim of my knickers.

'Don't do this, Lester,' I said, turning to him, my eyes pleading. 'Don't do it, for Anna's sake.'

He took no notice of my last-ditch attempt to prevent us from doing something which I knew we would deeply regret later, or at least I would. Instead he started stroking my pussy through my knickers.

'Oh Ellie, Ellie,' he sighed. 'Don't stop me now. We're doing nothing wrong. I'm a Pisces, remember? You need me.'

I sat there in limbo for a few moments, my legs open, welcoming the feel of Lester's hand on my pussy. It would be so easy to succumb. One quick shag and I would have completed my task. My father's money and his large house would be mine. There would be no more financial worries and I could do everything in my power to get Ryan back.

Lester knew he had won. He pulled his hand away from my treacherous pussy and started up the car. 'I'll drive us somewhere a bit more private,' he said confidently.

I said nothing. My tacit agreement was enough. Ten minutes later he drove into a small, quiet car park on Wimbledon Common and stopped the car. I could hear

211

the sound of my heart thudding in the deathly silence. Was I doing the right thing?

Lester reached out and pulled my skirt up round my thighs. I sat there, watching his pudgy fingers as they probed inside my knickers and began to pull them down. Once they were off, he quickly pulled my legs open and thrust his hand up to my pussy, slipping a finger inside. It was warm, slippery. The sudden penetration after a few weeks' abstinence made me moan out loud.

He sighed with pleasure. 'You feel so beautiful inside, Ellie. Oh, how I've longed to fuck you.'

I looked down at the top of his head as he leaned over my body. His grey hair was thinning on top and he had chronic dandruff. A vision of Anna in the hospital bed – smiling up at him adoringly, opening her arms for the flowers, doing everything she could to save his baby – suddenly sprang into my mind, and I knew there was no way I could go through with it, or even wanted to go through with it.

'No, no!' I cried, pushing hard at his chest with my hands.

He looked up at me in surprise, his fingers still exploring my pussy. 'What's the matter?'

'I can't do it. I don't want to hurt Anna.'

Lester's expression turned nasty. 'We agreed she'll never know.' His hand continued to grip my naked pussy tightly.

I yanked at his wrist and tried to pull his hand away. 'Please, Lester. Let me go. We've both got to think of Anna. She's having your baby, for Christ's sake.'

Lester seemed to ponder on my words for a few seconds, then he gave me a look of utter contempt and jerked his hand away.

Inwardly, I sighed with relief. For one brief moment I thought he was going to resist and try to force me. Coolly, so as not to antagonise him any further, I pulled my skirt down and asked him to take me back to the hospital car park. My knickers were somewhere in the car, but I didn't dare start looking for them.

Lester immediately started up the car and zoomed like a maniac out of the car park onto the main road.

I cringed in my seat. 'Please, Lester. Don't drive so fast. You'll kill us both.'

Lester slammed on the brakes to make a point and turned to me savagely. 'Just in case you change your mind, Miss High-and-Mighty, I'll have you know that there's no way I'd ever fuck you now. Anna's ten times better than you.'

Silently I agreed with him. I decided to take the road of least resistance and say nothing. The whole, sordid mess was as much my fault as Lester's.

Neither of us said another word until we reached the hospital.

He drove into the main driveway, leaned across my chest, cruelly squashing himself against my breasts, and flung the passenger door open. 'Get out!' he hissed.

I scrambled out but before I could slam the door in his face, he threw something at my feet. 'You've forgotten these,' he sneered.

I looked down to see my knickers sitting in the gutter. As I stooped to pick them up, he slammed the door and raced away. I stuffed them into my bag, looking around with embarrassment to see if anybody had noticed, but luckily all was quiet. Slowly I walked back to my car. I had been humiliated, but it was no more than I deserved. I could never have forgiven myself if I had betrayed Anna. Now, I had to look on the bright side. At least I was finally free of lusty Lester's attentions.

I was halfway home when I remembered I had intended to call in and see my Piscean estate agent. I hastily turned the car round and headed in the opposite direction, towards town.

* * *

213

I strolled into the offices of Steadman and Skinner the estate agents feeling quite confident and very sexy in my knickerless state. My man wasn't there; his desk was empty.

'Can I help you, Miss?' a young lad sitting in the adjacent desk asked.

'I wanted to speak to Mr Bayliss. Is he around, please?'

''Fraid not. He's on his honeymoon. Left for the Caribbean about ten days ago, lucky man.'

I felt myself go cold. Honeymoon? He'd told me he didn't have a girlfriend when he'd flirted with me relentlessly eight months ago.

'Can I get him to call you when he comes back next week?'

I turned in dismay towards the door. 'No, no thank you. It doesn't matter,' I said, a lump already forming in my throat, and made a hasty exit.

My mood plummeted from way above zero to way below zero. I wandered around the town like a zombie, looking in shop windows, not buying anything, too depressed to go home and too broke to buy anything. I could see my father's money slipping away as my challenge came to a grinding halt. I even began to wish I'd let Lester shag me. Then the heavens opened. I didn't have an umberella with me, so I took shelter beneath a shop awning, but after a while I got fed up with waiting for the rain to stop and foolishly strolled out into the streaming torrent. Ten minutes later I was soaked to the skin, and shivering with cold. My knickerless state didn't seem so sexy now. I thought of going into a shop and buying some new ones, but I couldn't be bothered. My apathy was increasing by the minute.

My steps took me to the outskirts of town. As I was approaching a large, old church, a couple came out of the main entrance. They stood together in the church porchway, arms linked, staring at the rain. Then the man pulled his jacket over the girl's head and they ran out into the downpour together, laughing with wild abandon. I envied them their happiness. I walked to the church door and opened it. It was cold inside, but at least it was dry. Nobody was about as I shuffled down the aisle, leaving a wet trail in my wake, before collapsing into the front pew. I wasn't religious and never had been. I didn't even know what denomination the church was, but as I sat there, my clothes soaked, my hair dripping large spots of water onto the bench, I found myself closing my eyes and praying to God to make everything better.

When I opened my eyes, a man was standing close by, watching me. 'Hello,' he said kindly. 'Are you all right?'

I shook my head, too frightened to speak in case I started to cry. When I looked at the man again, I noticed the dog collar round his neck. But he was only about thirty and looked quite normal in his thick, patterned sweater and jeans.

'Can I help you in any way?' he asked.

I laughed rudely. As if a vicar could help me!

He sat down on the pew next to me, ignoring the wet patches. 'What's your name?'

'Mariella.' I lowered my head and stared at my dirty shoes.

'It's all right, Mariella.' His voice was soothing. 'I can tell you are troubled. Do you want to talk about it?'

I looked into his eyes for the first time. They were big and soulful, a beautiful shade of brown. I burst into tears.

He reached out and took my hand, gently squeezing it between his own large hands. 'Don't cry. Talk to me. That's what I'm here for.'

'I'm not a Catholic,' I said, sobbing.

'Neither am I. This is the Church of England. But I can still listen to you. I promise I won't judge you.'

I stared at him, but all I could see was genuine empathy, so I opened my mouth and it all came tumbling out. I started at the very beginning, going all the way back to the loneliness I had felt as a child after my beautiful, young Italian mother had been killed in a tragic road accident when I was just two. My father had brought me up by himself, loving and spoiling me dearly, but I had missed that special bond that only a mother can create. I spoke about my difficulties at school, the teachers who didn't seem to understand me and how hard I had found it to pay attention even though I had a good brain and wished to follow in my father's footsteps and become a successful astrologer. I rambled on about my teenage years, and my past boyfriends, before mentioning my on-off relationship with Ryan and my love for him. Then I told him about my father's death and the conditions of his will. The kindly vicar did not bat an eyelid when I told him how I had nearly fulfilled my obligations but had so far failed to find a suitable Piscean. He listened intently to my emotional outbursts and the intimate results of my monthly challenges. I didn't pull any punches or try to make him feel sorry for me. I told him how much I had enjoyed the sex but in the end it had all turned sour on me when Ryan found out I had lied to him. I emphasised how much Ryan, Anna and Zoe had helped me, realising as I spoke that I had sometimes been very naive and selfish in my desire to get what I wanted. I finished my tale by telling him how I had nearly succumbed to Lester a few hours previously and had risked betraying one of my closest friends, just because I was desperate to finish my challenge and get my hands on my father's money.

When the shower of words dried up, I looked into my companion's eyes, daring him to challenge me and tell me I had sinned, but I could see only kindness mirrored in his large, soulful eyes.

'You've had quite a year,' he said softly.

'I don't expect you to understand,' I said defensively. 'Somebody like you doesn't need sex the way I do.'

He smiled. 'Don't you believe it. I'm not a priest, you know. I'm a vicar, a normal man with normal desires, who also happens to believe in the love of God.'

I nodded and managed a wry smile. 'But you have to get married before you can have sex, don't you?'

'Ideally, yes. But it doesn't always work that way. Sometimes the power of the flesh takes over and we find ourselves making love to a woman without being committed.'

I opened my eyes wide with surprise. 'Really? And I thought that vicars were all holier-than-thou.'

He laughed and shook his head. 'Far from it. I'm not much different from you when it boils down to it.'

I stared at him, fascinated, my own misery forgotten. 'Have you, er, you know, been with a woman lately?'

'There's no need to mince your words, Mariella. Just because the word "shag" isn't in the Bible it doesn't mean we can't use it. But in reply to your question, the the answer is "no". I was engaged for a long while, and yes, we did have premarital sex, but she eventually left me for another man. Then a year ago I had a fling with a very sexy girl, but she gave me the boot too. In between these relationships and for a whole year now I have been celibate.'

'Oh.' I suddenly felt sorry for him. 'Don't you get frustrated? Surely you'd like to do it more often?'

He looked at me so intently that I acutally blushed, and started stammering a little. 'D-don't get me wrong. I-I'm not offering my services. I'm just curious, that's all.'

He smiled sweetly at me. 'Yes. I do get frustrated. But

don't worry that I've got the wrong impression. I would feel very flattered if you offered yourself to me.'

'Even after everything I've told you?'

'It's not up to me to make judgements. That's one of the things Jesus tried to teach us. He forgave Mary Magdalene and loved her as much as he loved everybody else.'

My eyes brimmed over with tears again. 'You're a very kind vicar.'

He took my left hand and placed it between his hands. 'My name is Owen.' He reached out and stroked my straggly, wet hair. 'Would you like to come to my apartment and dry yourself off?'

I nodded.

He helped me up and led me to the back of the church, through a door into a small passageway, then through another door into a warm and cosy, but sparsely furnished, room.

'This is where I live,' Owen said proudly. 'I've got a bedroom, kitchen, bathroom and this room, which is my living room. It's not very big, but I like it, and it's very handy for my work.'

I stood in the middle of the room, my soggy clothes sticking to me, my shoes making dirty marks on the carpet.

'The bathroom's here, if you want to clean yourself up,' Owen said, opening an an adjoining door.

'Can I have a shower?'

'Sorry. I don't have such a luxury. But I do have a bath. The water is hot. You can put your wet clothes on the radiator to dry and borrow my towelling robe when you've finished. It's on the back of the bathroom door.'

'Thanks, Owen. You're an angel.' Before I had a chance to think about what I was doing, I went up to him and planted a big, fat kiss on his cheek.

He smiled and rubbed his cheek playfully. 'I'll treasure that, Mariella.'

Half an hour later, feeling clean, warm and dry in Owen's towelling robe, I emerged from the bathroom.

'Are you feeling better now?' Owen asked solicitously. He was sitting on the sofa reading a book.

I sat down beside him. 'What are you reading?'

'Part of the gospel of St Mark which I am aiming to read out in my sermon on Sunday.'

'Oh. Serious stuff.'

He laughed and put the book down. 'Would you like a tea or coffee?'

'I'd love a coffee. Lots of milk and two sugars please.'

'Coming up, ma'am. Make yourself at home, put your feet up and I'll be back in a minute.'

I did as he said, wrapping the towelling robe tightly round my naked body and raising my bare feet onto the sofa. I was beginning to feel much happier. There was something very nurturing about Owen's presence.

A few moments later Owen returned with two cups of coffee and sat down by my feet at the end of the sofa.

'You're looking a lot brighter now, Mariella,' he said, gently stroking my right foot with one hand and drinking his coffee with the other.

For once I didn't mind being called by my full name. Owen made it sound so pretty. 'Thank you for listening to me, Owen,' I murmured.

Owen put his cup down and placed his other hand on my left foot, so that he was clasping both feet in his hands. 'Your feet are cold. They need warming up,' he said, massaging them lightly.

I lay back, closed my eyes and allowed the pleasant warmth of his hands to permeate my feet. It felt as if he was giving me healing, but I wasn't sure whether it was for my feet or for my soul.

'You have beautiful feet, Mariella,' Owen said after a while.

I opened my eyes just in time to see him reach down

and tenderly kiss the arches of my feet with his warm, dry lips.

A bolt of lightning shot through me. Amazed at my incredible reaction to the feel of his lips, I immediately covered up my confusion by saying brusquely, 'No they're not, they're ugly, just like the rest of me.'

Owen looked at me reprovingly. 'Please don't put yourself down, Mariella. You are one of the most beautiful women I have ever had the pleasure to meet. Why not acknowledge it yourself?'

His fingers carried on manipulating my toes and gently squeezing my insteps and ankles.

'Do you like your feet being massaged?' he asked.

'Mmm. It's lovely.'

He bent over. This time he kissed the big toe on my right foot and then slowly took it into his mouth.

I was stunned. The movement was so fluid, so gentle, yet filled with such passionate longing, that it rocked me to the core. He wanted me sexually. When he turned to my other foot and did the same thing, this time gently nibbling all my toes in succession, my heart started to beat faster.

He sat up and looked deeply into my eyes.

I started to tremble. He was asking me to give myself to him. After everything I had told him, he still found me desirable. Was he using me, though? Did he think he was onto a good shag? I stared back into his kindly, soulful eyes which were now burning with passion, and knew instinctively that the answer was 'no'. He wanted Mariella the person, not Mariella the body. He was a good man who would give much more than he would take. I was entranced. I wanted him too. But then I remembered I needed a Pisces man to fulfil my quest, and it wouldn't do me any good to be sidetracked by a horny vicar. I lowered my eyes and pulled away from him slightly.

He stood up immediately, full of apology. 'I am so

sorry, Mariella, it was very wrong of me. I've offended you, haven't I? You told me your story, you trusted me, and I threw it back in your face by asking you to do the same thing with me. Please forgive me.'

He looked desperately unhappy and suddenly so was I.

I jumped up from the sofa and took his hand. 'No! You've got it all wrong. You're a lovely man. You haven't offended me at all. I feel honoured that you want me.' I reached for the belt on the towelling robe and undid it, revealing my naked body.

Owen stared at me in wonder. The gratitude and pleasure in his eyes brought tears to mine. He moved towards me and gently traced a finger across my face and onto my neck before moving silently downwards to my tingling breasts. I stood immobilised as he stripped the robe from my body, leaving me naked and vulnerable. He crushed me into his arms and we slid to the floor. His hands quietly explored my body, making contact with every part of me, turning my blood to fire.

Some time later he took his own clothes off, scooped me up into his arms and took me to his bedroom, where we continued our exploration of one another, our hands in mutual harmony as we caressed each other longingly. When I reached down and cupped his balls in my hands and stroked his cock so that it stood rigid and proud, he probed my wet pussy with his large, sensitive fingers, making me swoon with delight. For the first time in my life I felt truly loved.

With sensuous slowness we made love using our hands, bodies and tongues, lingering in each other's most sensitive parts, imbibing as much as we could of each other's nectar, making each moment last until we could bear it no more. When he finally thrust into me, I felt the communion of our souls as well as our bodies. We climaxed together in a shuddering crescendo which took us both to heaven and back. We were one.

* * *

I stayed with Owen for a week. We ate, slept, talked and made love together. I couldn't bear to be parted from him. Our love-making increased to such an intensity that we were fucking each other in every spare moment of the day. Owen couldn't keep his hands off me. It was as if he was trying to make up for all his years of celibacy in the space of one week. When he gave his sermon on Sunday I sat in the front pew listening to the rich, sweet sound of his voice, imagining his cock was inside me, pulsating with life and giving me pleasure. My pussy was so wet I nearly came. When the sermon was over we rushed to his apartment, flung off our clothes and made savage love. This was a different Owen. He thrust into me unmercifully, making me scream out for more. He bit my nipples and clawed my back and I loved every minute of it. The next day we made love in every room of the apartment in the space of a few hours, ending up on the sofa in a mindless orgy of laughter and limbs. We began to wander about the apartment with nothing on so that we could touch and probe each other more easily. One day Owen rubbed honey all over my body and licked it off. He was my saviour. I loved everything about him. Then one morning after we had made love, he quietly told me to get dressed because we needed to talk.

I sat twiddling my fingers in nervous apprehension at the kitchen table. Owen sat opposite me.

'This can't go on,' Owen said at last.

'Why not?' I wailed, tears coming to my eyes.

Owen sighed and gently wiped my tears away with his fingers. 'Because of so many things, my darling.'

'You don't want me any more, is that it?'

Owen shook his head sadly. 'I want you as much as ever, Mariella. I love you. You know that.'

My heart fluttered with pleasure and hope. 'If you love me, surely we can stay together?'

'No, I don't think so. Firstly, you don't love me; you

still love Ryan.' He saw me shaking my head wildly and motioned me to sit still. 'And secondly, you have a very important project to finish which needs your immediate attention.'

My heart went numb. Surely he didn't mean my father's challenge? I had almost forgotten about it.

'You mean you actually want me to go out and find a Pisces man and shag him so that I can claim my father's money?' I said in bitter disappointment.

He smiled, and my heart lurched, despite my anger.

'Not exactly. But I do think you should finish the book and take it to the solicitor's.'

'But that would be cheating.'

'Would it?' Owen looked at me seriously.

'Yes. I haven't met a Pisces. You know that.'

'Haven't you?'

I looked at him intensely, my heart beginning to thud loudly as it suddenly dawned on me what he was trying to say. 'D-do you mean –'

'Yes,' he interrupted. 'I'm your Pisces.'

'Why didn't you tell me before,' I cried, but even as I said it, I knew the answer.

'I didn't want you see me as just another statistic to help you finish your challenge. I wanted you to want me – Owen – not me the Piscean.'

I nodded slowly. 'I know. I understand. I'm glad you didn't tell me. But I'm not interested in finishing the book now that I've met you.'

'You must, Mariella. When you poured your heart out to me in the church, it meant everything to you. You've worked hard and put yourself on the line, even though you enjoyed most of the experiences. You've also lost Ryan because of it. Finish your book and take it to the solicitor as soon as possible. Then you can try and get it published and earn more money. I'd love to see a copy of it in print.'

'Would you?' I said, my eyes shining.

'Yes. But to do it, you'll need to go home and work hard for the next few weeks.'

My face fell. 'But what about you and me?'

'I think you should finish your book and then try to get Ryan back. I'm sure he still loves you.'

I shook my head. 'He doesn't. Not any more. Besides, I'm not sure I want him. But I'll do as you say. I'll finish the book and take it to the solicitor, and when I've done that, I'll come back here to you.'

Owen smiled soulfully and reached out to stroke my face. 'Mariella, I want more than anything for you to be happy. If you love Ryan – and I think you do – you must go to him. I love you too, but it's what you want that counts. You've given me more happiness than I deserve this past week. I'm a very lucky man to have known you.'

I stared at him in wonder. He was a saint. Such unconditional love was almost unbelievable, and for that I loved him deeply. But did I love him enough? Or was he just a substitute for Ryan? To be honest, I didn't know. I needed time by myself to find out. Owen had recognised this and was allowing me the freedom to discover the needs of my true, inner self. I would be eternally grateful to him, whatever the outcome.

I leaned forward and kissed him tenderly on the lips. His response was so sweet, so poignant and full of yearning that I didn't want it to stop. Eventually I found the courage I needed and pulled away.

'Thank you, Owen, thank you for everything. You picked me up when I was at my lowest ebb and made me very happy too. I'll never forget that.'

I left a short while afterwards. When I glanced back at him, Owen blew me a kiss with his hands. His eyes were full of tears.

Chapter Fourteen
The Outcome

I turned off the computer, sank back in my chair and gave a whoop of delight. I had finally done it! The book was finished and I had three days to spare before my appointment with Bernard Enright, the solicitor, on 21 March.

I decided I owed myself a treat. I went to my bedside cabinet and brought out the only booze left in the flat: half a bottle of vodka. I didn't have any tonic so I mixed the vodka with a little orange juice and downed it in one go. Then I finished the rest of the bottle.

When the phone rang later in the afternoon, I was on the kitchen table swinging the empty vodka bottle precariously in the air whilst gyrating my hips to the glorious sound of Ricky Martin blaring away on my CD player. I staggered down from the table, my head spinning, and tottered to the phone.

'Hi, Ellie.'

The familiar voice made me cry out in delight. 'Zoe! Where are you?'

'Back home, trying to get organised. But I'm pissed off with it. I'm longing to see you, Ellie. I've got so much to tell you. You won't believe the things I've seen and done over the last few weeks.'

'Oh, Zoe. I'm so glad you're back. I've got lots to tell you too.'

'Shall we meet up tonight for a drink?'

I giggled. 'I've just finished off a bottle of vodka, so I'm half-cut already, but I want to get totally sloshed. I've finished the book, Zoe.'

'Marvellous, Ellie. Well done!'

'Shall we make it the Flying Horse, as usual, about eight?'

I thought we might go to one of those new, trendy wine bars in town. If we do, we need to get there pretty early. They're packed by half eight.'

'OK. You name it, I'll be there.'

'Make it Nemo's Bar at seven, then.'

'You're on.' I put the phone down and did a little jig around the room. Things were looking up. I felt really positive. My book was finished. Zoe was back and Anna was out of hospital. All that was missing from my life was a man.

Zoe and I chatted away excitely as we caught up with each other's news. She was still seeing Tony – just. They'd had a few arguments on their travels and were having a cooling-off period at the moment, but reading between the lines, I thought it was almost inevitable that they would get back together.

Zoe reeled off loads of fascinating tales about the countries she had visited. I listened, rapt and envious, and decided there and then that travel would be number one on my agenda when I received my father's money.

Eventually I managed to get a word in edgeways and bring Zoe up to date with my tangled love-life. When I reported that there was no news from Ryan, she got mad, but when I told her about Owen, her eyes shone with approval.

'Who do you really want, Ellie? Ryan or Owen?' Zoe asked when I finally shut up.

I shrugged. 'I don't know. I thought these last two weeks would make it clear but I've been so engrossed in finishing the book, I haven't really missed either of them.'

'Perhaps you should move on to pastures new. Oh, my God, talk of the devil. Look who's just walked in with that awful bit of crumpet on his arm.'

I looked up and saw Ryan and Gemma at the bar. Gemma said something to Ryan and he nodded with irritation. Any other onlooker would have thought he was responding to her normally, but I knew him better than anybody else, all those little quirks of character which gave the game away. I could see that Ryan was not a happy man. Surprisingly I felt very little. There had been one quick flutter in my heart when I had first seen him, but that had quickly settled down into a kind of numbness. It was as if he wasn't really there and I was watching him in a movie.

'Are you all right, Ellie?' Zoe asked. 'Do you want to go?'

'No, I'm fine. They haven't seen us yet.'

'She's a right slag, that Gemma. I remember her at school. She always had her eyes on other girls' boyfriends.'

I smiled. 'Don't be wicked, Zoe. I used to hate her but I don't any more. I think she really loves Ryan, and she did help me find my Cancerian.'

Zoe aggressively stubbed her cigarette out in the ashtray. 'Well, I don't like her. Look how she's holding on to Ryan. She's like a bloody limpet.'

I laughed loudly.

Ryan must have heard me. He immediately spun round and stared straight into my eyes.

As our eyes locked I still felt very little.

Then he was moving towards our table, with Gemma hanging on to his jacket behind him.

'Hello, Ellie, Zoe. How are you both?'

Zoe gave him a venomous look.

'I'm fine, Ryan,' I said coolly. 'How are you and Gemma?'

'We're fine.'

'Good.'

Gemma pulled on Ryan's sleeve. 'Ryan, we ought to go. The film will be starting soon.'

Ryan ignored her. 'How's the book coming along, Ellie?'

'I finished it today. That's why we're here. We're celebrating.'

'And I'm just back from Asia. I've been backpacking with Tony,' Zoe interjected proudly.

'That's nice, Zoe.' He turned his attention back to me. 'So you found a Piscean all right?'

'Yep. No problem.'

Gemma was getting impatient. 'Ryan, we really must go.' She tucked her arm into his and smiled smugly at Zoe and myself. 'He's never on time for anything, is he, Ellie?'

I looked at her coldly. 'He was always on time for me.'

Gemma scowled and pulled at Ryan's arm again.

'Sorry. I have to go. We're booked in to see a film,' Ryan said, looking poignantly at me.

My icy heart began to thaw a little. I realised I didn't want him to leave. 'Oh. You'd better go then,' I said, not wanting him to see me weaken.

'See you sometime, then?'

I shrugged my shoulders. 'Perhaps.'

Gemma dragged him off. I stared after him, my eyes suddenly filling with tears.

'Forget him, Ellie. He's not worth it,' Zoe said, putting her arm around my shoulders protectively.

'I already have,' I said, my voice hard. 'Let's have another drink.'

The next day I had a massive hangover. I was rudely woken from my groggy state by the front-door bell. I tried to ignore it, but whoever was there wouldn't go away. I opened my eyes and peered at the clock. It was gone 1 p.m.

'Jesus!' I cried, jumping out of bed. I flung my dressing gown on. I had a dental appointment at 2.30.

The doorbell rang again, a long, insistent peal.

'All right, all right, I'm coming,' I groaned, rushing unsteadily to the door.

I opened the door and gasped. Ryan was standing there with tears in his eyes.

'Ryan. What are you doing here?' I tried to keep cool.

'Let me in, Ellie. I need to talk to you.' He pushed his way in before I had a chance to say no, and sank into the sofa.

I stood glaring at him, my arms folded across my chest. I felt awful, looked terrible and had no desire to get into a heated emotional debate with my ex-lover.

'I didn't say you could come in,' I said angrily.

He looked up at me, the eyes I knew so well soft and pleading. 'Please, Ellie, just give me a little of your time.'

'I've got a hangover and I feel grotty. Whatever you've got to say, I'm not in the mood to hear it.'

He stared at me, his eyes brimming with tears again. 'I love you, Ellie. I want you back.'

A few weeks ago I would have rushed into his arms. These were the words I had longed to hear during my lonely hours before I met Owen. Now they left me cold. 'Have you ever thought that I might not want you back?'

'Yes. All the time. That's why I left it so long. But seeing you last night . . . I, I can't bear it any more. I'm so unhappy. I need you, Ellie.'

I sighed. 'Perhaps I don't need you anymore, Ryan.'

He stared at me. 'You've changed, Ellie.'

'Perhaps I've finally grown up. You hurt me, Ryan. I know I deserved it. I shouldn't have lied to you, but you cut me off dead without listening to my side of the story, even though you claimed you still loved me. That's not love. Love is accepting somebody for who they are, what they do . . .' I suddenly stopped as a powerful vision of Owen in the church doorway, blowing me a kiss with tears in his eyes, came to my mind. But Owen had insisted I was still in love with Ryan.

'I know,' Ryan said. 'I treated you badly, Ellie. I'm sorry.'

I didn't have the energy or the desire to fight back anymore. My head was pounding and I felt sick. A large eruption of vomit suddenly rose to my throat.

''Scuse me,' I cried and ran to the bathroom, reaching the toilet just in time.

When I came out a few minutes later, Ryan silently handed me a black coffee.

'Thanks. It's just what I need.' I sat down in the armchair, pulling my dressing gown tightly across my body. For some reason I didn't want Ryan to see that I was naked underneath. He might get the wrong idea.

Ryan sat back on the sofa and looked at me kindly. 'Where do we go from here, Ellie? Is there any chance of us getting back together?'

I was no nearer to answering his question than I was a few weeks ago in Owen's apartment. It all really hinged on whether I still loved him or not. Owen was convinced I did, but I wasn't so sure. It was the feel of Owen's large, sensitive hands on my body that I still hankered after, not Ryan's. But then I didn't yearn to be with Owen the way I'd yearned to be with Ryan when he wasn't around.

'I don't know,' I said at last.

'Do you want me to leave?'

'I don't know.'

Ryan sighed and held out his hand. 'Come here, Ellie. Come and sit with me.'

Old habits die hard. Mindlessly I stood up and went to him. He pulled me into his arms and kissed me, lightly on the lips.

I didn't respond, nor did I push him away. I felt too ill to do anything.

I vaguely remember falling asleep in his arms and then nothing else until I woke up several hours later, naked in bed. I could hear Ryan whistling and banging crockery about in the kitchen. I closed my eyes contentedly and fell asleep again.

'Ellie, Ellie, wake up.'

I groaned and opened my eyes. Ryan was standing over me with a tray in his hands. 'I've made you some dinner.'

I pulled myself up, revealing my bouncing boobs, before I remembered I had nothing on. I half-heartedly dragged the duvet up to my neck but it wouldn't stay where it was, so I gave up. Ryan had seen it all before anyway.

Ryan looked longingly at my breasts before he put the tray into my lap.

'This is a rare treat,' I said. 'I'm surprised you could find anything in the fridge. Oh, mushrooms, my favourite. I didn't think I had any.'

'You didn't. I've been to the shops and stocked up for you.'

'Thank you.' I stared at Ryan. He was really trying. The amount of times he had cooked me a meal in the past could be counted on one hand. As for shopping: it had always been his worst nightmare.

He looked at me almost coyly. 'Just tell me when you

want me to leave, Ellie, and I'll go. I don't want to be a nuisance.'

I grinned at him as I tucked into the meal. 'No. You can stay. Aren't you eating?'

'No. I had a sandwich earlier.'

The meal was really good even if it wasn't particularly adventurous. Perfectly cooked chicken, with broccoli, mushrooms, onions and a jacket potato. I wolfed it down. I hadn't realised how hungry I was. Ryan sat on the edge of the bed, watching me. Every so often I would look up and smile and he would smile back at me.

When I'd finished, he got up. 'I'll go and get the dessert,' he said.

He came back with a bowl of strawberries, lightly dusted with caster sugar.

'Strawberries,' I squealed. 'This time of the year?'

'I know how you love them. Cost me an arm and a leg.'

I put one in my mouth. 'Mmm, they're delicious. Would you like one?' I leaned forward, the duvet uncovering my body completely, and popped a strawberry into his mouth.

Before I could sit back, Ryan grabbed my wrist and held me close to him, his eyes gazing into mine.

Suddenly, I felt a great gush of emotion and the floodgates finally opened. As the ice started to melt, tears of happiness streamed from my eyes.

Ryan pulled me towards him and kissed me again. This time, our lips parted automatically and our tongues probed hungrily into each other's mouths. Ryan found another strawberry and pushed it into my mouth. I chewed it a little then transferred it to his mouth. Together we finished off the strawberries, sharing every single one. When we had finished, Ryan took off his clothes and we sank back onto the bed together, laughing.

Ryan playfully tweaked my nipples. 'I've missed these handfuls,' he said, cupping my breasts lovingly.

I responded at once to his touch, feeling all the old familiar urges. My pussy was already wet with its welcoming juices as it opened up, ready for him.

Ryan pushed me onto my stomach and started to caress my buttocks. 'And I've missed these rounded beauties,' he said. 'You are so lovely, Ellie. It's no wonder that every man who sees you wants you.'

I smiled happily into the pillow as Ryan parted my cheeks and ran his fingers teasingly down the crease of my bottom.

'Am I better than Gemma, then?'

He snorted with derision. 'Ten times better, a hundred times, a thousand times even. There's no comparison. I never loved her, you know that.'

'Yes. I think I always knew, but last night at the bar confirmed it. You looked so miserable with her.'

Ryan pushed a finger into my arse, making me sigh with pleasure.

'I thought we might go out tonight,' he said. 'Celebrate our getting back together in style.'

'Who said we're back on?'

'I did.' Ryan's hand came down hard on my bottom.

The sudden, sharp tingling in my buttocks made me shiver with delight. 'OK,' I said humbly. 'I agree, we're back on. Where are you going to take me?'

'There's a fair opening up for Easter on the Common. I thought we might take a few rides there.'

I wriggled my arse appreciatively and he slapped me hard again. 'Get up, lady, we're going out now. Before the fair closes.'

He took his hands away from my backside and I sat up pouting then laughing. This was the old, familiar Ryan who was full of surprises and always seeking out new ways to make our sex life more exciting. This was the man I knew and loved. And, thankfully, I was back to my old self too. I suddenly realised that my time with Owen, although very precious, had not been real. I had been living in a fantasy dreamworld, in which I was a different person, someone more loving, kind and thoughtful than the real me. Someone who was willing to give up being her true self in order to follow the ways of the church and live happily ever after with a man of the cloth. Naturally, the bubble would have eventually burst, leaving me bored and resentful of all that Owen represented. Owen had known all along, of course. He had understood me so much better than I had understood myself. Wonderful, clever Owen, who would always have a place in my heart. But right now I wanted to give the remaining ninety per cent of my heart to Ryan, because he and I were two peas in a pod. We would have many more ups and downs before we finally settled down and had that child we'd spoke about, but at this moment in time, I was more concerned that we lived life to the full and expressed our own unique personalities. I looked at his very familiar naked body, his less-than-perfect physique with the small rolls of fat round his stomach and his overlarge thighs, and I loved him dearly. Everything about him was right for me.

I sprang up and poked him in the ribs. 'Let's see who can get their clothes on first,' I cried, and immediately dashed to the wardrobe where I flung on a very short skirt and an old warm jumper. Ryan was still looking for his trousers.

'Finished!' I yelled triumphantly, running over to Ryan.

Ryan laughed and put his hand up my skirt to feel my pussy. 'You'll be cold going on those rides with no underwear on.'

'No I won't. I'll have your hands to keep me warm.'

Ryan's eyes glazed over with lust. He pulled me to

him roughly and straddled me across his lap. I could feel his cock pulsating, gloriously hard.

'Can't we just have one quick fuck before we go?' I pleaded.

For a moment I thought he was going to give way. Then he changed his mind. 'Not yet, Ellie. We're going to paint the town red. I want us to do lots of different things again, like we used to. Shag ourselves silly, anytime, anywhere. I want you to be so hot for it that you'll drop your knickers – if you've got any on, that is – every time I crock my little finger. I want us to blow our minds, if that's OK with you.'

I shuddered with anticipation and nodded. 'That's fine by me, Ryan.' I clasped his head in my hand and kissed him. 'I do love you, Ryan,' I murmured into his open mouth.

'I know. I never really doubted it.'

I plonked the manuscript on Bernard Enright's desk and beamed at him triumphantly.

He gave me a funny look. 'Well done, Miss Hathaway. You have been busy. Do sit down.'

I did as he said, and leaned across the desk impatiently. 'Well? Do I get my father's inheritance now?'

'Of course you do. There was never any question that you would receive it eventually.'

'Oh? You didn't doubt I'd go through with it, then?'

Bernard Enright gave a little frown. 'I certainly did not think you would go through with it, young lady. I thought you would think better of it.'

'But if I'd done that, I wouldn't be sitting here now, claiming my father's money, would I?' I said, looking at him as if he were stupid.

Enright opened my father's file which was on the desk in front of him, took out a copy of my father's will, and handed it to me. 'Have you ever read that will properly, Miss Hathaway?'

I looked at him, puzzled. 'Of course I have. I read it here last year. Don't you remember?'

'Yes, I remember. You came here. I gave the will to you. You read it all – or so I thought – and then you left, very quickly, determined to carry out the silly conditions in the first half of the will.'

My mouth went dry. The first half of the will? Was there more which I hadn't seen. 'What do you mean, Mr Enright? Are you saying I haven't seen all of it?'

'Apparently not, Miss Hathaway. Otherwise you would know that your father went on to say that the physical experiments were not obligatory, only the writing of the book was. If you chose not to, or did not like the idea of er, um, liaising with a man of each sign, he gave you two years to finish the book and claim the money.'

Stunned, I flicked through the pages of the will until I came to the last section. Sure enough, there was another paragraph stating exactly what the solicitor had just told me.

'Why didn't you show me this before?' I said accusingly.

'I did. It was there all the time. You just didn't bother to read it.'

I stared at him angrily for a few moments. Then suddenly I saw the funny side of it and burst out laughing.

He tutted. 'I don't see that there's anything to laugh about,' he said primly. 'You've been a very silly girl, in my opinion. If you'd read the will properly in the first place, you wouldn't have needed to do anything you didn't want to do.'

I felt myself growing angry with him again. How dare he lecture me. 'When I want your opinion, I'll ask for it,' I said rudely. 'And just for the record, I enjoyed every minute of my "physical experiments", as you call them, and what's more, I don't regret a single minute. I learned more about sex than you'll learn in your whole lifetime. I'm glad I didn't read the rest of the will, because it would have taken me two years to write a book which would have been nowhere near as good. And I can assure you, Mr Enright, that this book is not for the fainthearted. It's extremely graphic. So you'd better not read it, or it might give you an erection, something I don't imagine you've experienced for quite a few years.'

Bernard Enright stared at me furiously throughout my angry tirade, his face turning more and more purple by the second. When I had finished, he gathered himself together and said very coldly, 'That was totally uncalled for, Miss Hathaway. I suggest you leave my office immediately and don't come back until you have learned some manners.'

I was so angry I was past caring. 'When do I get my money and my father's house?' I shouted.

'All the monies left from his estate will be in your bank within the week. You can move into his house any time. I'll write you a letter confirming everything.' He picked up my manuscript from the desk and thrust it into my hands. 'You can take that with you. I have no desire to read it, thank you. Now goodbye, Miss Hathaway. I hope we don't have the misfortune to meet again.'

'So do I, Mr Enright. Do you know, I wouldn't shag you for a million pounds, you dried-up old prune.'

I stormed out of his office, clutching my manuscript tightly to my chest.

Ryan was waiting for me outside. 'How did it go? Everything in order?'

I smiled up at him, my eyes full of tears.

'Ellie, what's the matter? Won't the old bastard give you the money?'

'Oh, yes. There's no problem there. I'll get the money very soon and can move into my father's house any time.'

'So why the tears?'

'Oh, nothing. Enright and I had a little set-to, that's all.'

'What about?

I turned away. 'It's not important, Ryan. Let's forget it, shall we?'

Ryan grabbed my arm. 'Tell me the truth, Ellie. Don't shut me out again.'

I looked up at him and knew I had to tell him about the extra clause I hadn't read in my father's will, and Bernard Enright's pig-headed reaction.

When I finished, Ryan stared at me in disbelief. 'Do you mean we've put ourselves through the mill for the last twelve months for nothing?'

'No. Not for nothing. We've both learned a lot, Ryan, about each other and about ourselves.'

Ryan remained quiet. He looked stunned.

'Please, Ryan. I know it was careless of me not to read the will properly, but at least I can see the funny side of it, can't you?'

Ryan suddenly relaxed and tousled my hair. 'You silly, silly girl, Ellie.'

I smiled up at him hesitantly. 'Do you think you can still love a silly girl like me?'

Ryan's face burst into a grin and then he started laughing. 'Of course I can, Ellie. I'm not giving up on you now.'

I smiled happily and looped my arm through his. 'Bernard Enright didn't want to read my book,' I said sadly as we strolled along.

'The silly old coot. Tomorrow you and I are going to take that book to a publisher. I've a feeling in my bones that it's going to make it, big time. You wait and see.'

I smiled up Ryan at adoringly. He stopped in his

tracks, a familiar look of lust crossing his face, and crushed me against the wall. His hands moved under my coat, down the back of my trousers and cupped my buttocks.

'I can't wait to shag you again,' he said, breathing heavily. 'Why don't we take a walk in the park?'

BLACK LACE NEW BOOKS

Published in October

ALL THE TRIMMINGS
Tesni Morgan
£6.99

Cheryl and Laura, two fast friends, have recently become divorced. When the women find out that each secretly harbours a desire to be a whorehouse madam, there's nothing to stop them. On the surface their establishment is a five-star hotel, but to a select clientele it's a bawdy fun house for both sexes, where fantasies – from the mild to the increasingly perverse – are indulged.

**Humorous and sexy, this is a fabulous yarn of women
behaving badly and loving it!**

ISBN 0 352 33641 2

WICKED WORDS 5
A Black Lace short story collection
£6.99

Black Lace short story collections are a showcase of the finest contemporary women's erotica anywhere in the world. With contributions from the UK, USA and Australia, the settings and stories are deliciously daring. Fresh, cheeky and upbeat, only the most arousing fiction makes it into a *Wicked Words* anthology.

By popular demand, another cutting-edge Black Lace anthology.

ISBN 0 352 33642 0

PLEASURE'S DAUGHTER
Sedalia Johnson
£6.99

It's 1750. Orphaned Amelia, headstrong and voluptuous, goes to live with wealthy relatives. During the journey she meets the exciting, untrustworthy Marquis of Beechwood. She manages to escape his clutches only to find he is a good friend of her aunt and uncle. Although aroused by him, she flees his relentless pursuit, taking up residence in a Covent Garden establishment dedicated to pleasure. When the marquis catches up with her, Amelia is only too happy to demonstrate her new-found disciplinary skills.

**Find out what our naughty ancestors got up to in this
Black Lace special reprint.**

ISBN 0 352 33237 9

Published in November

THE ORDER
Dee Kelly
£6.99

Margaret Dempsey is an Irish Catholic girl who discovers sexual freedom in London but is racked with guilt – until, with the help of Richard Darcy, a failed priest, she sets up The Compassionate Order for Relief – where sexual pleasure is seen as Heaven-sent. Through sharing their fantasies they learn to shed their inhibitions, and to dispense their alms to those in sexual need. Through the Order, Margaret learns that the only sin is self-denial, and that to err is divine!

**An unusual and highly entertaining story of forbidden lusts and
religious transgressions.**

ISBN 0 352 33652 8

PLAYING WITH STARS
Jan Hunter
£6.99

Mariella, like her father before her, is an astrologer. Before she can inherit his fortune, she must fulfil the terms of his will. He wants her to write a *very* true-to-life book about the male sexual habits of the twelve star signs. Mariella's only too happy to oblige, but she has her work cut out: she has only one year to complete the book and must sleep with each sign during the month of their birth. As she sets about her task with enthusiastic abandon, which sign will she rate the highest?

A sizzling, fun story of astrology and sexual adventure.

ISBN 0 352 33653 6

THE GIFT OF SHAME
Sara Hope-Walker
£6.99

Jeffery is no more than a stranger to Helen when he tells her to do things no other man has even hinted at. He likes to play games of master and servant. In the secrecy of a London apartment, in the debauched opulence of a Parisian retreat, they become partners in obsession, given to the pleasures of perversity and shame.

This is a Black Lace special reprint of a sophisticated erotic novel of extreme desires and shameful secrets.

ISBN 0 352 32935 1

Published in December

GOING TOO FAR
Laura Hamilton
£6.99

Spirited adventurer Bliss van Bon is set for three months travelling around South America. When her travelling partner breaks her leg, she must begin her journey alone. Along the way, there's no shortage of company. From flirting on the plane to being tied up in Peru; from sex on snowy mountain peaks to finding herself out of her depth with local crooks, Bliss doesn't have time to miss her original companion one bit. And when brawny Australians Red and Robbie are happy to share their tent and their gorgeous bodies with her, she's spoilt for choice.

An exciting, topical adventure of a young woman caught up in sexual intrigue and global politics.

ISBN 0 352 33657 9

COMING UP ROSES
Crystalle Valentino
£6.99

Rosie Cooper, landscape gardener, is fired from her job by an over-fussy client. Although it's unprofessional, she decides to visit the woman a few days later, to contest her dismissal. She arrives to find a rugged, male replacement behaving even more unprofessionally by having sex with the client in the back garden! It seems she's got competition – a rival firm of fit, good-looking men are targeting single well-off women in West London. When the competition's this unfair, Rosie will need all her sexual skills to level the playing field.

A fun, sexy story of lust and rivalry ... and landscape gardening!

ISBN 0 352 33658 7

THE STALLION
Georgina Brown
£6.99

Ambitious young horse rider Penny Bennett intends to gain the sponsorship and the very personal attention of showjumping's biggest impresario, Alistair Beaumont. The prize is a thoroughbred stallion, guaranteed to bring her money and success. Beaumont's riding school is not all it seems, however. Firstly there's the weird relationship between Alistair and his cigar-smoking sister. Then the bizarre clothes they want Penny to wear. In an atmosphere of unbridled kinkiness, Penny is determined to discover the truth about Beaumont's strange hobbies.

Sexual jealousy, bizarre hi-jinks and very unsporting behaviour in this Black Lace special reprint.

ISBN 0 352 33005 8

To find out the latest information about Black Lace titles, check out the website: www.blacklace-books.co.uk or send a stamped addressed envelope to:

Black Lace, Thames Wharf Studios,
Rainville Road, London W6 9HA

Please note only British stamps are valid.

BLACK LACE BOOKLIST

Information is correct at time of printing. To avoid disappointment check availability before ordering. Go to www.blacklace-books.co.uk

All books are priced £5.99 unless another price is given.

Black Lace books with a contemporary setting

THE TOP OF HER GAME	Emma Holly ISBN 0 352 33337 5	☐
IN THE FLESH	Emma Holly ISBN 0 352 33498 3	☐
A PRIVATE VIEW	Crystalle Valentino ISBN 0 352 33308 1	☐
SHAMELESS	Stella Black ISBN 0 352 33485 1	☐
TONGUE IN CHEEK	Tabitha Flyte ISBN 0 352 33484 3	☐
SAUCE FOR THE GOOSE	Mary Rose Maxwell ISBN 0 352 33492 4	☐
INTENSE BLUE	Lyn Wood ISBN 0 352 33496 7	☐
THE NAKED TRUTH	Natasha Rostova ISBN 0 352 33497 5	☐
ANIMAL PASSIONS	Martine Marquand ISBN 0 352 33499 1	☐
A SPORTING CHANCE	Susie Raymond ISBN 0 352 33501 7	☐
TAKING LIBERTIES	Susie Raymond ISBN 0 352 33357 X	☐
A SCANDALOUS AFFAIR	Holly Graham ISBN 0 352 33523 8	☐
THE NAKED FLAME	Crystalle Valentino ISBN 0 352 33528 9	☐
CRASH COURSE	Juliet Hastings ISBN 0 352 33018 X	☐
ON THE EDGE	Laura Hamilton ISBN 0 352 33534 3	☐

------ ✂ ------------------

Please send me the books I have ticked above.

Name   ....

Address   ....

            ....

            ....

            .... Post Code ....

Send to: **Cash Sales, Black Lace Books, Thames Wharf Studios, Rainville Road, London W6 9HA.**

US customers: for prices and details of how to order books for delivery by mail, call 1-800-805-1083.

Please enclose a cheque or postal order, made payable to **Virgin Publishing Ltd**, to the value of the books you have ordered plus postage and packing costs as follows:

UK and BFPO – £1.00 for the first book, 50p for each subsequent book.

Overseas (including Republic of Ireland) – £2.00 for the first book, £1.00 for each subsequent book.

If you would prefer to pay by VISA, ACCESS/MASTER-CARD, DINERS CLUB, AMEX or SWITCH, please write your card number and expiry date here:

....

Please allow up to 28 days for delivery.

Signature ....

------ ✂ ------------------